J.C. FIELDS

A MATTER OF PAYBACK

vinci
BOOKS

By J.C. Fields

The Michael Wolfe Saga

A Lone Wolf

The Last Insurgent

A Matter of Payback

A Cloak of Deceit

Vinci Books

vinci-books.com

Published by Vinci Books Ltd in 2026

1

A CIP catalogue record for this book is available from the British Library.
Paperback ISBN: 9781036706562

The EU GPSR authorised representative is Logos Europe, 9 rue Nicolas Poussion, 17000 La Rochelle, France
contact@logoseurope.eu

Part I

Chapter One

HAIFA, ISRAEL

December 2, 2001

Mohammad Al-Qaedi lifted the explosive-laden vest onto the shoulders of Ahmed Hadid. The nineteen-year-old slumped slightly with the addition of twenty kilograms to his slender frame.

"It is heavy."

"Ahmed, to accomplish our task today it has to be."

The young Palestinian nodded. "I know."

"Make sure it is secure to your body."

Hadid pulled on the two straps and cinched them tight. A trickle of sweat leaked from his hairline toward his temple. He slipped his arms into the black ankle-length coat. As he buttoned it, Al-Qaedi placed a black Fedora on his head. Black curled sidelocks, attached to the hat, hung in front of his ears, blending perfectly with the color of his hair and beard. The young man observed himself in the mirror. "I look exactly like one of those Zionist Hasidic Jews."

"Yes, Ahmed, you do. That is the point. You will be able to walk onto the bus without anyone harassing you and then all you have to do is activate the detonator in your coat pocket."

The young man continued to gaze at his image. "Then, I will be a martyr in paradise."

Al-Qaedi nodded. "Yes, Ahmed, you will." The older man's expression did not betray his thoughts. He kept his disdain for the ignorant fool to himself.

Michael Wolfe held his young wife's hand as he escorted her to the bus station for a trip to visit her parents in Tel-Aviv.

"I wish you were going with me, Michael."

"Sara, we've discussed this numerous times, I have to work. They don't care if my wife is taking a holiday. I have to report for duty tomorrow."

"I know, but it would be nice to spend a few days together without responsibilities."

"Yes, it would."

She leaned closer to him and whispered, "I heard from my doctor this morning."

Wolfe squeezed her hand. "And?"

"I'm pregnant."

He took her into his arms and held her tight. "When you get back, we will celebrate properly. Are you telling your parents?"

"Of course. They will be excited to know they're going to be grandparents." She paused and gave him a sad smile. "I'm sorry, Michael. I sometimes forget your parents are dead."

"Me, too. They would have loved being grandparents."

The bus pulled into the station. She watched it stop and then kissed Wolfe. "I'll call you when I get there."

"You'd better."

She hurried to the bus door and waited to board. She liked to travel light with only items she needed in a backpack. Once she climbed the three steps and disappeared inside, he started to walk to their car. Wishing to see her one more time before she left, he returned his attention to the bus. She waved at him from a window in the front. When he returned the wave, a tall young man dressed in the traditional clothing of a devout Hasidic Jew passed him, heading for the bus. He noted the man sweating heavily on a cool cloudy day.

Ahmed Hadid resisted the urge to scratch the back of his neck. Sweat, plus the rough material used to construct the vest he wore under his frock, irritated his skin. The itch became so pronounced, he shivered at the same time his forehead grew damp with perspiration.

He approached the steps leading into the bus and prepared to board. His irritated neck would soon not bother him.

The sweat Wolfe observed on the Hasidic man seemed out of place and troubled him. As a trained black-ops operator, now working for the Israeli Mossad, he could not shake the sense of foreboding. He started toward the bus just as the man clad in black climbed the three steps to the vehicle's interior.

He glanced at the window where Sara sat and noticed her stiffen. His pace quickened when his wife faced the window and placed the palms of her hands on the glass. Her eyes were wide and his name frozen on her lips.

The fireball and concussion of the blast propelled him backward. His head struck the parking lot asphalt, and the world went black.

Screams and sirens dragged him back from the darkness. He witnessed the burning hell before him. Staggering to his feet, he felt a sudden despair and emptiness.

"Sara!"

Black smoke rose from the inferno. He madly dashed toward the heat and fire. Flames shot from the vehicle's shredded carcass. Shards of glass crunched under his feet as blood dripped from his forehead.

He ignored the severe ringing in his ears as he rushed toward the flames.

"Sara!"

As he got closer to the vehicle, he slipped on something. When he looked down, it was a human hand. A woman's left hand. The fourth finger bore a simple gold band with a solitary diamond. Sara's wedding ring.

Chapter Two

TEL AVIV, ISRAEL

March 28, 2002

Michael Wolfe handed Uri Ben-David an envelope. The Israeli commander asked, "What's this?"

"My resignation."

"Why?"

Wolfe shrugged. "It's time."

Ben-David stood and handed the envelope back to Wolfe. When he did not accept it, the Israeli let it fall unopened onto his desk. "Israel does not have time for these kinds of theatrics, Michael. We have a crisis on our hands. Do you know how many died yesterday at the Park Hotel?"

"I haven't been listening to the news."

Leaning over his desk, Ben-David placed his palms on the top to support himself. "Thirty. Thirty individuals went to Netanya to celebrate Passover. Now they are all dead. All because of a suicide bomber."

Narrowing his eyes, Wolfe's face grew hard. "I am aware of what a suicide bomber can do, Uri."

"I'm mindful of that, Michael." He straightened and folded his arms. "Israel is going into Ramallah tomorrow morning. We will be placing Arafat under house arrest. I need someone with your skills to protect our boys."

Shaking his head, Wolfe kept his eyes on the unopened envelope on Ben-David's desk and said, "Not my concern anymore."

"Is the person who planned the bombing of Sara's bus your concern?"

Wolfe's eyes rose slowly to meet Ben-David's. His expression cold. "What about him?"

"His name is Mohammad Al-Qaedi. He is Iranian. We learned his name a week ago. Our source told us he had another bombing planned. Where, the source did not know. When we did learn where, it was too late to stop it."

"Where is he?"

"Do I have your attention?"

"Yes."

"What about this letter?" He pointed to the envelope on the desk.

Picking it up, Wolfe folded it and placed it in his jeans back pocket. He returned his gaze to Ben-David. "I'll reconsider. Where is he?"

"Ramallah."

"Do you have a picture?"

Ben-David opened a file on his desk and withdrew a picture. He handed it to Wolfe. "This was taken five years ago in the Gaza Strip."

Without taking his eyes off the picture, Wolfe said, "Where do I report?"

Operation Defensive Shield
Ramallah, West Bank
March 30, 2002

Twenty-one kilometers north of Jerusalem, in the West Bank, lies a city called Ramallah. Within the city limits is a Mukataa, Arabic for a headquarters, built in the 1920s by the British during their occupation of the area. This particular one became Yasser Arafat's West Bank headquarters in 1996. For Operation Defensive Shield, Israeli Defense Forces occupied and surrounded the compound, basically isolating Arafat and placing him under house arrest.

Outside this compound on a rooftop nearby, Michael Wolfe and his Israeli spotter, Josef, surveyed the streets surrounding the Mukataa. Having just celebrated his thirtieth birthday without his beloved Sara by his side, he relished the thought of avenging her death.

At the young age of nineteen, Wolfe had attained the distinction of being one of the best snipers ever produced by the United States Marine Corps. Serving with distinction during the brief 1991 Operation Desert Storm, he emerged from his stint with the Marines as a decorated combat soldier. Afterward, he attended Georgetown University, earning a degree in international business management. Recruited by the Israelis to work at their embassy in Washington, he later moved to Israel, with the blessing and encouragement of the Mossad. There he met Sara Sobus, a second-generation Israeli descended from Polish immigrant parents.

Josef tapped him on the shoulder. "Ten o'clock. Five bogies with AK-47s."

Wolfe aimed his Barrett M99 .50 BMG sniper rifle toward the location indicated by Josef. The crosshairs of his scope centered on the lead Palestinian whose face and head were covered by a tactical desert keffiyeh. "What's in front of them?"

"Couple of our guys, keeping tabs on the compound."

"Do they see them?"

His spotter grew quiet. Wolfe maintained his concentration on the five Palestinians. Finally, Josef said, "No. They are sneaking up on our patrol from the rear."

Without responding, Wolfe increased the pressure on the Barrett's trigger. With the massive suppressor installed on the weapon, the rifle shot would not be heard by the men advancing on the Israeli patrol.

An enormous hole opened in the chest of the lead Palestinian. Surprise and shock triggered his comrades to abandon their quest and retreat at a full run.

Josef said quietly, "Got him."

Wolfe's mouth twitched as he aimed at the retreating men. He released another round, which ricocheted off a wall ahead of the running men. This encouraged them to run even faster.

Raising his head from the scope, he surveyed the scene. "See anything else?"

"No. Good shot, Michael."

Without a response, Wolfe returned his attention back to Arafat's compound. A man stood outside a building within the walls. Getting back behind the scope, he centered the crosshairs on the man's face. A chill went up his spine as he studied the person's features.

"Josef, there's a guy standing outside a door on the east side of the building where Arafat is sequestered. Use your scope to see if you can identify him."

"I see him." The spotter grew quiet as he scrutinized the

man. "Michael, the picture you showed me this morning, I think it's him."

Wolfe did not divert his scope from the target. "That's what I thought. Radio in and let them know I have Al-Qaedi in my sights. Request permission to fire."

Studying the man, Wolfe memorized his features. He appeared to be in his mid-to-late thirties. A tan-and-brown keffiyeh covered only his head, leaving his face unobscured.

The next thing Wolfe heard was Josef saying, "Take the shot."

As he increased the pressure on the trigger, the man turned his gaze directly at Wolfe and gave him a half grin. Just as the Barrett fired, the terrorist ducked back into the building.

By May, 2002, Israeli Defense Forces no longer occupied Palestinian cities, and the number of suicide bombings tapered off. With one of their invasion's missions accomplished, Israel steeled itself for the forthcoming condemnations of its actions by the rest of the world.

Michael Wolfe reappeared in the office of Uri Ben-David. Standing at attention in front of the desk, the Israeli commander studied a report while the man standing in front of his desk waited. Finally, he said, "Once again, you managed to distinguish yourself in Ramallah. Congratulations, Michael."

With a grim expression, Wolfe said, "I had Al-Qaedi in my sights. I hesitated and lost the shot."

"That's not what I read. You followed procedures. The delay in granting permission for you to fire is what lost the shot."

"He saw me."

"You specifically, or you the sniper?"

"Me the sniper."

"So, he wouldn't be able to recognize you?"

"I don't see how. My face was behind the scope. Plus, I was over 500 meters away."

"But he knew someone was there."

"Yes."

"We have reports of him being spotted on the streets of Tehran, a week ago."

"Figures. Men like Al-Qaedi are basically cowards. They want the other guy to die for the cause."

"What about your resignation?"

"What resignation?"

"Good, kind of what I thought. Ready to track down Mohammad Al-Qaedi?"

Wolfe nodded.

"Why are you still standing there?"

Wolfe immediately walked out of his office.

Chapter Three

TEL-AVIV, ISRAEL

September 14, 2004

Uri Ben-David kept track of Michael Wolfe as he approached his location in the small café in central Tel-Aviv. The American did not walk directly to the table but circumvented the area several times before finally sitting down across from the Mossad assistant director.

"I understand you wanted to see me, Uri."

The Israeli motioned for the waiter to take Wolfe's order. "Coffee, Michael?"

"Yes."

When the waiter left, Ben-David leaned over the table. "I got a call from a friend of mine in the United States, Joseph Kincaid. Do you know him?"

"We've met."

"He wants to borrow your talents."

Raising an eyebrow, Wolfe remained quiet as the waiter placed a cup of coffee in front of him. When the man walked away, the sniper said, "Why?"

"It seems a car bomb exploded in Baghdad this morning. Forty-seven souls lost their lives, and the wounded count has climbed over one hundred. Rumors are that Mohammed Al-Qaedi is responsible."

Sipping his coffee, Wolfe remained silent for a while. Finally, he asked, "Why now?"

"Good question, Michael. I asked Joseph the same thing. He said the war was not going well for the American coalition. It seems this Mohammad Al-Qaedi is orchestrating more and more suicide attacks, and the body count is climbing."

"That's not how it's being reported in the news."

With a nod, Ben-David kept his eyes on his guest. "When has any government admitted to bad news?"

"Never. What do they have in mind?"

"You seem to be the only person alive who has seen Al-Qaedi in person. He's as elusive as a sand cat."

"And that means?"

"They want you to lead a team of snipers to find him."

"There are plenty of well trained—"

"That's not the only reason."

Taking another sip of coffee, Wolfe tilted his head.

"There is a faction within the Knesset that want all non-Israeli contractors out of the Mossad."

Wolfe's mouth twitched.

"They say anyone who works for the Mossad and is not a naturalized Israeli citizen will be automatically considered a security risk."

"So, all of a sudden, I'm a security risk, and Joseph Kincaid miraculously asks for my assistance. Does that sum it up?"

Ben-David nodded.

"So much for loyalty."

"That's what I told them."

"Tell Joseph I'll be happy to help."

Southern Syria
October 26, 2008

Abu Kamal sits on the Euphrates River in eastern Syria near the border with Iraq. Military leaders in the US and within the coalition considered it a major conduit for foreign fighters, money, and arms entering Iraq to join the insurgents. On October 26, 2008, CIA paramilitary personnel from the Special Activities Division and US Joint Special Operations Command sent a team into the area. Four American aircraft, two Blackhawks, and two AH-6 Little Bird attack helicopters deposited a team of operators to attack the main building supposedly used by the smugglers as their headquarters.

CIA black ops sniper Michael Wolfe and his spotter, Rick Flores, kept a close watch over the area prior to and during the raid from an adjacent building a block away.

Flores asked, "You ever get tired of babysitting these types of events?"

Wolfe, lying prone behind the scope of his trusty Barrett M99 BMG said, "Nah. Somebody's got to do it. Might as well be me."

"I do. When my tour's up, I've been asked by the FBI to take over their sniper training school."

Wolfe turned his attention to his spotter. "Sounds like a nine-to-five gig."

"Yeah, the wife's happy. She says I'm gone too much."

"You've been doing this since we infiltrated Kuwait back in 1990. You'll get bored."

"Let's hope so." Flores paused for a second. "You've been doing this for a while, too."

"Not really, I went stateside and got my degree at Georgetown."

"That's right, I forgot. So why did you come back?"

"It's a matter of payback. There's an Iranian who owes me."

The two old friends fell into silence. Thirty minutes later, the sound of distant helicopters approaching their position grew louder. Flores said, "Heads-up. They're coming in."

Wolfe asked, "See anything?"

Peering through his binoculars, Flores did not answer right away. As the helicopters grew closer, he said, "Second floor, north window. We've got a bad guy sticking his head out. Apparently, he hears them, too."

"Keep an eye on him. If he starts getting hyper, let me know."

"Got it."

The helicopters slowed as their noses pitched up. The two UH-60 Black Hawks then hovered several feet off the ground, and five men from each jumped out and ran toward the building guarded by Wolfe and Flores. Flores glanced at two AH-6 Little Bird attack helicopters circling the area. "Someone must be expecting trouble."

"I noticed that." Wolfe's concentration centered on a man running from the rear of the building under attack. He followed him with the scope. The figure had the same type of tan-and-brown Keffiyeh and body build as the man standing outside Yasser Arafat's compound in Ramallah five years prior. He applied pressure to the trigger just as the figure disappeared behind another building. He muttered to himself, "Damn."

Flores asked, "What'd you say?"

"Nothing." He trained the Barrett back on the four-story building they were assigned to protect as weapons fire could be heard.

One of the AH-6 Little Birds landed just outside the structure they occupied. Flores tapped Wolfe on the helmet. "Time to go, buddy. Our ride's here."

"I saw him, Joseph."

"In Abu Kamal?"

"Yeah. He ran out of the building the guys were targeting just before the helicopters started hovering."

"Huh." He studied the cup of coffee he held. "The Syrians are claiming all the casualties in the building were civilians. If Al-Qaedi was there, it means we got the right target."

"I would agree."

"You sure it was him."

"Positive."

"How?"

"Same tan-and-brown keffiyeh and the same smirk he had in Ramallah."

"Okay, that's why you were there. Too bad you didn't get a shot at him."

"I hesitated."

"I doubt it."

The two men were silent for a while. Finally, Wolfe said, "I need to go back to the States for a while."

Raising an eyebrow, Joseph said, "You giving up?"

"No, my grandfather passed. He left me some land in Missouri I need to check on."

"Never thought of you as a farmer, Michael."

"Trust me, I'm not. When I was young, he and I would go there a lot. It's secluded and beautiful. My grandfather built an earth-sheltered home on it some years ago that I've never seen." Wolfe took a deep breath and let it out slowly. "He was the last living member of my family."

"I thought your parents were still alive."

"No."

"I'm sorry. When?"

"A year before Sara's murder. Drunk driver."

Joseph tilted his head. "Why didn't you come home then?"

Narrowing his eyes, Wolfe stared hard at his friend. "I was in Turkey taking care of Mossad business."

"Ah." Joseph sipped his coffee. "You taking off wouldn't have anything to do with rumors about William Little being spotted, would it?"

"Didn't hear that."

"Michael, I would suggest you leave him alone."

"I have no interest in William Little, Joseph. It's ancient history. But I do have unfinished business with Mohammad Al-Qaedi. Unfortunately, it will have to wait."

"You've spent four years searching for him, and he finally shows up in Syria. I'm surprised you're giving up so easy."

Wolfe raised an eyebrow. "I'm not giving up, Joseph, I simply have other things to do right now."

"So, when you complete whatever it is you need to do stateside, what then?"

Wolfe shrugged. "Don't know."

"When you're ready, call me."

"Why?"

"I always have requests for someone with your talents, Michael."

"We'll see."

Chapter Four

August 2010

FBI agent Sean Kruger ducked under the yellow tape surrounding the crime scene and paused. He studied the buildings surrounding the area, observing thousands of windows and multiple rooftops. He drew a breath and let it out slowly as he walked toward the body covered by a blue tarp. The task ahead would be daunting.

"What've you got, Preston?"

NYPD Police Detective Preston Alvarez stood from kneeling by the body and shook Kruger's hand. "No one heard the shot. Witnesses are telling us the man's head just exploded." Alvarez spoke with an accent Kruger couldn't identify, probably a combination of the diverse cultures of New York City. He stood even with Kruger's six-foot frame but several years younger. His blue-gray eyes had seen a lot in his sixteen-year career as an NYPD detective. This was the second time Kruger had the privilege of working with him.

Kruger surveyed the buildings in the area surrounding the body. He remained quiet for several moments. "Any idea where the shot came from?"

"From the placement of the body and splatter pattern, we think it came from the Marriot." Alvarez pointed to a tall structure across the busy street and down three blocks. "I've got uniforms over there searching."

Kruger nodded. "Makes sense. Easy access, easy egress." He returned his attention to the body. "Any ID?"

"I was waiting for you."

"Why, so you can slide the case over to me?"

Alvarez studied the FBI agent with a sly grin. "I would do no such thing. However, if you are so inclined, I would not complain."

Laughing out loud, Kruger patted Alvarez on the shoulder. "Preston, I appreciate the professional courtesy. This will make the fifth similar incident in three different states. If your guys are done taking pictures, let's find out who he is."

Kruger accepted the latex gloves handed to him by Alvarez and pulled back the tarp. He took a sharp breath when he saw the damage to the man's head. He ignored the carnage and searched the inside of the man's suit coat and pants pockets. When he located a wallet, he stood and extracted a driver's license. "I was afraid of this."

Alvarez raised an eyebrow. "What?"

"They've all been ex-military officers."

Kruger considered the window of room 29112 on the twenty-eighth floor of the Marriot. A small circle, eight inches in diameter, had been cut into the glass pane. City sounds and wind swirled from the small opening.

Alvarez handed Kruger a piece of paper. "Hotel manager told me the individual who rented the room used a credit card."

Kruger took the paper and read the name. "Are you kidding me? Really?"

"Yeah, really."

"Ima Goode Shotski." He chuckled as he studied the page. "At least he has a sense of humor." He paused for a moment. "No one questioned the name?"

Alvarez shrugged. "Hey, man, it's New York City."

Kruger returned his attention to the small opening in the glass.

"How far would you say the shot was, Preston?"

Alvarez walked over to the window and peered down. "A long-ass way."

"Yeah, I'd say at least 800 yards or more." Kruger paused as he studied the scene. "Plus, all the eddies from wind swirling around the buildings."

"Hell of a shot."

Kruger crossed his arms and placed his hand on his chin. "Yeah, a hell of a shot." He grew quiet for several moments. "I doubt there are many individuals with the skills to make a shot like that. It's probably time to ask an expert."

FBI Training Facility, Quantico, VA

Kruger shook the hand of Special Agent Rick Flores as they stood in his office just outside the long-range sniper training facility at Quantico.

"Agent Sean Kruger, it's an honor to finally meet you."

"The honor is mine, Agent Flores. Please call me, Sean."

"Everyone around here calls me Flores, but I prefer Rick. What can I do for you today, Sean?"

"I'm sure you've heard of the five retired military officers killed by long-range rifle shots?"

Flores nodded.

"This last one was a tricky one."

"How so?"

"When we measured the distance, it totaled 904 yards."

"That's not too difficult a shot."

"It came from the twenty-eighth floor of a Marriot in the middle of Manhattan on a warm and windy day."

Flores gave a long whistle. "Huh."

"That was my reaction as well."

"Let me think about that for a second. What time did the shot occur?"

"Around 1:30 p.m."

"Okay."

"The sidewalk was busy, lots of pedestrians. Our victim was hit as he exited a restaurant."

After a small pause, Flores asked, "Where did the bullet hit? Center mass?"

"Head shot."

"Uh, boy."

Kruger raised an eyebrow. "What?"

"Not many guys have that skill set. The shot is possible, with the right equipment, but the thermals and wind vortices make it difficult."

"How so?"

"Think about it for a second. A bullet is a physical object. While its forward inertia is substantial, the total mass isn't that large. Wind, thermal eddies, and the downward trek make calculating the trajectory challenging. It's feasible, but I would say damn near impossible."

"So, you're saying only a few individuals might possess the skills to make a shot like that?"

"I'd say there are fewer than a dozen men in the US with those kinds of skills."

"Narrows our suspect file."

Flores gave Kruger a grim expression. "Not necessarily."

The FBI agent contemplated Flores for several seconds. "And that means?"

"What about individuals we don't know about? Men and women trained in Russia, China, England, France, Germany, etc. I'd say your list of suspects would be more than a dozen."

Silence dominated the room.

"Shit."

"Sucks, doesn't it?"

The call from Alan Seltzer, Kruger's immediate supervisor, informed him a courier would deliver a packet to the hotel for him early the next day.

After room service delivered the envelope along with coffee, a bagel, and strawberry jam, Kruger opened the package. It contained seven files with the words *Your Eyes Only* stamped on each.

The information provided profiles and personnel records on current United States snipers. Two were Green Berets, one a Marine, three were Seals, and the last, a member of the FBI Hostage Rescue Team. Kruger dialed Seltzer's office phone.

"Did you get a chance to read the documents?"

"That's why I'm calling. Why these particular guys?"

"They all have the talent and training to make the shot from the Marriot."

Kruger was silent. "Do they have alibis?"

"No. That's why we included them. We eliminated military men who are overseas and anybody from the FBI currently elsewhere."

"Alan, there have been four other killings besides the one yesterday."

"We know that, but you need to talk to each of them. It might help you develop a profile."

"Have you read the investigation summaries of each incident?"

"No."

"I'm not convinced it's one person doing the shooting."

"When did you come up with this theory?"

"Autopsies indicate a different caliber in each case."

"So?"

"It's an inconsistency I don't like."

"That's why you're the one leading this investigation, Sean. You don't take the easy route."

Kruger took a deep breath. "Alan, I'm going home for a few days. I haven't seen my son for three weeks. I'll get back on this Monday."

"I won't mention the longer the delay, thc colder the trail will be."

"The trail's already cold. A few more days won't make a difference."

Silence was his answer. Finally, Seltzer said, "Very well, call me Monday."

After checking the time, Kruger called the Bureau travel agency.

Monday morning found Kruger at his home office desk reading the sniper files for the third time. Having put the investigation on hold, he used the weekend to enjoy seeing his son play in an exciting baseball tournament, prepare steaks on his grill, and get a few chores completed around the house. Now, he poured over the case with renewed enthusiasm.

Accessing the Bureau's phone directory on his computer, he found the number he needed and punched it into his cell phone.

"Flores."

"Rick, Sean Kruger. You got a second?"

"Sure, what's up?"

"I've been thinking about what you said last Wednesday."

"I said a lot of things Wednesday. Remind me."

"You thought there might be more than a dozen men with the right skill set. How many men over the course of the past few decades were trained as snipers by the military?"

Silence.

Kruger waited. He heard Flores take a deep breath.

"Not sure I could answer your question with any certainty. I did my training at Camp Pendleton while I was a Marine. The other training sites for the Marines are Camp Lejeune in North Carolina and here at Quantico. The Army does their training at Fort Benning. A lot of guys have been through those facilities in the past three decades."

"Kind of what I'm thinking."

"You have an epiphany over the weekend?"

Kruger chuckled. "No. I went over some files this morning and needed some clarification, that's all."

"I also thought about your problem over the weekend."

"Really, and?"

"I know a former sniper you need to talk to."

"Where and when?"

"Well, he's not too far from Kansas City."

"Oh?"

"Yeah. He's got a cabin somewhere in Southern Missouri, I believe it's near the Mark Twain Forest. It's isolated and hard to find. I know how to get in touch with him, so I'll let him know you're coming. I've been a spotter for him numerous times over the past two decades."

"Really."

"Yep. He's the best I've ever worked with."

"Thanks, Rick."

"No problem. I'll call you when it's arranged and give you directions."

The call ended, and Kruger drummed his fingers on his desk. An actual sniper as a consultant. Interesting. His gut told him the investigation was going in the wrong direction. He punched in another number on his phone.

"Seltzer."

"Alan, the men in the files you gave me are not our shooters."

"How do you know?"

"Logistically improbable."

"Okay, walk me through it."

"First, the five shootings have happened in five major cities across the country. Dallas, Houston, LA, San Francisco, and now New York City. The files you sent are for individuals still on active duty. It would be practically impossible for anyone on active duty to be in that many cities in so close a time frame."

"Okay, I'll buy that."

"Plus, I just spoke to Rick Flores. Thousands of men have been through sniper training in this country over the past three decades, not counting the ones from the Vietnam era. Although those guys are getting up in years, there were a lot of them. Somewhere, in the past, our sniper has crossed paths with his victims. I need a deep dive on them."

"Well, we already have a couple of agents doing background on the victims. So far, they haven't found a connection between them."

"They're looking in the wrong direction."

"Okay, I'll assign a researcher to you. Not sure who it will be right now, but they'll be in touch."

"Make it a Forensic CPA."

"Why?"

"A hunch."

"Okay, your hunches are usually correct. Anyone in particular?"

"Yes, Sharon Crawford."

"Thought so. Why?"

"All of the victims were officers, majors and above. I need her to dig into their finances."

"I'm not following you."

"I think we've been looking at this all wrong. The victims are the key."

"Okay. Are you going to call her?"

"Yes."

Chapter Five

SOMEWHERE IN SOUTHERN MISSOURI

August 2010

Sharon Crawford stopped studying the map she held. She rode in the passenger seat of Kruger's Ford Mustang as he drove east on Highway 60.

"Have we passed Birch Tree?"

"No, we passed a mileage marker a minute ago. We're about five miles away. Why?"

"You'll need to take Missouri 99 south."

"Okay." Kruger glanced over at her. Sharon Crawford was in her early thirties and a five-year veteran of the FBI's forensic accounting department. After working several cases together, he found her to be intelligent and highly skilled at her job. A job he would have found tedious and boring. Slender and tall, she stood an inch shorter than Kruger's six-foot frame. She wore her dark-brown hair short, which accentuated her slightly oval face and hazel eyes. During work hours, she was professional, wore little if any makeup, and had a stern demeanor with blocky unflattering glasses.

Today, the glasses were gone. She wore tight-fitting jeans, an open-collar silk blouse, and a hint of makeup. Kruger found her extremely attractive.

He said, "Have you ever been in Missouri?"

"No." She did not take her eyes off the map.

"I have a GPS unit. You don't have to use the map."

She furrowed her brow. "I like knowing where I am."

"I can tell you exactly where you are. You're approaching the middle of nowhere." He returned his attention to the road as he slowed the Mustang to make a right turn onto Missouri 99.

"Sorry, I've never been in a place like this."

"Beautiful, isn't it?"

"If you like hills, trees, towns that are basically wide spots in the road, and a total lack of civilization, then it's beautiful."

"Sharon, this is rural Missouri. Have you ever been in Upstate New York?"

She hesitated for a second. "No."

"It's similar."

She sighed. "Sean, we've been in the car for over six hours. When will we get there?"

He glanced at the GPS unit attached to the front windshield by a suction mount. "We're about fifteen miles from our next turn. That's when our journey will finally get to the middle of nowhere."

The gravel road sloped down. When the Mustang reached the end, Kruger stopped, shifted to first, and set the parking brake. He did not see a structure, only a mound of dirt covered with grass. The land left of the mound held a row of solar panels and a tall wind turbine. He opened the door and stood. To the right, a grove of oak trees blended into the surrounding woodlands. Over the top of the mound, Kruger saw a long grassy clearing rising toward the south.

Sharon exited the car. "Are you sure this is it?"

"No, but those solar panels and turbine are powering something."

A man of average height appeared on the right side of the berm. His lean and deeply tanned face featured a week-old beard. He wore jeans, an olive-green T-shirt, and scuffed hiking boots. Kruger recognized him from a picture sent to him by Flores. This was Michael Wolfe.

When the man was twenty feet away, he stopped. "You Kruger?"

"Yes." He motioned toward Sharon. "This is Agent Sharon Crawford. We appreciate you talking to us."

Wolfe looked at Sharon. "Ma'am." He returned his attention back to Kruger. "Only reason I agreed to talk to you is because Rick Flores asked."

"I understand. All we need is your assessment of several shootings."

Staring at Kruger, Wolfe remained a statue for several moments, his face a blank canvas. Finally, he motioned for them to follow him toward the rear of the small rise.

When they got to the far side of the mound, it revealed the front of a structure buried into the side of a hill. An overhang shielded the door and windows. Wolfe led them inside and pointed toward a room off the entrance. "We can talk in there. Want some coffee?"

"Yes, we would. It's been a long drive."

Sharon said, "Excuse me. Can I use your restroom?"

Wolfe pointed to a hall. "Down the hall, second door on the left."

When she returned, Kruger and Wolfe were seated at a small table occupied by three mugs of steaming coffee. The two men sipped the brew and considered each other intently.

Sharon interrupted the staring contest. "Thank you, Mr. Wolfe."

"Name's Michael."

"Thank you, Michael." She sat down next to Kruger.

"Okay, Agent Kruger." Wolfe sipped his coffee. "What do you need assessed?"

"Name's Sean."

Wolfe's face softened. He leaned back in his chair. "Flores said you're okay. I don't get a lot of visitors out here."

"I can understand why. Is this house self-sufficient?"

"Yeah. Solar and wind provide enough power to eliminate the need for propane. Because it's an earth-sheltered structure, the temperature inside is usually a constant sixty-seven degrees. When I do need heat or cooling, I have a geothermal pump. Water comes from a deep well."

"What do you do, Michael? Flores didn't tell me."

"I'm a consultant."

Kruger fought to hide his smile. "What do you consult on?"

"International Business and stuff."

Remaining quiet for a few moments, Kruger folded his arms. "Did Flores fill you in on why we're here?"

"Yeah. Who were the targets?"

Keeping his gaze locked on Wolfe, Kruger said, "Retired General Howard Carlson, Colonel Adam Sherman, Colonel Rachael Frazier, Major Nathan Tucker, and Lieutenant Colonel John King."

Wolfe threw his head back and laughed out loud. "Have you checked their backgrounds?"

"We have several agents working on it."

"Well, they won't find the reason they were the targets."

Sharon tilted her head. "Why do you say that?"

He remained silent while he drank coffee. "Because, during Desert Storm, those five were part of a group of officers who ran an underground operation that got a lot of our guys killed."

Kruger studied his host for a few moments. "Should I consider you a person of interest, Michael?"

"Probably. I have the skills and the motivation. But not the opportunity."

"How's that?"

"I've been in Venezuela for the past month."

"Doing what?"

"Consulting."

Kruger raised an eyebrow. "Can you substantiate your alibi?"

Wolfe nodded.

"Okay, tell me about the operation."

"They were smuggling antiquities, mostly out of Kuwait and some out of Iraq."

"Did you report it to the authorities?"

Wolfe cocked his head. "I was a sergeant, Agent Kruger. Those individuals were the authorities."

"Wrong choice of words."

Sharon leaned forward on the table. "How did it get our guys killed?"

"Not only our guys but members of the coalition. I heard the British were pissed about it."

Kruger leaned forward. "Can you give us more details, Michael?"

Wolfe stood and went to the coffeepot. While he poured, he said, "There were seven of them. The five you mentioned were underlings. A three-star general was supposedly the brains behind the operation. His name was William Little. They called him Big Bill behind his back and General to his face." Wolfe studied his cup of coffee and fell silent.

"You haven't told us how it got our guys killed."

"I'm getting there. Big Bill would identify a location and send a unit in to capture it. He didn't give a shit if the location was heavily fortified or not. He wanted it captured. Lots of our guys died because of his orders. Once they secured the location, he would send in members of his team to liberate the antiquities they found. He picked the locations by how much stuff he could loot. The majority of the spots had zero strategic value."

Kruger remained silent. Sharon said, "The army didn't say anything about it?"

"Hell, no. Schwarzkopf didn't give a shit. He was more interested in his hundred-hour ground offensive."

Kruger asked, "Did this occur during the offensive?"

Wolfe shook his head. "No, these little operations were conducted during the so-called air offensive. It was all hands-on deck for the ground war. Which, by the way, wasn't much of a war. It was just a lot of vehicles racing through the desert, shooting at sand. By that time, Big Bill and his team had their fortune stashed off the coast of Kuwait in a cargo ship headed for Switzerland."

Kruger sat back in his chair. "Do you think these five assassinations are related?"

"Yeah, Big Bill is tying up loose ends."

"Would one man be responsible?"

"Probably not. I'd say you have five different shooters.

Those guys and gal made more than a few enemies over there."

"How do we find out?"

"Follow the money."

Kruger and Sharon talked to Wolfe for another hour and left just before five in the evening. Dark clouds rolled in from the northwest.

Wolfe followed the Mustang with a series of security cameras placed every hundred feet along the gravel driveway. When it reached Highway 90, it headed back north. After switching off the monitors, he rubbed his face with his hands. "My alibi in Venezuela should hold unless you get too curious, Agent Kruger."

One Week Later

Kruger parked his Mustang at the end of the gravel road next to the grassy mound. Wolfe stood outside the house, waiting. When Kruger walked up to him, they shook hands. No words were spoken as they went inside.

"Michael, I appreciate you talking to me again."

Wolfe remained silent.

"Did you know William Little is living in an estate on the Island of Madagascar near the city of Toamasina?"

Wolfe kept his face neutral and lied. "I'd heard rumors. Why?"

"The FBI can't touch him."

Wolfe tilted his head. "No extradition treaty, right?"

"None. No extradition treaty between the United States and the island. I haven't told anybody about this, but I was able to confirm four large transfers of money out of a bank account in the Caymans to four separate numbered bank accounts in Switzerland."

Wolfe kept his expression neutral even though his mind raced with these new revelations.

"The account in the Caymans belonged to retired Major Nathan Tucker. As you know, Tucker was the man shot in New York City."

Again, Wolfe did not respond.

"We think Tucker's assassination was separate from the first four."

"Oh, and why is that?"

"We can't find a trace of the shooter in New York. However, information has come to light suggesting the other assassinations were conducted by foreign nationals who entered the country legally a few days before a shooting and immediately left the same day. Not really evidence, very circumstantial, but it does indicate a pattern. Wouldn't you agree?"

Wolfe nodded.

"The other piece of evidence we found was a transfer of funds to the account owned by Tucker two weeks before the first shooting. Those funds came from a numbered account in a Swiss bank known to have received money from a private auction of antiquities in 1992."

Wolfe tilted his head. "Why are you telling me all this, Agent Kruger?"

"Professional courtesy. You pointed us in the right direction, and I wanted to thank you."

"You could have called to say thank you. Why drive six hours to tell me all this?"

"Six and a half, actually." Kruger shrugged. "I didn't have anything else to do today."

"Somehow, I doubt that."

"I checked your alibi in Venezuela."

Wolfe's expression remained neutral.

"Very convincing. Well planned and well thought out. You only made one mistake."

"Oh? Tell me."

"The credit card account you used at the Marriott in Manhattan was cloned from an American Express account last used in Caracas, Venezuela by a Mexican diplomat. The name on the card was bogus, but the card worked. I liked the name, by the way: Ima Goode Shotski. I got a good laugh over it."

"I have no idea what you are talking about. But if I did, how would I have done all of this?"

"Easy. Do I need to explain?"

Tilting his head slightly, Wolfe crossed his arms. "What are you planning to do with all of these assumptions, Agent?"

"Not a damn thing."

Wolfe displayed a puzzled look. "Why?"

"I can't touch Little. He's out of my reach. You can."

"I'm a consultant, Sean."

Kruger gave Wolfe a knowing smile. "Yeah, so you've said."

Chapter Six

SOUTHWEST MISSOURI

August 2011

Joseph Kincaid's dark-gray Range Rover sat parked north of the berm on Michael Wolfe's land. Inside the earth-shelter home, the homeowner made coffee while the guest sat at the breakfast bar. "I have a proposal for you, Michael."

Raising an eyebrow, Wolfe poured water into the coffeemaker's reservoir. "Do you want sugar?"

"Black."

"Good choice." Wolfe pressed the start button and turned his attention toward his mentor. "I'm listening."

"I spoke to Uri Ben-David yesterday. He is now in charge of the counter-terrorism division of Mossad."

"Good for him."

"He—uh—asked me to tell you he was sorry about your last meeting with him."

"No reason to apologize. Shit happens."

Joseph smiled. "Yes, it does. He did make a request."

"Let me guess. They need my assistance again."

"Kind of. It's more of a joint venture between the Mossad and the CIA."

Rolling his eyes, Wolfe walked to a cabinet and got down two coffee mugs. He placed one in front of Joseph and kept the other. "What kind of joint venture?"

"The two agencies, with new technology, have been able to trace and pinpoint the exact location of several known terrorists."

Wolfe poured coffee into Joseph's mug. "That's helpful."

"Very."

Taking a sip of the coffee in his own mug, Wolfe asked, "So, you guys want me to utilize this information—how?"

"By doing what you do best."

"Who would I work for?"

"You'd be based here with an apartment in Tel Aviv. Expenses and compensation would be paid by one of the CIA's numerous payroll accounts."

"That didn't answer my question, Joseph. Who would I report to?"

"Uh…"

"I work for you, Joseph, and you only. Otherwise, I'm not interested."

"That's a fair request. I can make that happen."

"What's my cover?"

"Same as it has always been: international business consultant."

Tel Aviv
December 2011

After the death of Wolfe's parents and the murder of his wife, Sara, Wolfe rarely celebrated Christmas or Hannukah. Since less than 3 percent of the citizens of Israel were Christian, Christmas was more of a private affair for those who observed the day. Celebrations in Israel during this time of year centered around the Festival of Lights and the eight days of lighting the menorah. Plus, all the festive food.

Christmas day found him in his apartment waiting for his next assignment. At six in the evening, someone knocked on his door. Holding his Walther PPK in his hand behind his back, he checked his security camera feed and then opened the door.

A slender woman, of average height, stood outside. Her long dark-brown hair flowed unbound around her stunning oval face. She wore tight jeans, flat canvas shoes, and a white silk blouse open at the collar with the top three buttons undone. Despite himself, he stared without comment at the beautiful lady before him.

She tilted her head. "I am Nadia Picard. I have a package for you."

Wolfe remained silent as he stepped aside, and she entered his apartment.

The woman took in the sparsely furnished space. "I assume you are Michael Wolfe?"

"Yes."

He hid the Walther in his belt at the small of his back before reaching for the manila envelope she offered him. "This is the first time someone's hand delivered it."

She folded her arms. "Uri Ben-David suggested I bring it to you."

"Do you work for Uri?"

"Yes."

Wolfe opened the envelope and read the note clipped to the file. Then he returned the file to the package. "Did he tell you he attached a personal note suggesting I ask you out for dinner?"

"Mr. Wolfe, I have heard a lot of pickup lines in my life, but that one is unique."

Reaching into the envelope, he pulled the note out and showed it to her. "Not a pickup line."

After reading it, she smiled. "Well, I do not have anything else to do. Do you?"

Tel Aviv
December 2012

Nadia Picard reached over the table and placed her hand on Wolfe's. "You have been quiet tonight. What is wrong, Michael?"

"Nothing. I was just thinking it's been a year since we had dinner together for the first time."

As she squeezed his hand, she said, "It is hard to believe. It does not feel like a year. I am glad Uri wrote the note."

"Me, too." He paused and squeezed her hand back. "I asked him, but he denies knowing anything about it."

"It was his handwriting."

Wolfe tilted his head. "It appeared to be his handwriting." He paused and studied the woman he was falling in love with. "Or was it?"

She gave him a mischievous grin.

"Nadia Picard, you wrote the note, didn't you?"

"I am surprised it took you a year to figure it out, Michael."

"Did he ask you to deliver it?"

"No, I volunteered."

"Why?"

"You were alone during Hannukah, as was I. I took a chance. During this past year, I discovered your reputation as a tough guy is a façade. You are actually a kind and compassionate man." She held his hand with both of hers. "Are you upset with me?"

He shook his head. "Not even a little."

Tele Aviv
December 2013

Wolfe lay in bed waiting for Nadia to finish her nightly shower. He heard her singing softly in French. A sign she was content and happy. When she emerged from the bathroom, she slipped under the covers and snuggled up next to him. He automatically placed his arm around her shoulders.

After several silent moments, he said, "I need to ask a favor."

"Sure, Michael. What is it?"

"How difficult would it be for you to do an inquiry on an individual in Madagascar?"

She raised up on one elbow. "Depends on who it is."

"An American expat named William Little."

"What do you want to know about him?"

"I need to know as much as possible. I know he lives on

an estate near the town of Toamasina, but exactly where is unknown."

"Why do you need to find him?"

"It's a matter of payback."

She remained silent for a moment. "What did he do?"

Wolfe proceeded to tell her.

Two weeks later, just before the New Year's holiday, Nadia extracted a flash drive from her purse. "Everything I was able to learn is on this." She held it up for him to see. "It seems he is quite the philanthropist. He gives to charities, helps raise money to build hospitals, and has been a member of the National Assembly for the past twelve years. In addition to all of his charitable work and public service, he takes kickbacks to the tune of millions of dollars per year."

"Really."

"Yes, he is considered one of the most corrupt politicians on the island."

"How does he keep getting reelected?"

"From what I could find, the people love him because he gets things they need done. But businessmen, law enforcement, and other politicians can't stand him."

"Huh." He paused as he contemplated these revelations. "Did you find out where he lives?"

"Yes, he has an enormous estate on the eastern coastline where he hosts huge parties on a regular basis." She paused. "Guess where he holds these gatherings?"

"I would have no idea."

"On a large open-air veranda attached to his house, which is next to the beach. There isn't a neighbor for kilometers. Plus, in that section of Madagascar, the beach is flat for thousands of meters in both directions."

"How about that."

Island of Madagascar
May 2014

The crosshair of the Leopold Scope centered on a tall man entertaining several guests on his expansive patio. Security guards patrolled the grounds next to the party. The patio hid behind a ten-thousand-square-foot mansion on the island's east side, south of the coastal city of Toamasina. The sniper's hide lay in a sand dune off the beach sixteen hundred meters from the patio. A gentle inland breeze drifted off the Indian Ocean. Michael Wolfe adjusted his scope to compensate for the wind.

The tall man entertaining on the porch was retired three-star General William Little who had basked in his wealth for twenty-two years and no longer worried about five ex-colleagues and his late trusted co-conspirator, Major Tucker, spilling their story to the FBI. Now in his mid-sixties, he was a politically powerful man on this island off the southeast coast of Africa.

Wolfe knew all of this. Four years earlier, FBI Agent Sean Kruger had revealed the man's location, a fact he had not known at the time. Time and planning were his allies. Officially, he was at a conference in Dubai. Unofficially, he was in Madagascar under one of his many false identities.

Little laughed at something when the trigger broke on the Barrett M82A1 sniper rifle. The .50 BMG round reached its target 1.87 seconds later and the general's head disappeared in a cloud of mist.

Satisfied with his efforts, Wolfe crawled down the

mound and ran toward a Jeep hidden in the dunes one hundred meters from his hide. Minutes later, he drove toward a small airport south of Toamasina where a Lear Jet owned by the Mossad waited for him. Payback for William Little, even twenty years after the fact, left him with a sense of peace he had not felt for years.

Chapter Seven

RURAL SOUTHWEST MISSOURI

Late Fall 2018

"Oh, Michael, it is a beautiful piece of land."

"I thought you might like it."

The newly engaged couple walked beside the asphalt runway, hand in hand, as he showed her the features of the twenty-five-acre plot. Pointing toward the west, he said, "It's basically a rectangle with trees extending 200 yards to the west. The runway extends, as you can see, almost to the southern tree line." He paused for a few moments as they continued their exploration. "I was a little surprised Rhonda called so fast with an offer on our land in Howell County."

"I wasn't. When we left her office, she said she already had several inquiries."

"Yeah, but that's standard real estate agent hyperbole."

"Be happy, Michael. The offer was more than the listed price." She drew closer to him and placed her head on his shoulder. "Are you sorry you sold your land?"

"A little, but not to the point I want to cancel the deal. It was the last connection I had to my grandfather."

Raising her head, she grasped his hand tighter as they walked. Nadia glanced back at the small hangar on the northern end of the runway. "I take it you have plans for a newer hangar."

"Yeah, and a bigger house. As soon as we close on the land next week, I have a contractor scheduled to erect a metal building with a second floor for an office and gun room."

"You said we." She turned to him.

"Yes, I said we. We're buying this together, Nadia. I really don't want to close on the property until we're married."

With a sly smile, she said, "And when will that be?"

"We have an appointment with a judge tomorrow."

She raised her eyebrows. "What if I want a traditional wedding?"

"Who would you invite?"

"You."

"Already planning to attend."

"I was teasing. I spoke to Joseph. He said he would like to host our wedding at his house and take care of the guests." She took a deep breath and let out a sigh. "I wish our parents were alive."

"So do I. Mom and Dad would have loved you."

Both continued to walk, their attention on the ground. After a few moments, she said, "Mine would have been honored to know you, Michael. My father was just like you. Stoic and quiet."

"If you want a traditional wedding, we will have one. Tell Joseph thank you and to go ahead and arrange it."

Silence ensued for a few minutes. Finally, she squeezed

his arm. "Thank you, Michael." She paused for a heartbeat. "I never want to leave this land. I love it here."

"Good because you're in charge of the house. I'll take care of the hangar, but the house is your project."

"I thought we were going to live in the one already here?"

"We will, at least until your new one can be built."

She actually jumped into his arms and squeezed him around the neck.

Five Days before Christmas, 2018

"Michael Wolfe, wilt thou have this woman to be thy wedded wife to live together after God's ordinance in the holy estate of matrimony? Wilt thou love her? Comfort her, honor and keep her, in sickness and in health, forsaking all others, and keeping thee only unto her as long as you both shall live?"

"I will."

"Nadia Picard, wilt thou have this man to be thy wedded husband to live together after God's ordinance in the holy estate of matrimony? Wilt thou love him? Comfort him, honor and keep him, in sickness and in health, forsaking all others, and keeping thee only unto him as long as you both shall live?"

"I will."

The minister paused. "Michael, do you have a ring?"

"Yes." He slipped the slim gold band on her finger and gazed into her eyes. "I am my beloved's, and my beloved is mine."

Nadia gave a slight gasp as she looked up from the ring

to Wolfe. As a tear slid down her eye, she whispered, "Thank you, Michael. That is the Jewish commitment. Something I did not expect."

The minister waited for her to finish speaking. He then said, "Nadia, do you have a ring?"

"Yes. I, Nadia, take you, Michael, to be my husband. I promise to be true to you in good times and in bad, in sickness and in health. I will love you and honor you all the days of my life."

He smiled as Nadia recited the words from his own childhood faith. She then slipped an identical ring to her own on his left ring finger.

The minister said in a louder voice, "Then by the authority entrusted to me by the State of Missouri, I pronounce you husband and wife." He raised his arms to address the small group gathered on Joseph's back deck. An unusually warm December evening allowed the simple ceremony to occur outside. "Be joyous, my friends, as I introduce for the first time, Mr. and Mrs. Michael Wolfe."

As everyone clapped, Nadia whispered into Michael's ear, "This is much better than a judge. Thank you for a traditional wedding."

"It was traditional in that we had friends and a real minister. Sorry, there aren't a lot of rabbis in Christian County."

"It is okay, Michael. We are married. That is all that matters."

Rural Southwest Missouri
Early Spring 2019

Wolfe parked the 1979 Beechcraft B55 Baron in its new hangar at the northern end of his two-thousand-foot newly resurfaced runway. Having stored the plane at a private airport near Branson, Missouri, he finally had easy access. The event created a sense of contentment and closure for him.

After purchasing the plane, sight unseen, from an estate sale in Atlanta in 2015, he had it shipped to an aircraft restoration company in Wichita, Kansas in several sections via flatbed trucks. Wolfe commissioned them to fully restore the plane and install modern avionics, electronics, engines, and props. With all the modifications, the plane flew better than when new.

He exited the aircraft and noticed Nadia standing off to the side, a worried expression on her face. When he had the plane secured, he exited and hurried to her side. "What's wrong?"

"Joseph called. He wants to meet with us at his place as soon as we can get there."

Wolfe did not respond immediately as he contemplated the implications.

Joseph's home, where Wolfe and Nadia were married, sat on a sprawling parcel of land in Christian County, south of Sparta and forty-five miles east of Wolfe's new property. The house, a modern rustic log structure with two stories and a wraparound wooden deck featured a massive front door. Rock pillars supported a deck surrounded by roughhewed railings. Sleeping quarters were on the second floor, with the living and kitchen areas on the first. A gazebo-like structure containing a breakfast nook featured prominently on the right side of the house.

Wolfe parked his Jeep Grand Cherokee behind Joseph's dark-gray Land Rover on the asphalt circle driveway in front of the residence.

Joseph Kincaid, currently the National Security Advisor for President Roy Griffin, rarely visited his property due to his commitments in Washington, DC. Tonight, though, would be an exception, as he stood on the porch and waved to his visitors when they stepped out of the Jeep. As always, Joseph, a man who resembled the actor Morgan Freeman more than a little, wore his trademark Navy blazer, white Dover dress shirt, sans a tie, khaki chino pants, bright socks, and scuffed brown loafers.

Concern filled Wolfe's thoughts about the sudden invitation as they approached the man on the porch.

"It's good to see you two." He shook Wolfe's hand and gave Nadia a peck on the cheek. "I appreciate both of you coming tonight on such short notice."

Nadia asked, "When did you get back, Joseph?"

"This afternoon. Something's come to my attention, and I believe both of you can be of assistance."

Wolfe glanced at his wife and then returned his attention back to his friend. "Okay, what is it?"

"Let's go in and I'll tell you."

Once inside, Joseph asked, "I just made a fresh pot of coffee. Can I get either of you a cup?"

Nadia shook her head, and Wolfe said, "Sure. What came to your attention?"

As he poured two mugs of coffee, Joseph said, "Mohammad Al-Qaedi."

Accepting the cup, Wolfe remained quiet, waiting for more information.

Joseph continued. "There is considerable Internet chatter going on right now about him. The CIA briefed me yesterday concerning the matter. After consulting with the president, I took a few days off to meet with you."

Wolfe folded his arms. "You're stalling, Joseph. You could have sent Jerry."

"I could have, but he doesn't have the clearance level for this information."

Both Wolfe and Nadia narrowed their eyes. "How can Jerry have a lower security clearance level than Nadia or me?"

"Because I bumped both of your levels up after the Gerald Reed affair."

Nadia said, "I am not sure that was a good thing."

Their host said, "Yes, it was a good thing. It means I can use both of you for more critical assignments."

She tilted her head and glared at Joseph. "I don't remember being asked if we wanted a higher security clearance. It could be bad for both of us."

"You two thinking of retiring?"

Wolfe said, "It's crossed our minds a few times."

"But?"

Nadia crossed her arms. "It did not stick—yet."

"Good." Taking a sip of his beverage, Joseph said, "The chatter concerning Al-Qaedi indicates he is planning something inside the United States."

Wolfe stopped, his coffee mug halfway to his lips. "Does the chatter indicate where?"

"No. Just a date."

"Great, when?"

"First two weeks in July."

"That narrows it down." The retired Marine raised the coffee mug and just before he took a drink, said, "What happens the first two weeks of July?"

Joseph said, "The Fourth of July comes to mind."

Wolfe said, "And the All-Star baseball game. It's in Cleveland this year."

Chapter Eight

CLEVELAND, OHIO

July 2019

The Great Lakes Waterway is a series of natural channels and manmade canals flowing from Lake Ontario to the Gulf of St. Lawrence connecting the upper North American lakes to the North Atlantic Ocean. Although the lakes are naturally connected, at one time, water travelers faced obstructions such as Niagara Falls and the rapids of the St. Mary's River.

One or more US Coast Guard icebreakers keep the water passage open during the fall and early winter. Afterward, shipping comes to a grinding halt during the coldest months of winter. During the summer months, the waterway possesses few obstacles for shipping.

On the first day of July, a bulk cargo vessel named *Shining Star* entered the causeway on its journey to Cleveland and other Great Lakes ports. In one of its holds, it carried a load of semolina for a local fresh pasta company. Buried in the middle of this wheat, placed there during a stop at the

Port of Alexandria in Egypt, lay a cache of weapons and explosives. The captain of this particular vessel held certain sympathies with the plight of disadvantaged groups around the world. It did not hurt that a large sum of money would be transferred into his bank account with the safe delivery of the package.

The intended recipient of this cache observed the ship through binoculars as it made slow progress through the Welland Canal on its journey from Lake Ontario to Lake Erie and its final destination of Cleveland.

The man watching *Shining Star's* progress was pleased. His careful and meticulous planning allowed the ship to sail into these waters without scrutiny.

His clean-shaven face hid the blackness of his beard. A round face and a thin aquiline nose hinted at his ancestry. His normally coal-black hair appeared light brown, thanks to a bottle of *Just for Men* hair coloring.

Mohammed Al-Qaedi finished studying the ship and then walked back to his rental car on the west bank of the Niagara River near the town of Fort Erie, Ontario. It would take him three and a half hours to drive across the Peace Bridge to the town of Buffalo, New York and then the two hundred miles on to Cleveland, Ohio.

The unloading of the ship and its clandestine cargo would be handled by others who were paid not to ask questions. Besides, being discovered in the United States might be dangerous for someone of his nationality and political persuasion.

Cleveland, OH
July 3

Jerry Griggs sat across from Wolfe and Nadia in the hotel breakfast area. He leaned forward and said in a low whisper, "Internet chatter is intensifying on a daily basis about something going to happen here in Cleveland."

Taking a sip of coffee, Wolfe contemplated Joseph's assistant. "Specifics, Jerry. We need specifics."

"Trust me, I'm trying to get them for you, Michael."

Nadia said, "Jerry, Cleveland is a big town. Unless we have more detailed information, Michael and I are basically looking for a needle in a hay bale."

Griggs frowned.

Wolfe said, "Stack, Jerry, haystack. I'm tired of sitting on my thumbs waiting for someone to come up with some intelligence. What about the docks? Any chatter about them?"

After a shake of his head, Griggs said, "No."

Wolfe folded his arms. "What exactly is the chatter saying, Jerry?"

"It keeps talking about something big. A big crowd is mentioned."

"Jerry, the only big crowd will be tomorrow night at the fireworks display and then on the eighth and ninth at the Major League Baseball All-Star Game."

"What did you say about the eighth? I thought the game was on the ninth?"

"It is. The home-run derby is the night before on the eighth. It is usually televised."

Griggs frowned at Wolfe. "Several of the intercepts mention Allah sending a fierce wind out of the north on the eighth to cleanse the Earth."

Wolfe closed his eyes and shook his head slightly. "Jerry, one of the hadiths of Islam concerns the wind."

"Okay, I know I'm supposed to know this, but what is a hadith?"

"A tradition or saying attributed to the Prophet Muhammad. The wind is considered one of Allah's creatures and one he controls. It can be a mercy or a torment. In this case, I would assume the reference indicates a torment."

"Well, now we know the date. But I don't understand what a fierce wind could reference."

"Think about it for a second. What does an explosion cause?"

"Ahh, crap. A fierce wind."

Wolfe nodded. "Exactly."

July 5, 2019
Friday

Robert Cormick, second generation Irish deputy dockmaster, known to his buddies as Bobby, studied the manifest for the cargo ship, *Shining Star*. Semolina, as a rule, did not get exported by Egypt. Few, if any, countries bordering the Mediterranean exported wheat. Olive oil, yes, but not wheat.

Also, as a rule, ships like *Shining Star* seldom, if ever, asked for specific dock workers to unload their cargo. The whole affair did not smell right. He picked up his phone and dialed his boss, dockmaster and fellow Irishman, Darin Sweeney.

"Darin, it's Bobby. What the hell is going on with the *Shining Star*?"

"Good morning to you, Bobby. Haven't got a clue what you're talking about. Want to explain?"

"Sorry, I'm looking over the manifest for the *Shining Star*. It's carrying wheat from Egypt and docked Wednesday. Because of the July 4th holiday it isn't scheduled to be unloaded until today. Plus, they are requesting a specific crew to unload their cargo."

"I'll grant you the request for a specific crew is unusual, but what's wrong with a cargo of wheat?"

"Egypt doesn't export wheat."

There was silence on the phone for about fifteen seconds. "Huh. Didn't know that."

"What do you want done?"

Sweeney said, "Have port security check it out."

"Thanks, that's what I hoped you would say."

July 6, 2019
Saturday

Bureaucratic regulations and the occurrence of a national holiday in the middle of the work week delayed port security from expediting an inspection crew to examine the wheat shipment. By the time a security guard from the Port Authority checked the cargo, the *Shining Star* had left the dock and was already halfway through the locks of Welland Canal on its way back to the North Atlantic.

Billy Monroe, a guard with the Cleveland Port Authority conducted a preliminary check of the wheat with his German shepherd. Almost as soon as the dog got within two feet, she flagged the load as suspicious. Monroe, a veteran retired military police sergeant with four tours in

Afghanistan, and his explosive-sniffing partner, Murphy, knew immediately something was wrong. He activated his radio. "Base, this is Billy, I'm at dock seven. I've got a 10-89."

"Billy, you've got what? Repeat."

"I have a 10-89. I need the bomb squad."

The Next Day

When Wolfe and Griggs were allowed to interview the security guard, the wheat delivered by the *Shining Star* remained in quarantine while Homeland Security clamped a gag order on any news or announcement about the incident.

Using his ID as US Marshal Patrick Ryan, Wolfe introduced himself to Monroe. After shaking hands, Wolfe asked, "Where'd you serve?"

"Afghanistan."

With a nod, Wolfe said, "So, you knew what your partner signaled?"

"Yeah, when I retired, they let me adopt Murphy. We both had a few years of service left in us, so we went to work for the Cleveland Port Authority. Murphy hit on the load immediately."

"Do they know how the explosives got out of the port?"

The sergeant handed Wolfe a printout of a security camera video. "The crew loaded it into the back of an old Chevy pickup with a camper shell and then someone drove it out the front gate. Right in front of God and everyone."

"How's that possible, Sergeant?"

"Happens all the time."

Studying the photo, Wolfe said, "Sometimes doing it that way works best. Don't hide it. Just do it out in the open." He paused. "Do they know how much the explosives weighed?"

"Five hundred pounds."

"That much?"

"Yeah. That's the difference between the registered weight of the load and what the wheat weighs now."

"Thanks, Sergeant. We'll need access to the original video."

"No problem."

With the information gleaned from the port security cameras, the Cleveland Police Department issued a BOLO order for the silver 2000 Chevy Silverado 1500. Numerous false alarms were received, but the real truck did not expose itself to scrutiny. This, Wolfe expected.

"They aren't going to drive it around Cleveland until they need it."

Griggs frowned. "The FBI is starting to believe it's a false alarm. They don't believe the truck exists. They think it left the area."

"The truck exists and it's here, Jerry. It's sitting in a garage somewhere waiting for the night of the eighth."

"So, what do we do?"

"The only thing we can do. Find it before it reaches the stadium."

July 8, 2019

Monday

Wolfe walked the perimeter of Progressive Field several times. With each pass, he judged the vulnerability of the various entrances. The main one at Ontario and Carnegie provided concrete bollards to prevent vehicles from charging through this vulnerable spot. Unfortunately, there were two which offered a determined suicide driver the opportunity to penetrate the stadium with a bomb-laden pickup. Only one entrance on Carnegie allowed easy access to a truck traveling at high speed on the main thoroughfare. The other vulnerable access point on Ontario could work, but it did not allow a vehicle to gain the necessary speed to breach deep into the building. He chose the one on Carnegie.

Jerry Griggs consulted with the Cleveland Police Department and the owner of the Cleveland Indians. He reported back to Wolfe neither believed the threat to be viable.

"You're kidding me, right?"

"The police have not spotted the vehicle and believe it is out of the area. Therefore, risk assessment has been downgraded."

"What did they expect, someone driving around Cleveland with five hundred pounds of high explosives in the truck bed?"

Griggs shrugged. "I have no comment."

"So that means, if I need to do anything, I'll have to be stealthy."

"Invisible would be a more accurate term."

Wolfe stared at a point over Griggs' head. "I think there's only one way to come in and have the speed needed to penetrate the stadium."

"Southeast?"

"Yeah, if I position myself too far away, I could run the risk of missing him. No farther than East 14th would be my guess."

"Not a lot of places between there and Carnegie to set up a sniper hide, Michael."

"I know." He paused and opened his phone. He started checking the area on Google Maps. "There's an air quality testing site on the northwest corner of Orange and 14th. If I remember correctly, it has a wood deck on top where all the equipment is exposed to the elements. There's a wood railing around it that will give me a little cover. Not much but a little. I could set up there and keep tabs on 14th to the north and Orange to the east."

"What if you're wrong?"

"I can't think that way, Jerry. I'm not wrong."

"What are you going to do?"

"Take out the driver and then the motor. If it explodes, there isn't a lot around there to damage."

"Except an air-quality testing site."

"Yeah, well, there is that."

Chapter Nine

INTERSECTION OF ORANGE AND 14TH, CLEVELAND, OH

July 8th

Wolfe settled behind his trusty .50 BMG Barret M82A1 sniper rifle with the factory-installed suppressor. His presence on the wooden deck of the air-quality testing site obscured by a woodland ghillie suit. Positioning himself early on the deck had been hampered by the presence of a City of Cleveland-owned white Chevy pickup.

As the festivities before the home-run derby commenced, Wolfe lay in the tall weeds west of the area, waiting for the driver of the pickup to leave. As seven o'clock approached, he waited as the man exited the chain-link compound and padlocked the entry door. After the truck drove away, Wolfe crawled closer and paused for a break in traffic on 14th Street. Once it occurred, he rushed to the gate, snipped the lock with his bolt cutters, and slipped inside. After quickly ascending the stairs to the deck above the station, he positioned himself facing the southeast.

He tapped his headset and said, "In position. Update."

Griggs asked, "What's traffic like your position?"

"Nominal, everyone's already at the stadium."

"Nothing on east 14th."

Wolfe said, "Nadia?"

"One and a half kilometers southeast of your location, nothing."

"Good. Keep me posted."

Fifteen minutes passed as Wolfe steeled himself to a long wait. The crowd from the stadium could be heard cheering as the players fought for the title of home-run king for 2019. Sunset would occur at 9:03 p.m. Light faded as the time grew near. At 9:10, he heard a squelch in his ear.

Nadia said, "Target is one kilometer, your position. Repeat, one kilometer, followed by two CPD vehicles."

"How far back?"

"Four hundred meters."

"Roger."

Griggs said on the radio, "Lots of CPD traffic converging on your location."

"Roger."

Ten seconds later, Wolfe detected the first sirens approaching and the sound of a vehicle motor under strain coming closer.

He took a breath and let it out slowly as the silver 2000 Chevy Silverado first appeared in his scope. He focused on the driver and, as the trigger broke, he moved the scope to the front of the vehicle and let the rifle bark again. Not stopping to admire his work, he crawled toward the stairs and made good his exit from the deck atop the air-quality testing station.

Rushdi al-Sami felt sweat leaking down his forehead as he accelerated the truck toward the stadium. Three Cleveland police cars followed, their sirens blaring. Using his sleeve, he wiped the perspiration from his brow and briefly entertained letting them catch up and stop him. Almost immediately, he dismissed the idea as he knew he would not survive an encounter with the American police. Particularly when they discovered what was underneath the camper shell. The imams at his mosque assured him he would be in paradise at the end of his drive. But a figment of doubt still tickled his subconscious. His biggest fear centered on failure. If he did not finish his mission now, he would be chastised by the members of his congregation for the rest of his days. This caused him to press the accelerator to the floor.

His thoughts and doubts ended suddenly as the glass of his windshield shattered and blackness overtook him. Less than two seconds later, a fifty-caliber BMG round passed through the radiator and cracked the block. As hot coolant hissed out from under the hood, the engine ceased. The truck veered to the right at the intersection of 14th and Orange. Unimpeded by any obstacles or other vehicles, it crashed headlong into the concrete pillars of an overpass north of Orange on 14th.

Wolfe watched as the truck plowed into a bridge support column under the overpass at full speed. He flinched at the expected explosion, but other than the sound of metal impacting concrete and screaming sirens, he heard nothing. Emerging from the air-quality testing facility, he raced to the street as Nadia screeched to a halt at the curb. He scrambled into the passenger seat of their rented Ford Explorer, and she accelerated west, away from the scene. Turning to him, she smiled. "Nice shot."

He nodded, residual adrenalin triggering rapid breathing. "Thanks for the ride."

"Any time."

Following at a safe distance behind the police cars chasing the truck, Mohammad Al-Qaedi observed their brake lights flare and then move to the right. He slowed as he approached an intersection two thirds of a kilometer from the stadium. His anger grew as he passed the horrific crash. He realized the money, time, and planning spent getting the explosives into the United States were a wasted effort. The truck had not detonated on impact. If the explosion had occurred at the overpass, he could have claimed responsibility. This would have given him a small victory in his fight against the United States. Even that outcome was denied him. Slapping his palm against the steering wheel, he drove forward.

Exiting Orange Avenue onto east 9th street, Al-Qaedi observed the speed limits and drove away from the thwarted terrorist plot.

Cleveland, OH
July 9th

Daylight leaked through the curtains of their hotel room as Nadia nudged her husband. "You are snoring."

"I don't snore."

She laughed. "If you say so." She threw the covers back and walked to the bathroom. Still groggy from a hard sleep, Wolfe found the TV remote and hit the power button. Scrolling through the channels, he found a local news station and then checked the digital clock on the nightstand, 6:47 a.m.

Nadia crawled back into bed. "Any news?"

"Don't know. Just started watching."

"Michael, why did the truck not explode?"

"No idea." On the TV screen appeared a reporter standing in front of the air-quality testing station. "Maybe this will tell us."

The report said, "Last night after a lengthy police chase, the driver of a stolen pickup truck crashed into the pillars under the I-77 exit near Progressive Field. The driver died on impact, and his identity has not been released."

Wolfe frowned. "I suspected they would whitewash this. No mention of the explosives and no indication the guy died from a gunshot."

She snuggled against him. "In other words, it never happened."

"Nope, and we were never here."

"Joseph?"

"Probably. The FBI and the Cleveland police were never on board with the story, so they'll cover it up to hide the truth. If the real story came out, they'd look bad."

"In other words, it's time for us to go home."

"Yes, we'll head to the airport as soon as we can get ready and check out."

Three hours later, Wolfe's Beechcraft B55 Baron lifted off from Cleveland Burke Lakefront airport on their journey back to southern Missouri. With a scheduled refueling stop in Champaign, Illinois, Wolfe felt a sense of relief to be out of Cleveland.

As they flew over the rural countryside of Ohio, Nadia asked, "What's next, Michael? We are getting a little old to be acting like we're in our twenties."

"I tend to agree with you, Nadia. But Jerry indicated he had another request for my services when we get back. They want me to travel to Mexico."

"Why?"

"Something about someone causing trouble down there."

"Wonderful. Am I involved?"

"It didn't sound like it."

"Good, I have things to do at the house."

Wolfe grew quiet as he piloted the plane on a southwesterly course. "They're still a threat, Nadia. We got lucky in Cleveland. If the explosives in the truck had gone off, there would have been unacceptable casualties. Traffic was heavy on the overpass above the crash."

"I know." She glanced over at him and smiled. "I am French, Michael. I like to complain."

He returned the smile. "I know, one of the many things I love about you."

Later That Same Day

Wolfe finished his post-flight maintenance on the Beechcraft, closed the hangar door and walked toward the house. Just as he approached the back door, his cell phone alerted him of a text message. He checked. A number appeared and the words, *secure phone 10 minutes press 1 for yes, 2 for no.*

Pressing the number one, he entered the house, went to his office and opened their laptop. Exactly eight minutes later, a VoIP call came in.

"This is Wolfe."

The familiar voice of Joseph Kincaid said, "Congratulations on a successful trip to Cleveland."

"Who came up with the stolen pickup story?"

"That was actually Jerry's idea. FBI liked it, and the CPD went along. Both agencies wanted to avoid any bad press."

"Which they would have received. Did they determine why it didn't detonate on impact?"

"Yeah, they missed a bullet on that one. Whoever set up the wiring on the explosives did it wrong. Even if he had crashed into the stadium, it wouldn't have gone off."

"Why the call, Joseph?"

"Two things. The president sends his thanks about Cleveland, and I have an urgent request from the National Security Agency."

"What about Al-Qaedi?"

"He's disappeared off everyone's radar."

After several moments of silence, Wolfe finally said, "Alright, what's the urgent request?"

"The NSA has intercepted several phone calls concerning POTUS. That's why we need you in Mexico. It seems there will be a meeting in the Sierra Madre mountains between two cartels about joining forces. They want to figure out how to assassinate the president of the United States."

Part II

Chapter Ten

SOUTHWEST MISSOURI

Present Day

Sweat drenched his forehead as he bolted upright, the darkness of the bedroom broken only by the faint glow of the digital clock on his nightstand, 3:34 a.m. Nadia stirred next to him. She mumbled something unintelligible but remained asleep. Taking a deep breath, details of the images faded, but the theme he knew all too well. Quietly pushing the covers aside, he walked out of their bedroom to the kitchen.

The new house, replacing the previous one destroyed by a crazy Irishman and his daughter, still seemed unfamiliar to him. Nadia supervised the final construction process while he and Ian McGill were in Iran for three months. The fact Nadia designed it and handled every aspect of building the home made it even more precious to him.

After filling a glass with cool water from the dispenser in the refrigerator door, he walked out onto the back deck and gazed at the stars. The passage of time slowed. How long he stood there, he had no idea. Reality returned as the back door opened. He turned to find Nadia there with a furrowed brow.

"Are you okay?"

He nodded.

"I heard you get up, but when you didn't come back to bed, I got worried."

"No need. Just a dream."

She folded her arms. "Michael, you are having more and more of those types of dreams lately. Maybe it is time you talk to your doctor?"

Shaking his head, he said, "No, what I need to do is stop going to Iran."

"You have never told me about what happened."

"Nothing to tell." He paused, took a deep breath, and let it out slowly. "That's not exactly correct. There's nothing I want to talk about. I would just as soon forget the whole experience."

She walked over to him, placed her arms around his waist and leaned her head against his chest. "If you ever want to, I'm here to listen."

He returned the embrace. "I know."

They stayed in each other's arms for several minutes. The peace and calmness of her touch allowed his mind to clear as he inhaled the familiar scent of her shampoo. The nocturnal sounds of katydids and tree frogs provided a familiar background symphony to their embrace. He did not want the moment to end.

She interrupted by whispering, "Is it time for us to retire from this silly game we play?"

The stillness of the early morning hour and the sounds

of the nocturnal creatures inhabiting the surrounding woodlands helped ease his troubled mind. Wolfe said, "Yeah, it probably is."

"How often do these events occur, Michael?"

"I haven't experienced any for a long time. But now they're occurring frequently."

"How long ago?"

"After I got back from Desert Storm in the early 90s, they eventually went away."

"How frequent are they now?"

Taking a deep breath, Wolfe let it out slowly. "Nightly."

Doctor Vince Harmon, a retired Marine Corps physician, studied the computer monitor in the examination room. "Your blood pressure is elevated."

Wolfe nodded.

"I hate to start you on medication. Once you start, they're hard to stop."

"Then, let's not."

"When was the last time you took a vacation?"

"What's that?"

Harmon chuckled. "Kind of what I thought." He studied Wolfe for a moment. "I can put you in touch with a doctor I know with Veteran's Affairs. He specializes in PTSD."

"No." Wolfe shook his head. "I prefer talking to you."

"I'll take that as a compliment. But I don't have the expertise he does."

"That's okay, I'll still stick with you."

"Okay." He typed something on the keyboard of the in-room computer station. "There doesn't seem to be any physiological reason for your sleep disruptions, except possibly the high blood pressure. What I would like to see you do is start a regimen of physical activity and take a vacation. Plus, I'm also going to prescribe ten days of a mild sleeping aid."

"I've got some trees on the property I need to clear."

"Perfect. Now, what about the vacation?"

"I'll stop answering my phone."

"Even better."

Numerous trees at the southern end of Wolfe's runway posed a potential problem during landing procedures in a strong wind. His solution? Take them down. The wood from the fallen trees would not be wasted, owing to Nadia's foresight. A Buck Stove capable of heating the entire house made it into the final construction plans. With twenty acres of land, of which 75 percent were thick Ozark woodlands, there would be plenty of fuel for the woodburning stove for the foreseeable future.

With solar panels installed on the hangar's roof and the geothermal heating and cooling system, the home could stay off the grid indefinitely, if needed. Water from a deep well and Internet via satellite finished off the system. This allowed Wolfe and Nadia to be independent of any utility company, except the one providing their satellite service.

The physical exertion required to fell seven mature oak trees and the mild sleep-enhancing prescription allowed Wolfe to have several uninterrupted nights of sleep. On the third night, Nadia woke him at 2:19 a.m.

She rose to one elbow and gently shook his right arm. "Michael—Michael."

"Huh?"

"You are having a bad dream again."

His eyes blinked several times trying to emerge from the fog of sleep. "I was?"

"Yes, you almost kicked me out of bed."

"Sorry, wasn't on purpose."

She lay down and snuggled against him. "I know. After the last two nights, I thought you had them under control."

"Guess not." He placed his arm around her shoulder. "I keep seeing the bus explode over and over. The locations are always different, but the face in the window is always the same."

"Sara?"

"No, yours."

She did not respond immediately. "I'm sorry, Michael."

"Not your fault." He grew silent as they lay in each other's arms. "I haven't told you, but it's been such a long time, I can't even remember what Sara looks like."

She rose to one elbow again. "What about pictures?"

"When I was told to leave Israel, I left them behind. I don't have one anymore."

She remained quiet with this revelation, not sure how to respond. It was the first time since their marriage he had even mentioned his long-dead first wife. Lowering herself, she placed her head on his chest. They remained like that until she felt his breathing slow and grow more rhythmic. Soon, she, too, drifted off to sleep.

The following morning, Wolfe remained asleep as she left their bed to make coffee. When she returned, she found him sitting on the side, his head in his hands.

"Michael, what is wrong?"

Looking up, he smiled. "Nothing. I felt like I actually got some rest last night."

Sitting next to him, she leaned her head on his shoulder. "You did. After I woke you from your nightmare, you settled down and slept soundly."

"You woke me up?"

"Yes."

"When?"

"Around two."

Taking a deep breath, he shook his head. "I don't remember. This is starting to get annoying, Nadia. I've never experienced anything like this in my life."

"We are both getting older, Michael. Age can affect sleep."

"I know, but this was a sudden onset. It's not supposed to happen that way."

"It did not start until you returned from Iran."

"I'm aware of that."

"So, what are we going to do to help you?"

Wolfe took his eyes off Nadia and concentrated on a point on the wall. "It's something I'll have to work out myself."

She folded her arms. "Michael Wolfe, I am your wife. Do not dismiss me like I am not here."

He faced her once again. Long dark hair framed a scowl and fell provocatively around her shoulders. Her beauty shocked him and gave him a sudden insight into the cause of his sleeplessness. "I'm not dismissing you, Nadia. It just dawned on me why I am having these dreams. I'm scared of losing you."

The scowl softened, and she moved closer to him. Putting her arms around his waist, she placed her head against his shoulder. "There is very little chance of that happening."

Returning the embrace, he took a deep breath and buried his face in her hair. "Even a small chance scares me."

She raised her head to look him in the eyes. "Let's make that no chance." She paused and gave him a soft smile. "Coffee is ready, and I've warmed some croissants. Let's go sit on the deck."

Chapter Eleven

SOUTHWEST MISSOURI

Wolfe wiped his brow with a towel and leaned the wood maul against a stack of firewood. He paused from splitting logs to observe the dark-gray Range Rover turn onto his asphalt driveway from the county road in front of his house. He knew only one individual who owned one of these sleek, sturdy SUVs: Joseph Kincaid.

He wiped his hands as he walked toward the vehicle now parked in the paved area between his house and the hangar. Joseph stepped out and waved as Michael approached.

"Thought you were in DC, Joseph."

As the two men shook hands, Joseph said, "Taking a few days off. Mary is growing tired of Washington and wanted some peace and quiet. So, here we are."

Chuckling, Wolfe said, "Do you really expect me to believe that?"

"No, but it is the truth." He paused for a moment and surveyed the new house. "This is the first time I been here since you finished the place. It appears Nadia made a few improvements."

"She finished it while I was in Iran. But you knew that." He paused. "She made a few changes I totally agree with, plus she added a few upgrades."

"I like the planters in front. I assume they are hardened concrete and rebar."

"You would be correct to assume so. We decided having someone drive their SUV into the front of the house was not something we wanted to repeat."

Joseph walked toward the deck attached to the rear of the house. "Is it off the grid?"

"Completely. Solar power, geothermal heating and cooling, deep well, and wood heat back up. Plus, we're using tricks JR taught us several years ago with the satellite Internet."

Joseph continued his walk around the house as if inspecting it. They were both quiet during the trek. When they were near the parking area again, he spoke. "What happened to you and McGill in Iran?"

"Why do you ask?"

"Chapman called and told me he is concerned about Ian."

"How so?"

"He's bordering on catatonic."

"It wasn't the best trip I've ever taken."

"Someone told me you aren't sleeping well."

"Nadia?"

"No, she would never betray your trust. Your doctor called me."

"How…" Wolfe shook his head. "Never mind, I forget you know everyone. What about HIPAA law confidentiality?"

The only answer Wolfe received was a sly smile.

"Don't worry, I'll work through it."

Placing his hand on Wolfe's arm, Joseph asked, "Are you two thinking about retiring?"

"The thoughts crossed our minds."

"Don't. At least, not yet. McGill is flying over and will be here tomorrow. You and Nadia need to pick him up at the airport. Then bring him out to my place for dinner. Chapman is already there."

"I thought Mary—"

"She and Chapman's wife went to Branson today."

"I've never met Jonathan Chapman."

As Joseph walked back to his Range Rover. He said, "You will tomorrow."

Before he could shut the door, Wolfe asked, "What happens if we don't show up?"

"You will." Joseph gave Wolfe a half grin and closed the door to the Range Rover.

Ian McGill threw his duffel bag onto the driver's side rear seat as he slipped into the Grand Cherokee behind Nadia. "Bloody nice of you to pick me up, Michael."

"My pleasure, Ian. How've you been?"

"I imagine about as well as you have."

Nadia twisted in her seat and glared at the retired SAS sergeant major. "He hasn't been doing well at all. Maybe you'll tell me what happened in Iran."

McGill gave her a tired smile and then directed his attention out the passenger window. "Just where the hell in this huge country are we?"

Nadia threw her hands up and started spewing French expletives.

Wolfe waited until his wife grew quiet. "About 650 kilometers southwest of the geological center of the country."

"Kind of what I figured. It took almost five hours to get here from JFK." He continued to observe the countryside. "What we flew over was beautiful."

"This part of the state can be pretty. However, there are sections that aren't."

"How far to your place?"

"About forty-five minutes. We're kind of isolated."

"Good."

"Did you know Chapman was here?"

McGill didn't answer right away. Finally, he said, "So I heard."

Wolfe checked his friend in the rearview mirror. They locked eyes for a knowing second, and Wolfe asked, "So, why is Chapman here, and why did they drag you seven thousand kilometers to meet him?"

"Because I bloody told him to take the job and stuff it."

Laughing out loud, Wolfe glanced at McGill again. "Good for you." Returning his attention to the highway, he continued, "How long you staying?"

"Might never go back." He paused for a moment. "Depends."

"Depends on what?"

"If I find someplace around here to buy."

Raising his eyebrows, Wolfe's eyes found Nadia, who was already studying him. When she nodded slightly, he said, "We know a good real estate broker who can help you. She's the same one who found our place."

"Is that the same thing as an estate agent."

Wolfe returned his attention to McGill's reflection. "Pretty much, only over here, they have to attend classes and get a license to do it."

"I'd like to meet this person. Bloody good."

Wolfe brought his Jeep to a halt behind Joseph's Range Rover parked in the log home's circle drive. He turned in his seat to face McGill sitting in the back. "You haven't said a word since we left the house, Ian."

"Nothing to say. This is bloody going to be a waste of time."

"Don't say that. Joseph always cooks on his grill for these types of occasions, and his steaks are among the best I've ever had."

"Hope he has lots of scotch."

"Glenfiddich as a rule."

"My opinion of Kincaid just went up a notch."

"He's a good man, Ian, and a good friend when I needed one."

"Have you ever met Chapman, Michael?"

"Haven't had the pleasure yet."

"Apparently, they are two of a kind. Only Chapman can be a bit overbearing at times."

"So can Joseph."

"Well…" McGill opened his door to exit the Jeep. "Let's get this over with."

An hour later, after introductions and McGill's second Glenfiddich, Jonathan Chapman took him aside and asked, "Now that you're here, are you still hell-bent on living in the States?"

"More so now than before."

Taking a deep breath, Chapman closed his eyes for a brief moment. "We should never have sent you back into Iran."

"It's time, Major. It wasn't just Iran. It's this whole bloody terrorist thing. We get rid of one, and two others pop up to take his place." He paused and took a sip of his drink. "Afraid you'll have to fight them without me."

"What the hell happened to you two over there?"

McGill studied his glass. "I need a wee bit more scotch. Can I get you another?"

Chapman shook his head, and McGill wandered back inside the house.

Wolfe noticed his friend heading toward the sliding glass door and casually moseyed over to where Chapman stood. He said, "Ian is beginning a search for land to buy. Did he tell you?"

"Yes." Chapman brought his attention away from the sliding glass door and studied Wolfe. "Joseph informed me you were thinking about retiring."

Wolfe said, "Thought crossed my mind."

"Ian won't tell me what happened in Iran. Will you?"

The corner of Wolfe's mouth twitched. "Nothing to tell. We went in, did our job, and got out. End of story."

"I understand your first wife's name was Sara, correct?"

Wolfe nodded.

"And that she was killed by a suicide bomber in Haifa."

"She was."

"We know that Mohammad Al-Qaedi built the bomb based on a design given to Hamas by Danny McCaffrey."

"So, I've been told."

"Then you and Ian have something else in common."

Taking a sip of his drink, Wolfe kept his eyes locked on Chapman. "What's that?"

"Ian was engaged to a Spanish woman he met in 1999. On March 11, 2004, she was one of the 193 souls killed in the Madrid train bombings."

An eyebrow rose as Wolfe listened.

"Jamal Ahmidan, also known by the name El Chino, bought the explosive, called Goma-2 ECO, illegally from a mine in northern Spain. He used it to fashion backpack bombs. They were based on a design given to him by Mohammed Al-Qaedi."

"Where are you going with this, Jonathan?"

"Let me finish. On Saturday, April third of the same year, Spanish police stormed a Leganes, Spain apartment where Ahmidan and another member of his group were building more bombs. Leganes is south of Madrid. They committed suicide by detonating the explosives. The blast also killed a policeman. McGill was acting as a consultant to the Spanish police at the time. The policeman killed was a friend of Ian's."

Wolfe blinked.

"So, you see, Michael, Ian has some unsettled business with Al-Qaedi, just as you have."

"Let me guess, MI6 knows where Mohammed Al-Qaedi is located, and you want both of us to go after him."

"Unfortunately, we have no idea where he is. There were rumors floating around claiming he died in a drone strike in 2013 near Tora Bora, Afghanistan."

"He didn't. He's alive."

"Yes, we know."

"Then, why the story?"

"Just a reminder that you both have unfinished business with him."

Wolfe did not offer an immediate response. Finally, he said, "I'll speak to him."

"Good. Joseph and I would hate to lose all of the experience you and Ian bring to the party."

"I said I would talk to him. Don't celebrate yet."

Chapter Twelve

SOUTHWEST MISSOURI

One Month Later

"What do you think, Michael?"

Wolfe noticed his friend McGill held the hand of a woman very close to his own age, Lori Shepard. The real estate agent who Nadia introduced McGill to four weeks earlier.

"It's beautiful, Ian. I particularly like the stream running through the middle. How many acres are here, Lori?"

"There's a total of 150, but the owner wants to sell it in fifteen-acre plots. This is the most picturesque of the ten. Plus, I think it possesses the best building lot."

Nadia walked back toward them from the crest of the ridge to the northwest.

"Oh, Michael, this is a beautiful piece of land. I am jealous." She turned her attention to Lori and said, "Why did you not show this to Michael and me?"

The real estate agent said, "Because it didn't have a

runway. I specifically remember Michael telling me he had to have room for a runway."

With a pretend pout, Nadia hugged Michael's arm. "I guess that means I can't be jealous now, can I?"

Lori continued, "Besides, it wasn't for sale when you two were looking."

Kneeling next to the stream, Wolfe put his hand in the water. "It's cold. Where does the stream originate, Lori?"

She pointed to the north. "About a mile from here. There are natural springs all over this area."

As he stood, Wolfe wiped his hands on his jeans and said to McGill, "That means there's a good chance you have an aquifer underground. Good for drilling a deep well. I also suggest geothermal heating and cooling."

Tilting his head, McGill asked, "Why would I need that?"

Pointing toward the south, Wolfe continued. "You have an open southern exposure. Solar panels can provide the electricity you'll need, and a geothermal system will replace a heating and air-conditioning system. It can pay for itself in a matter of years and will be a lot less expensive than having a propane tank filled every six months. You can supplement it with a woodstove if needed. Most of the winter storms in this region sweep off the plains of Kansas and blow in from the northwest. You have a natural windbreak with that crest. I'd say build a partially earth-sheltered home close to where we're standing. If you do, you'll have a self-contained house that can be kept off the grid."

Lori frowned. "Why would Ian want to stay off the grid?"

McGill patted her hand. "Privacy, me love. Privacy."

With a nod, Wolfe said, "If they can't find you, they can't surprise you."

"I still don't understand. Why would Ian not want to be found?"

The ex-SAS sergeant major sighed. "All my life, I've had to be available on a moment's notice. Available to fly to gawd knows where to protect her majesty's realm or whim. I'm tired of it. I don't want to be found anymore. Sorry, Lori. I hope you can live with that."

She wrapped her arms around McGill and placed her head on his shoulder.

Lori Shepard, a native of Southwest Missouri, whose paternal Scottish grandparents hailed from Inverness, stood three inches shorter than McGill's five-foot-ten frame. Her sandy-brown hair and green eyes were almost the same color as Ian's. During their first date, a dinner at a small bistro in Springfield, they learned her grandparents had known Ian's grandparents. This fact helped solidify their relationship. Where Nadia was slender and athletic in build, Lori trended more toward a healthy buxom figure.

During their first date, Lori learned Ian also hailed from the Scottish Highlands and was a retired sergeant major with the elite Special Air Service. While McGill did not go into explicit details, he told her he had been involved in every hotspot the members of Parliament had committed the United Kingdom to during the past two and a half decades. Now in his mid-forties, he maintained the appearance of a man ten years his junior. His light-brown hair, which he wore short, showed no signs of gray. A closely cropped beard adorned his oval face, and his green eyes observed the world through rimless glasses supported by a long and narrow nose.

Lori Shepard had been smitten with him at their first meeting. And he with her.

On the drive back to their place in Christian County, Wolfe asked Nadia, "Did you expect Lori and Ian to hit it off so well?"

"I am French, Michael. I am the perfect matchmaker."

"Bullshit."

With a laugh, she shook her head. "No, I didn't. But she is a beautiful woman, and he has a certain ruggedness women find attractive."

"Do you?" He said this with a grin.

With a deadpan gaze, she said, "I fell in love with a man who makes Ian's ruggedness appear feminine."

With a chuckle, he said, "I thought you loved me."

"Je parle de toi, imbécile."

Wolfe laughed out loud.

The drive returned to silence as they headed north. Five minutes later, Nadia said, "Are you expecting more surprises from our past?"

"I hope not, but you never know. Ian is concerned about it. He told me so the first night after we got out of Iran."

"What did he say?"

"Nothing specific, but he's been a troubleshooter for MI6 for the past decade. Like you and me, he's made his fair share of enemies."

"Michael, what happened to you two in Iran?"

He shot a quick glance at her and then returned his attention to the highway. After taking a deep breath and letting it out slowly, he said, "It's not what happened to us, it's what we witnessed. I'll tell you when we get home."

At that exact moment, Wolfe's cell phone chirped. He checked the multimedia LCD display, recognized the number, and pressed the accept call button on the steering wheel. "Hello."

"Are you two at home?"

"Good afternoon, Jerry."

"Are you home?" His tone was unusually serious.

"No. Why?"

"I'm in town and need to talk to you and Nadia."

"Again, why?"

"Are you at your house?"

"Not at the moment."

"When will you be back."

"An hour."

"See you then."

The call ended, and he glanced at Nadia. "Now, what the hell was that all about?"

She shrugged. "Who knows? I thought you told Jerry and Joseph we were retired?"

"I did. Obviously, nobody listened."

"Why did you say an hour? We're only a few miles from the house."

"We need to make sure we're ready."

An hour later, as Jerry Griggs sat at the kitchen table, Wolfe poured water into the Cuisinart coffeemaker. "What's the emergency, Jerry?"

Griggs sat with his hands clasped together in front of him on the table, his usual cheery expression absent. "Where's McGill?"

Removing his attention from the coffeemaker, Wolfe

said, "At this precise moment, I have no idea."

"But you've seen him."

"I didn't say that. I said, I don't know where he is right now. Why?"

"State Department is revoking his visa."

"Why?"

"Above my pay grade."

Folding his arms, Wolfe paused for a few moments. "Wrong answer, Jerry. Until you answer my question, I'm not answering yours."

Raising his arms with his palms out, Griggs sighed. "I'm just the messenger, Michael. They didn't tell me why."

"Here's a message for you, Mr. Messenger. Until whoever tells me why they revoked his visa, I'll never know his location. Is that clear enough?"

After a long pause while he studied Wolfe, Griggs clasped his hands again and took a deep breath. After letting it out, he said, "Chapman needs him in London. Chatter on the Internet is pointing toward an attack by Mohammad Al-Qaedi on Parliament."

"That wasn't so hard, now, was it?"

Without taking his eyes off Wolfe, Griggs continued, "The chatter also involves you."

"How?"

"It seems the Iranians know who destroyed their bioweapon stockpiles. And they are extremely pissed off."

"So?"

"Washington doesn't want some jihadist wandering around the US seeking to avenge Iran's loss. That could cause collateral damage."

"McGill's retired, or did everyone conveniently forget that?"

"You of all people should know by now that folks like us never actually retire from this business."

"What does Joseph say about it?"

Griggs tapped his finger on the table and pursed his lips but did not answer.

"In other words, this was his idea."

"Not really."

"Well, you helped me make up my mind. Nadia and I are now officially retired."

Chapter Thirteen

LONDON

Jonathan Chapman peered over his wire-rimmed glasses at his assistant. "Have you heard anything about McGill?"

"No, sir."

"Damn."

"I spoke to Mr. Kincaid's assistant, Griggs, this morning. Apparently, this Wolfe character is keeping mum on McGill's whereabouts."

"Not surprising." He paused for a moment. "They became quite the chums during their two trips to Iran."

Noah Anderson stood in front of Chapman's desk, at parade rest, his hands behind his back. He waited while the newly appointed director of MI6 tapped his index finger on his lips.

Returning his attention to a stack of files on his desk, Chapman said, "Thank you, Noah. Please close the door behind you."

This was the assistant's signal the interview was over. He briskly walked out of the office. As the door closed, Chapman studied the desk phone. After checking the small clock next to it, he picked up the handset and punched in a number he knew by heart. The call was answered on the third ring.

"Good morning, Jonathan."

"Afternoon here, Joseph."

"Heard you were finally made director. Congratulations."

"Sometimes, one needs to be careful of what one strives for. One might actually achieve the goal."

"I've heard that."

"I need your intervention in a developing delicate situation, old boy."

"And what might that be?"

"It is imperative we get in touch with Ian McGill. He has disappeared into the backwaters of your country."

Aware of the situation, Joseph asked, "It's a big country, Jonathan. Easy to find places to hide. Why do you need to talk to him?"

"Michael Wolfe seems to know where he is but is not sharing the information."

"Sounds like Michael. You didn't answer my question. Why do you need to talk to McGill?"

"One of the high-ranking Iranian ayatollahs has declared Jihad on McGill and has tasked Mohammed Al-Qaedi with carrying out the mission. We are not sure why, but it apparently has something to do with the 2004 Madrid train bombings. While there's no direct evidence of Iran being connected to the incident, McGill became involved with the investigation. His fiancée was killed in the attack, and he volunteered to help with the inquiry. This is where he and Mohammed Al-Qaedi first encountered each other. Plus, other chatter is indicating Al-Qaedi may be headed for London."

"This isn't the first time I've been told McGill and Al-Qaedi have a history."

"I'm sure it isn't."

"So does Michael."

"Oh dear. Care to enlighten me."

"Al-Qaedi built the bomb that killed his wife on a bus in Haifa, December of 2001."

"Do they know this about each other?"

"Jonathan, I wouldn't know. Michael has never spoken to me about it. The only reason I know is Uri Ben-David told me."

"McGill is the same way. I can't recall him ever mentioning it."

"Was Wolfe included in the declaration?"

"No, that's why we don't suspect it is due to their incursion into Iran earlier this year."

"Why McGill, then?"

"We don't know that, either. Thus, the reason we need him back in London. We need to understand what he knows and why, after all these years, the Iranians suddenly have their hair on fire about him."

"I'll talk to Michael."

"Thank you, Joseph."

Wolfe checked the caller ID on his cell phone and accepted the call. "Hello."

"Michael, it's Joseph. How are you today?"

With a chuckle, Wolfe answered, "I don't know where McGill is."

"How do you know that was what I called about?"

"Well, Griggs has called me every hour on the hour,

asking the same question. I figured you would eventually call."

"They need him in London."

"Did anyone bother to ask him if he cares what they need?"

"It's more critical than we were originally led to believe."

"What could be that critical? He's retired."

"An ayatollah has declared Jihad on him and his family."

Wolfe laughed out loud. "Seriously, Joseph. You think that will concern him? Besides, he doesn't have any family left. His brother is dead, as are his parents. They're going to have to come up with something more menacing than that to get him back to London."

"You remember the Madrid train bombing?"

Wolfe hesitated. "Yeah. What about it?"

"McGill lost his fiancée in the event. While I don't have the details on how, he became involved in the follow-up investigation. That was his first encounter with Mohammad Al-Qaedi."

Silence filled the phone call as Wolfe flashed back to the images seared in his brain of the bus in Haifa exploding. The image in the window of his long-dead wife replaced by that of Nadia's. Taking a deep breath, he let it out slowly.

Joseph said, "Ben-David told me a few years back, you lost your first wife in Haifa to a suicide bomber."

Refusing to comment, Wolfe let Joseph continue.

"That information is nowhere in your file."

"With good reason. It's nobody's business."

"I'm a little disappointed you've never mentioned it."

"Well—get over your disappointment, Joseph. The incident is ancient history."

"Mohammed Al-Qaedi was credited with building the bomb that destroyed the bus, am I right?"

"Yes."

"Where do you think Al-Qaedi learned to build those bombs, Michael?"

"An ex-Irish Republican Army loyalist named Danny McCaffrey."

"Correct. The CIA doesn't know a lot about Al-Qaedi except he was a young student during the 1979 takeover of the American embassy in Tehran."

Wolfe interrupted. "That would make him in his fifties."

"Yes. Remember, Danny McCaffrey had been known to spend time in Iran."

"Canfield told me all about it."

"CIA speculates the two men crossed paths several times in 2000 and 2001. The Mossad, in cooperation with MI6, has confirmed the design of Hamas suicide bombs are direct copies of the ones used in Northern Ireland during the 1990s."

"I've been aware of that for some time, Joseph. What does all of this have to do with Ian?"

"That's what Chapman wants to find out. They need to talk to him."

"Again, Joseph, why?"

"Al-Qaedi may be on his way to London."

"Let me see what I can do."

"I'm not bloody going back to London, Michael." Ian McGill sat at the breakfast bar in Wolfe's kitchen watching him make coffee. Nadia sat next to the retired SAS sergeant major.

"Don't blame you. It's a long flight."

"That's not the reason. I'm done with this terrorist nonsense."

"Does it have to do with your new relationship with Lori?"

"It has everything to do with her."

Wolfe pressed the start button on the Cuisinart. "Al-Qaedi is supposedly enroute to London."

"Good for him."

"Chapman thinks you have information that will help them stop him."

"They're bloody daft. How would I know anything about him?"

"Because he was responsible for the death of your fiancée in 2004?"

McGill studied the tabletop and remained quiet. Nadia put her hand on his forearm. "Ian, Michael's first wife was killed by a suicide bomb built by Al-Qaedi. You two have a common bond."

McGill stared at Nadia for more than a few heartbeats before returning his attention to Wolfe. "Is that true?"

A nod was Wolfe's response.

"Bloody hell."

"I have a solution for us, Ian."

"What's that?"

"Nadia and I know a computer expert who can set up a Zoom video meeting and disguise where it originates."

"How does that solve anything?"

"They know I live here, but they don't know where you are. I can tell them you will only concede to a Zoom meeting. I will not be involved. This computer expert can make it appear you are somewhere else in the US."

"And they won't know where I am?"

Wolfe shook his head.

"Set it up, Michael."

"Already have." Wolfe glanced at the clock on the microwave. "We need to be at JR's office in two hours."

"Awful cocksure about me agreeing to this, aren't you?"

"Not really. Your sense of duty to the queen and England still runs deep, Ian."

"I'm from Scotland."

With a knowing smile, Wolfe remained silent.

"Who's this JR person?"

"You'll find out."

Chapter Fourteen

SOUTHWEST MISSOURI

McGill stepped out of Wolfe's Grand Cherokee and took in the southwest section of Springfield where they were parked. "This is it? Doesn't look like much."

"This is JR's office."

"There's no name on the building. It's just a plain buff brick two-story structure."

"That's how JR likes it. He's not a flashy person, so neither is his office. But it's one of the nation's premier computer security companies. His desk is on the second floor."

They reached the top of the stairs and saw in the northwest corner a soundproof conference room. JR already occupied it when McGill and Wolfe entered.

After introductions, JR said, "When we start the Zoom meeting, you will need to wear the headset with the microphone. That will isolate any extraneous noise. Michael and I will monitor the session with these." He held up two sets of white objects resembling apostrophes.

McGill pursed his lips. "If they try to backtrack the connections, what will they find?"

A slight smile appeared on the computer expert's lips. "Michael suggested making it realistic, so if they do backtrack, they'll find the call is originating in a small coffee shop in San Francisco."

McGill nodded. "Large city, easy to get lost in. Perfect."

"I could have put you in Sydney, Australia, but they probably wouldn't believe it."

"Probably not," McGill said to Michael, who stood across the table next to JR. "I'm glad you're staying in the room. They might ask something you can confirm."

"Happy to."

JR said, "Remember, don't look at us. You are by yourself in a coffee shop in San Francisco. I've blurred your background so they can't use it to locate you. Also, Michael and I will monitor the whole thing." JR pointed to a flatscreen at the end of the conference table. "We will be listening in but won't have a microphone."

"Got it."

"When you're ready, just click on the Zoom link they sent you."

McGill placed the headset over his ears, used the mouse, and waited. A few minutes later, he said, "What's so bloody important you had to bother me? I'm retired."

The computer screen showed three images: Chapman, a man Ian did not know, and, of course, his own image. Frowning, McGill said, "Who the fuck are you?"

Chapman smiled. "It's okay, Ian. This is my assistant, Noah Anderson."

Wolfe, watching from the end of the conference table, closed his eyes, and stifled a laugh.

McGill said, "I agreed to talk to you and only you, Major."

"Sergeant Major, I need him in this meeting. So, at ease for—"

"I don't work for you anymore, Major. It's just you and me, or I turn this bloody thing off. Your choice."

Chapman's stern expression softened. He turned to look at his assistant. "Noah, I would like to talk to the sergeant major in private. Thank you for being here this afternoon."

The image of Noah Anderson disappeared from the screen. Chapman said, "Happy?"

"Not really, but it's a start." McGill's Scottish accent thickened. "Now why are you so insistent about my returning to London?"

"It has to do with Mohammad Al-Qaedi."

McGill's blank expression did not change.

"Ian, can you enlighten me on why Internet chatter indicates he is searching for you?"

"Haven't got a bloody clue."

"Does it have anything to do with your and Wolfe's incursion into Iran?"

"Nae."

"Then what?"

The ex-SAS operative just stared into the laptop.

"Does it have anything to do with your activities after the Madrid train bombing?"

"You read me report, I assume."

"Yes, but there's nothing mentioned about Al-Qaedi in it, yet we know you had an encounter with him."

"If me report does not mention it, then it didnae happen."

"Ian, you are not being truthful with me. Your and Wolfe's post-action reports about your most recent incursion into Iran were dearth of details. Almost as if both of you were hiding what happened. Care to comment on that topic?"

"We accomplished our mission and destroyed their stockpile of the bioweapon, Major. Not sure what other comments were necessary."

Chapman clasped his hands in front of him on his desk. His expression grew grave. "Ian, I can't protect you from nearly nine thousand kilometers away. We need you here to make sure nothing happens to you."

McGill laughed. "Major, I've been protecting me self without London's help for decades. I believe I'll manage." He paused and tilted his head. "This conversation is starting to bore me."

"What can I say to convince you to return to England?"

"Nary a thing. Goodbye, Major." McGill clicked on the end icon and his screen went blank. He took off the headset and asked, "Did your trick convince them I was in San Francisco?"

JR nodded but continued to study the monitor as he typed. "So, it would seem, but they are backtracking the connection again." His fingers danced on the keyboard. "I'll shift the location to Cape Town, South Africa. They'll be scratching their heads over that one."

Wolfe said, "Do you have any idea why Chapman is so insistent about you returning to the UK?"

"Aye, I do."

"Care to tell us?"

"How much time ya got?"

London

Chapman took a deep breath and looked over at Anderson. "Did they locate him?"

"Unfortunately, he had someone helping him. While you were talking to him, our tech boys found the IP address he used belonged to a coffee shop in San Francisco. As soon as he ended the Zoom link, the IP address shifted to South Africa."

With pursed lips, Chapman contemplated his assistant for an extended period. "Huh." He paused and returned his attention to the computer screen. "I wonder." Without hesitation, the MI6 Director picked up his cell phone, found the number he needed, and pressed the send icon. Not long afterward, he said, "Kincaid, old boy, do you have a moment?"

Joseph hesitated before answering the call from Jonathan Chapman. He knew what the question would be, and he had no intention of betraying the trust of JR Diminski.

"Of course, Jonathan. What's on your mind?"

"That computer hacker fellow you know, what's his name, TJ or something like that?"

"His name is JR. What about him?"

"He lives somewhere close to that wonderful house you own in Missouri, right?"

"Yes."

"Does he know Michael Wolfe?"

"Not to my knowledge, why?"

"We had a strange call with Ian McGill a while ago, and it sure had JR's fingerprints all over it."

With a chuckle, Joseph asked, "What type of fingerprints?"

"When we traced the call, our tech boys discovered McGill may have been in a coffee shop in San Francisco. Then, all of a sudden, they said the IP address switched to South Africa. That sounds like something this JR fellow could accomplish."

"Yes, it does. But I happen to know JR is out of town at the moment."

"Unfortunate."

No comment came from Joseph.

Chapman also remained silent for a few moments. "Joseph, it is imperative Ian McGill return to London. If there is anything you can do to persuade Wolfe to convince him to come back, I would be forever grateful."

"Forever is a long time, Jonathan."

"It's that critical."

"If it's that important, why don't you tell him the reason?"

"Because it would compromise an MI6 source. A source we cannot afford to burn."

"For some reason, I don't think either Ian or Michael is a security risk or would endanger a source."

"It's more complicated than that."

"Jonathan, we've been through a lot together. But I will not endanger Michael for an unknown reason. Nor will I be complicit with compelling him to persuade Ian without full knowledge of why."

Chapman remained silent for a considerable amount of time. Finally, Joseph heard, "Mohammad Al-Qaedi has been an MI6 source for the last ten years. We need to bring Ian in from the cold to protect him."

With his usual unfailing ability to hide his emotions, Joseph said, "Now, was that so hard?"

"We need Ian in the UK. If Al-Qaedi does what he has pledged to do and hunts him down in America, MI6 will have no other choice than to give him assistance."

"He's that important a source?"

"Yes."

"Hmmm."

"This is not a matter open to discussion, Joseph."

"Well, Jonathan, I'm not sure how the president will react to MI6 giving aid to an Iranian terrorist on American soil."

"Remember, the State Department has revoked his visa."

"Not if the president intervenes. Be careful with your decisions on this matter. It could have horrific ramifications on UK and US relationships."

"That is what I am trying to avoid. We need Ian in the UK."

"So, you can allow Al-Qaedi to assassinate him?"

Chapman did not respond.

"From your silence, I will assume that is your intention."

"That is not the reason, Joseph. I want Ian here in England to help protect him from the possibility."

"Jonathan, men like Al-Qaedi will stab you in the back at the first opportunity. You are dealing with the devil. I will not be a part of it."

"Joseph—"

"Good night, Jonathan."

Chapter Fifteen

WASHINGTON, DC

Joseph Kincaid closed his eyes and pinched the bridge of his nose with his fingers. He turned to Jerry Griggs who had listened to the call. "What do you think?"

"Gee, boss. That didn't sound good."

"No, it didn't."

"Do you really think MI6 will send agents to help Al-Qaedi terminate McGill?"

"Unfortunately, it has happened before. I need to know if the CIA is involved. Any chance you can check with some of your sources?"

"I can try. But this may be above my access."

"What about Carla? She always knows what's going on."

"Not sure she will talk to me."

"Jerry, one cannot assume such matters. One has to ascertain the facts."

Griggs smiled. "You know me too well, boss."

"See what you can find out and then I'll ask the big boss to intervene."

With a whistle, Griggs put his hands on his hips. "This is getting weird."

"Amen, Jerry, amen."

Carla Webb's pencil-thin frame made her appear susceptible to being blown away by a strong wind. However, appearances could be deceiving as she could be as tough as nails and equally as deadly. Jerry Griggs knew her from his days at the CIA. She had saved his life more than once and he hers.

The smoky bar where they met on a seamier side of Washington, DC allowed for the clandestine meeting to hopefully go unnoticed by the ruling elite. Griggs, sitting at a table in an isolated corner of the establishment, kept his attention on the front door. When she entered, he raised his glass.

She curled a lip after sitting across from him. "You have got to find better places to meet."

He shrugged. "Spur-of-the-moment decision. How are you, Carla?"

She pointed to his glass. "I'd be better if you order me one of those."

He lifted his glass and studied it for a moment. "Not sure what it is, but I'll order one for you."

"Never mind. I'll order myself." She flagged a waitress down and asked for a Coors Light. After the woman placed the bottle in front of Carla and walked away, the diminutive CIA operative asked, "What was such an emergency you needed to meet right away?"

After taking a sip of his beer, Griggs said, "Any rumors

floating around about the UK having a highly placed Iranian source?"

Stopping with her beer halfway to her lips, Carla tilted her head. "Who's asking?"

"My boss."

"Why?"

"So, there is one."

Carla finished taking a sip of her beer. "I didn't say that."

"You didn't have to."

She placed the bottle back on the table. "Why did Joseph send you? He should still have contacts within the agency to find out for himself."

"Plausible deniability. Plus, this so-called source might have Michael Wolfe in his crosshairs."

Carla studied her beer bottle and started to peel the label off.

"I've seen that look before, Carla. You're debating with yourself on what to tell me."

"I like Michael. I'd hate to see anything happen to him."

"I feel the same way. Tell me."

Leaning forward, she dropped the tone of her voice so Griggs could barely hear her. "Rumors are running rampant about MI6 securing a highly placed mole within the Iranian Ministry of Intelligence. Some of us think it's BS."

"It isn't."

"What do you know, Jerry?"

"Ever hear of man named Mohammad Al-Qaedi?"

"Who hasn't?"

"We have it on good authority, he's the MI6 source."

Carla laughed out loud. "Do you know how ridiculous that sounds?"

"Trust me, I don't believe it, either. But I just attended a meeting where MI6 is threatening to help him find someone in the US if we don't turn that person over to them."

"Is that someone Michael Wolfe?"

"No, but Michael could be collateral damage."

She blinked several times as she took a sip of her beer. "We can't have that, Jerry."

"I would agree."

"What do you need me to do?"

White House

"Let me get this straight, Joseph. MI6 is threatening to help an Iranian terrorist find someone inside the United States. Is that what you're telling me?"

"Yes, sir."

"Who's the individual?"

"Ian McGill. He's a retired SAS sergeant who recently helped Michael Wolfe destroy Iran's stockpile of their new bioweapon."

"Where is he?"

"Michael has him stashed in the Ozark hills."

"Good." President Roy Griffin stood from behind the Resolute desk and walked around it so he could lean on the front. Joseph sat on one of the sofas in the Oval Office. "Why are they so worried about McGill?"

"Good question. A question Jonathan Chapman would not answer. What concerns me, sir, is that I don't see Mohammad Al-Qaedi as a viable source. It doesn't make sense. He is responsible for numerous terrorist attacks on British soil. Why would they trust him?"

"Have you discussed this with the CIA?"

"I, uh, have someone checking on it, sir."

Griffin smiled and then folded his arms. "I think it's time we have a chat with Dwight."

"I would agree."

President Griffin sat behind his desk and surveyed the two men sitting in front of him. "Thank you for coming on such short notice, Dwight."

CIA Director Dwight King sat next to Joseph Kincaid. "My pleasure, sir. What can I do for you today?"

The president motioned to Joseph. "My National Security Advisor had a very disturbing conversation with your counterpart at MI6 last night."

King raised his eyebrows, shot a quick glance at Joseph, and then turned his attention back to President Griffin. "Concerning?"

"A high-placed mole inside the Iranian Ministry of Defense."

King studied his notes. Finally, he said, "Yes, sir. They claim to have a source deep within the ministry. However, they have not identified the mole to us, I'm afraid."

The president looked at Joseph. "Would you tell Dwight what they told you?"

Joseph turned to face King. "Dwight, you realize Jonathan Chapman and I go a long way back."

"I'm aware of that, yes."

"Yesterday, he told me Mohammad Al-Qaedi is the well-protected source for MI6."

The director of the CIA did something neither Joseph nor the president expected. He laughed out loud. "He's delusional. He and I have had this conversation before. I'm a little surprised Chapman mentioned it to you, Joseph. The last time we spoke, he downplayed the importance of the information the individual has been providing."

"For instance?"

"With information gleamed from the source, MI6 helped the Belgian VSSE take down an ISIS led group in Brussels."

Joseph kept his emotions in check when he said, "Iran is a majority Shia country. ISIS is ideologically anti-Shia."

"I am aware of that, Joseph. That's why he downplayed the source's contributions."

"Why did the State Department withdraw Ian McGill's visa?"

King frowned. "I wasn't aware they had."

The president clasped his hands together, placed his elbows on the desk, and tapped his lips with his extended index fingers. "CIA did not make the request?"

"Not to my knowledge, sir."

Leaning forward in the sofa toward King on the opposite side of the coffee table, Joseph said, "Chapman threatened to send MI6 assets into the US to find McGill. Why would he risk the UK's relationship with the US over McGill?"

King's face turned crimson. "He what?"

"He told me, if we do not send McGill back to the UK, he would have to take measures to do so himself."

Turning his attention back to the president, King shook his head. "Sir, this is all news to me."

The president picked up his phone and said, "Nancy, please find the Secretary of State and tell him he has five minutes to call me."

Chapter Sixteen

SOUTHWEST MISSOURI

McGill stood and walked out of the conference room to the coffee service where he poured the hot liquid into his cup. When he returned to the conference table, he clasped the mug with both hands. "Chapman has utilized my services off and on for the past three decades. It started while I was still a master sergeant in the SAS and extended until you and I returned from Iran this last time, Michael. I returned to my home in Scotland and then immediately gave him my resignation."

Wolfe tilted his head. "What happened?"

"The place has been in me family for generations." He paused as he studied the coffee mug. After taking a deep breath, he said, "I've never told anyone this before. Guess I'm starting to feel my age. When I got there, I realized I was alone in the world, a stranger in my own home. Me brother's gone, as are me parents. There are memories there I didnae care to revive."

JR remained quiet as Wolfe said, "Your fiancée?"

"Aye, she lived there for a number of years while I was

overseas. Everywhere I looked, I could see her touch, even though it's been almost twenty years since her death at the hands of Al-Qaedi."

"What are you going to do with it?"

"I handed it over to an estate agent."

"You're selling it?"

"Aye." He paused for a few moments and sipped his coffee. "In fact, it's already sold. I'm going to use the funds to buy that piece of land Lori showed me the other day."

"Congratulations, Ian."

"Not sure that's in order, Michael. Chapman may have other plans for me. Plus, there is the problem of me visa being revoked."

JR spoke for the first time since the video meeting ended. "Not necessarily."

McGill raised an eyebrow. "Not following ya, laddie."

"How attached are you to your current name?"

"It's the only one I've got."

"I realize that. But if you purchase the land under your name, you can be located easily by Chapman or even Mohammed Al-Qaedi. We can either manufacture a new identity for you, or you can purchase it with various legal work-arounds, such as a blind trust. It would keep your name out of the public records."

After staring at the top of the table for a few moments, he looked at both JR and Wolfe. "How would you create a new identity for me?"

JR just smiled.

Secretary of State Albert Doyle entered the Oval Office

along with Chief of Staff Hannah Patton exactly four minutes and thirty-two seconds after the president's request.

Doyle said, "Glad I was in the building. What can I do for you, Mr. President?"

"Al, I don't expect you to have the answer at your fingertips, but I need you to find out why a visa was revoked for a man who just completed an important mission for this country. His name is Ian McGill."

"I am very aware of this issue. The British ambassador is the one who requested McGill's visa to be revoked."

Griffin considered his Secretary of State for a moment and then frowned. "What was the ambassador's reason?"

"Questioning about crimes committed against the Crown."

"Ambassadors do not make those types of requests without reason. Did he say on whose authority he was making the request?"

"Yes, sir. The prime minister."

The president remained quiet for a long time without responding. He said, "Somebody is lying. Find out who it is." He turned to Hannah Patton. "Postpone my afternoon appointments."

"For how long, sir?"

"For the day, I'm calling the British prime minister."

The president dismissed everyone in the room except his National Security Advisor. After the room emptied, he said, "What's going on here, Joseph?"

"At the moment, sir, I don't know. Wish I had a good answer for you."

"The question was more rhetorical. I didn't expect you to answer."

Joseph just nodded.

"Let's go to my private office to call the prime minister. I want you to hear her responses."

It took several minutes for the call to go through, but at 2:32 p.m. Eastern time, 8:32 p.m. London time, the new prime minister of Britain, Maxine Clayton, came on the line.

"Hello, Mr. President."

"Thank you for taking my call at this late hour, Madame Prime Minister."

"Nonsense, the night is still young, Roy."

Relaxing a bit, Griffin said, "Maxine, I need to ask you a sensitive question."

The speaker on the president's phone went silent for a few seconds. "Very well, what is it?"

"Several months ago, two clandestine agents, one from the US and the other from the UK, infiltrated Iran and destroyed their stockpile of a new bioweapon they had developed. Your agent is here in the US, and your ambassador has asked us to revoke his visa and send him back to the UK. I would like to know the reasons for this request."

The prime minister did not answer right away. Finally, she said, "Jonathan Chapman, the head of MI6, made the request. He did not give a reason, only to say it concerned national security."

"According to a conversation Mr. Chapman had with my National Security Advisor, he is threatening to send MI6 agents into this country to find your man if we do not abide by his request."

The silence grew longer this time. "I am sure we can persuade your State Department to help us with this request, Mr. President. Our two countries' best interests are far more important than protecting one man."

Griffin glanced at Joseph, who shook his head.

Returning his attention to the speakerphone, he said, "I am afraid, without further details, we cannot grant the request. This individual has done my country a service, and I am inclined to offer him sanctuary. Plus, sending MI6 personnel to force him to return to your country could threaten US and UK relations."

"Should I have Mr. Chapman contact your CIA director to clear up this matter?"

"Madame Prime Minister, I believe that would be the appropriate solution. Thank you."

"Very good. Tell him to expect a call at exactly eight, your time, in the morning. Good night, sir." The call ended suddenly.

Griffin drummed his fingers on the desk. "I believe I touched a nerve there."

"A raw nerve."

"Can you be with Dwight when the call comes in?"

"I wouldn't miss it."

CIA Headquarters, Langley, VA

Joseph sipped coffee as he sat in front of Dwight King's desk.

King said, "Do you know where McGill is?"

"At the moment, no. I knew where he was a week ago, but since then, I'm told he moved on."

"That will be Chapman's first question."

After taking another sip of coffee, Joseph only nodded.

"So, I can honestly tell him we do not know where McGill is."

"Yes, you can."

"Do you want to talk to Chapman?"

"No. I would prefer he not know I'm listening."

"Any particular reason?"

With a sly smile, Joseph said, "I believe he will be more honest with you. During our last conversation, I got the feeling he wasn't exactly truthful with me."

The desk phone on King's desk buzzed at exactly eight a.m. He touched a button and said, "Yes, Gloria."

"Jonathan Chapman on the line, sir."

"Thank you." King pressed a button and said, "Good morning, Jonathan."

"Dwight, I assume you know the reason for this call?"

"I do."

"Will you turn Ian McGill over to us?"

"At the moment, we don't know his location, so no."

"Unless the United States abides by our request, this could erupt into an international incident."

"Only if the UK makes it so."

"One individual should not be the reason for a conflict between the US and UK, Dwight."

"According to my president, not until we have due cause."

There was a sigh on the other end. "Dwight, I was hoping you and I could make this little problem go away without involving the civilians."

Joseph frowned, and King did the same. "Jonathan, President Griffin made it perfectly clear to me yesterday that until he has ample reason to abide with your country's request, he will not authorize it."

"Unfortunately, we have uncovered evidence that Ian McGill has been an undercover agent for a foreign government."

With a roll of his eyes, Joseph shook his head.

King said, "How can that be, Jonathan? He has been a trusted member of your country's armed forces and, from what I've been told, he has served with distinction during this period."

"He did and has. But we have been supplied evidence which informs us that when they were in Iran this past year, he and Wolfe met with members of the Iranian Ministry of Intelligence and Security. That is why his debriefing papers were so cryptic. We also learned they did not destroy the stockpile of bioweapons as they indicated they did."

"Jonathan, who or what is your source?"

"A very highly placed member of the Iranian MOIS."

"Who is it?"

"I am not at liberty to disclose this individual's identity."

"You are making accusations against a man who has served the United States with loyalty and dignity. I will not disparage his service without verified proof. And I mean substantiated physical proof."

"I cannot give you the proof you request without jeopardizing our source."

"Well, then we are at a stalemate."

Joseph slipped a note to King. The CIA director glanced at it and nodded.

"I'm sorry to hear this, Dwight. I was hoping we could work something out."

"Why is this the first time Michael Wolfe's name is mentioned in these conversations?"

"I'm not at liberty to discuss that."

"You brought it up, Jonathan. What are you dancing around?"

"You'll have to take my word for it at the moment."

"Something I am starting to question and not inclined to do right now."

"Your country will need to question Wolfe about his and McGill's activities in Iran."

"We will. But he will have ample opportunity to defend himself. Something you don't seem to be offering McGill."

"As I have said, we can't disclose our source."

"Then we are at an impasse."

"I will report our conversation to the prime minister."

"And I, to my president."

The call ended, and King turned his attention to Joseph. "That was weird. What do you think?"

The National Security Advisor stood. "Chapman's hiding something. I need to talk to Wolfe face-to-face."

Chapter Seventeen

SOUTHWEST MISSOURI

Wolfe folded his arms while he listened to Joseph Kincaid summarize the conversation with Jonathan Chapman. When he concluded, the retired Marine sniper remained quiet for an extended period.

Joseph said, "By your silence, I take it there is some truth to the accusations?"

"None whatsoever. My silence is my disbelief Chapman is actually entertaining this tripe."

"Okay, tell me what happened."

"The reason neither one of us wants to discuss our time there has more to do with what we witnessed than what we did."

Both men sat on the deck of Joseph's Christian County home. Joseph held a crystal glass with two fingers of Glenfiddich twelve-year-old scotch, and Wolfe held a bottle of beer from a local microbrewery.

"Michael, to put your mind at ease, I don't believe a word of what Chapman claims. I know you too well."

"Thanks, Joseph. The notion that Mohammad Al-

Qaedi is a double agent is ludicrous. More likely, he is posing as one to throw the Brits off his trail."

"That thought crossed my mind several times."

"It's the only thing that makes sense." Wolfe paused and stared off into the woods behind Joseph's house. "Unless Chapman is relying on someone else for his information."

"I didn't think of that, but it's possible."

Taking a sip of his beer, Wolfe focused on his old controller. "Maybe McGill needs to disappear and be spotted in, let's say, Brazil or Australia."

"JR?"

Wolfe nodded.

"I think that is an excellent idea. Both have enormous land mass with lots of places to hide."

"I don't know Chapman, but it occurs to me the only way to get him off McGill's back is to expose Al-Qaedi for what he truly is and take him off the game board."

"I believe President Griffin would agree."

Raising an eyebrow, Wolfe said, "How far up does this go, Joseph?"

"It is currently jeopardizing the congenial relationship between the US and the UK. Griffin had a rather contentious discussion with the British PM."

"Aww boy."

"Still want to retire?"

"Yes, but not right now."

"I take it you can deliver a message from me to Ian."

"Maybe. If I can find him."

Joseph remained quiet.

Wolfe noted the silence. "When are you going back to DC?"

After taking a sip of his cocktail, Joseph directed his gaze to the woods behind his house. "Like you, Michael, I am finding it harder and harder to pretend I care about the absurdities of the world. I've known Jonathan Chapman for over two decades. His behavior over the past few days has me wondering if I ever really knew him.

"Plus, Mary is growing tired of the Washington DC scene and will be spending more time here. She and I have wasted most of our lives pursuing our careers and not paying attention to each other. Griffin is well into his first term as an elected president, and I have asked him to start searching for my replacement."

After laughing out loud, Wolfe said, "Joseph, you can't help yourself. You will find it tedious and boring not being in the middle of things."

"That's what the president told me."

"When are you going back?"

"Couple of days, why?"

"Let me see if I can find McGill."

"Bloody hell."

"I would agree."

McGill paced in the conference room on the second floor of JR's office building. "I can't believe Chapman would accept anything coming out of Al-Qaedi's mouth, let alone think I would be a willing partner."

Wolfe tapped a finger on the conference table. "It doesn't make any sense. That's why I think you should let JR create a new identity for you and then make it appear you've disappeared into the Australian bush."

"I don't like running from a fight. But before I decided to come to the United States, the thought of Australia did cross my mind."

JR directed his attention away from the laptop on the conference table in front of him. "Actually, it would be easy to insert your arrival into the Australian Border Force records. Doesn't matter if anyone remembers you entering the country or not, there'll be a record of your passport on file. We can even postdate it for a week ago."

"How did I get there?"

"Qantas out of Atlanta."

"How'd I get to Atlanta?"

"Rental car."

"Records?"

"All can be created and easily discovered."

"Good." McGill stopped pacing. "Could ya tip off Chapman that I'm there?"

"Of course. What fun would it be if we didn't tell him?"

Drumming his fingers on the conference table, Wolfe pursed his lips. "This is a Band-Aid. How did Al-Qaedi persuade Chapman you were a threat? And why is Chapman even listening to him?"

McGill frowned. "I just realized I don't know much about Jonathan's history."

Wolfe raised his palms toward his friend. "Don't look at me. I've only met the guy once, and I wasn't that impressed."

JR's fingers were flying over the laptop's keyboard during this exchange. Finally, a small grin appeared. "Gentlemen, Jonathan Chapman has a hole in his resume. A rather large one, I might add."

"When?" McGill placed his hands on the top of a conference room chair.

"Right after his recruitment. He graduated from Cambridge and went right into training for MI6. His first assignment was to infiltrate Iraq during the buildup to Operation Desert Storm. He wasn't heard from until after the air war ended in early 1992. In fact, Vauxhall Cross classified him as MIA until April of that year. They found him in a Kuwaiti hospital. How he got there is subject to debate."

Almost to himself, McGill said, his bushy eyebrows pinched together, "Wonder why no one ever mentioned that to me?"

"Probably because Vauxhall Cross didn't want its prized Cambridge recruit to be washed out."

Both Wolfe and McGill turned their attention to JR. Wolfe said, "What does that mean?"

"Chapman was a legacy recruit. His grandfather worked for the SIS during the first and second world wars. His father served with distinction during the Indonesian Confrontation when Britain helped create Malaysia in the mid-sixties. You can't have a legacy with a question mark hanging over his head. So, his disappearance was sponged from his record."

Wolfe folded his arms. "How did you find it?"

JR gave him a slight grin. "You have to know where the bodies are buried. CIA speculated he might have been undercover in Iran. He is fluent in Persian. But when they found him in Kuwait, that particular theory lost favor."

McGill pursed his lips. "So, if Chapman was undercover in Iran, he could have encountered Al-Qaedi?"

JR said, "Correct. Like I said, the CIA report I found concerning the incident held the label *speculative*." JR turned his attention to McGill. "Want to know what your new name is going to be?"

"Aye, laddie."

"Can't hide your accent, so how about Ian Murdock."

"A right fancy name it is. I don't even have to get new monogramed shirts."

With a chuckle, Wolfe said, "You don't own any monogramed shirts."

"Me point exactly."

Nadia snuggled up against Wolfe after leaving the bathroom. The lights were out, but he lay in bed with his hands behind his head. She said, "So, Ian's buying the property?"

"That's what he told me today after we met with JR."

"How?"

"Proceeds from selling his land in Scotland. Lori is having the land held in escrow with money supplied by McGill. Once JR gets his new identity finalized, Ian will buy it under his new name."

She rose on one elbow. "How is changing his name from McGill to Murdock going to keep him from being found?"

"That's the simplicity of the plan, the name Murdock is more common in the US than in Scotland but not as common as the last name McGill here in the States. If someone starts searching for an Ian McGill in the US, it will take a while to narrow it down. Even then, they won't find him."

She lay back down, this time with her head on his chest. "So, what's next?"

"You and I need to have a meeting with Joseph. He's thinking about retiring soon, and I won't work for anyone but him. But I want to help Ian get his name cleared before you and I retire."

"So do I. Is Joseph still here?"

"Yes, through tomorrow. He leaves first thing Sunday morning."

Lifting her head off of his chest, she returned to her pillow. "Once we help Ian, we need to stop playing these silly games."

He rolled over and kissed her. "Including this one?"

She wrapped her arms around his neck. "This is not a silly game. This is important."

They finally got to sleep an hour later.

"What time are you leaving in the morning?"

"My flight is at eight. Mary's not returning until midweek."

"Want me to fly you back to DC?"

Joseph shook his head. "The offer is tempting, but the president is sending an Air Force Learjet. He wants me back by noon."

"If you change your mind, let me know."

"I will, Michael." He paused. "Now, what did you and Nadia need to see me about?"

"Chapman."

"A topic of many conversations lately. Have you spoken to Ian?"

A nod was his answer.

"And?"

"It seems he flew to Sydney, Australia out of Atlanta a week ago."

"That's convenient, how?"

"Apparently, he rented a car from Enterprise and drove."

"Can I inform the president?"

"Yes."

"Will the FBI be able confirm this information?"

"What do you think?"

"JR?"

Wolfe shrugged.

"Good, I'll let the president know."

After a few moments, Nadia said, "How well do you know Jonathan Chapman?"

Joseph folded his arms and raised a finger to his lips. As he tapped it, he said, "I have conducted business with him for over two decades. Do I know him?" He paused. "Apparently, not that well. Why?"

Wolfe asked, "Were you aware he went missing during Operation Desert Shield and did not resurface until April of 1992?"

"No."

"He was found in Kuwait in a hospital after an undercover assignment in Iran." He paused. "Did you know he is fluent in Persian?"

"Isn't that interesting."

"Kind of what Nadia and I thought."

Chapter Eighteen

VAUXHALL CROSS, LONDON

Jonathan Chapman sat in front of the Foreign Secretary's desk and listened to an unusually harsh lecture from the Right Honorable Anna Brooks.

"Honestly, Jonathan, the prime minister is extremely unhappy with you right now. She has never raised her voice to me before but, apparently, she and President Griffin had an extremely unpleasant conversation about your obsession with Ian McGill."

"He is a threat to the Crown, ma'am."

"So, you have said. But threatening to send MI6 personnel to the United States to find him, really, Jonathan. You overextended your authority on that statement."

"It was merely a way to express the need to find McGill."

"It did not work. It only infuriated the American president."

"Not my intention."

"I am sure it wasn't, but it did."

Chapman remained quiet.

Brooks took a deep breath and clasped her hands in front of her. "What proof do you have of McGill's guilt?"

"The word of a highly placed source within the Iranian intelligence agency."

"Has this so-called highly placed source given you proof?"

Chapman slowly shook his head.

"I'm skeptical about this accusation until he or she does. I've been instructed by the Prime Minister to tell you to drop the matter."

"And if I don't?"

"There are plenty of men and women within MI6 who are qualified to perform your duties."

"Do you wish my resignation?"

She considered him for a few moments with tight lips. She then shook her head. "Not at this time."

Chapman stood. "Is that all, ma'am?"

"For now. Are you dropping this obsession?"

"As you wish, ma'am."

"See that you do." She returned her attention to a stack of paperwork on her desk as Chapman exited the office.

After Chapman arrived back at his building and hurried down the hall to his office, Noah Anderson fell into step beside him. "We have news, sir."

Raising his hand and one finger, Chapman motioned toward his office door. Anderson knew to not say another word until they were behind closed doors.

Once inside the space, Anderson placed a piece of paper on Chapman's desk as the chief of MI6 sat. Putting his glasses on, Chapman scanned it and frowned. "He's in Australia?"

"Yes, sir."

"When?"

"Over a week ago."

"Have we confirmed this information?"

"The FBI sent our friends at MI5 a detailed report about his trip."

Chapman pursed his lips. "How detailed?"

"Where he rented a car, the stops he made to buy gasoline, and an electronic copy of his boarding pass on a direct flight via Qantas from Atlanta to Sydney."

"What about in Australia?"

"We checked, and there is a record of his passport being scanned by Australian Border Force."

"Did he have an Electronic Travel Authorization?"

"All of his paperwork was in order and approved through proper channels."

"I thought we canceled his visa to the US?"

"It seems his trip occurred before we notified the US State Department."

"Hmmm."

"Do you want us to ask the Australians to find him?"

Chapman did not answer right away. Finally, he said, "Yes, but have them do it quietly. Just tell them we would like to know his whereabouts."

"Very good, sir."

After Anderson left the office, Chapman continued to question the convenience of McGill disappearing into the vast expanse of Australia. After a few minutes of contemplating his options, he picked up the phone and asked for his car to return.

Washington, DC
Monday

Joseph Kincaid motioned for his assistant Jerry Griggs to follow him as he headed toward his office. Griggs shut the door behind him and asked, "What's up, boss?"

"How many times have I asked you not to call me that?"

"At this point, 231, boss."

Shaking his head, Joseph pointed toward a chair in front of his desk. "Sit."

With a mischievous grin, Griggs said, "Yes, boss."

"I need information."

"Concerning?"

"Jonathan Chapman."

Griggs whistled softly. "How deep?"

"The unpublished or not readily available kind."

"You searching for something illegal?"

"Don't know what I'm looking for. Chapman is not acting like himself, and I want to know why."

"Does this mean I get a fully expense-paid trip to London?"

"If that's what it takes, yes."

"I haven't been to London in years. But I don't think my wife will appreciate me going without her."

"Jerry, this is important."

"I know, just kidding." His demeanor changed. "What about the CIA? Wouldn't they have a better chance of finding the information you need?"

"I'm going to talk to a friend of mine. Did you ever hear back from Carla after your last meeting?"

"No, and that's unusual. I'll check with her while you talk to your friend.

Joseph Kincaid's long history with the CIA allowed him to be acquainted with more than a few individuals known in the business as *spooks*. However, those individuals were officially called operations officers by the agency. Normally, when they retired, these individuals would move to a quiet place and spend leisure time away from the craziness of the business. One of those individuals, who did not follow the norm, stayed in DC and now earned his living as a consultant. A fancy way of saying he charged a lot of money for information other people needed. Sitting in his car parked in the agency's Langley, Virginia lot, Joseph dialed a number committed to memory years ago. When the call was answered, he heard a voice grumble on the other end, "Haven't heard from you in a while. Did you get too big for your britches?"

Joseph replied, "If I did, I'm sure you would tell me about it. How are you, Will?"

"I was better before you called."

"Nonsense. I'd like to buy you a beer."

The gruff voice lost the annoyed tone. "When?"

"Now if you're available."

"Guinness?"

"Is there any other kind?"

"Not to my knowledge. Everything else is just watered-down piss."

"I agree with you, Will. Usual place?"

"I can be there in half an hour."

William Fischer, better known as Will to his friends, did

not possess the looks of a stereotypical Hollywood movie spy. On the contrary, Fischer possessed unruly dark-rusty-brown hair, bushy eyebrows he refused to trim, a round face accented by a broad nose and a red walrus mustache. Dark-green eyes viewed the world through the smudged lenses of his black horn-rimmed glasses. His normal wardrobe could best be described as thrift shop chic: rumpled corduroy sport coat, khaki pants two inches too long, scuffed loafers, and a wrinkled white Oxford shirt.

Joseph arrived first and secured a table in the far rear corner of an authentic Irish pub located in a strip mall on Chain Bridge Road. Five minutes later, Fischer entered the establishment and made a beeline for Joseph's table.

Just as he sat down, a college-age waitress arrived and placed a pint of Guinness in front of him.

He lifted the glass, inspected the dark-brown ale, and said, as he tilted the glass to his lips, "One of God's gifts to man." After consuming half the contents, he set the mug on the table and lowered his head to look over his glasses at Joseph. "What's on your mind, old friend?"

"You appear well, William."

"Bullshit. I'm fat and I drink too much."

"Easily remedied."

"Not in this lifetime. You buying the next round?"

"Of course."

"What do you need to know?"

"Jonathan Chapman."

"The chief of the Secret Intelligence Service?"

"One and the same. What do you know about him?"

Fischer raised the Guinness to his lips again and took a swig. "Who needs to know?"

"Me."

"Thought you knew him."

"I do, but you might know more."

Closing one eye and tilting his head, Fischer considered his answer. "Facts or rumors?"

"Either or both."

"The rumors are more interesting."

"Start there."

"Oops—it appears I have emptied my glass."

Joseph raised a hand, got the waitress' attention, and pointed toward Fischer. Within a minute, another freshly poured Guinness sat in front of the man.

"Now, where was I?"

"Rumors."

"Ah, that." He took a gulp of his drink and set it down. "Joseph, how well do you know Jonathan Chapman?"

"I've had dealings with him for over twenty years. But I realized I didn't know anything about his personal life, other than he is married. He's always been tightlipped about that part."

Fischer nodded. "From what I heard, he's that way with everyone."

"So, what are the rumors, Will?"

"Not actually a rumor. He had a nervous breakdown in the 1990s."

Joseph raised an eyebrow. "Early 90s?"

"That's what I heard. It happened when he was in Iraq. A close friend hid him in a hospital in Kuwait."

"He was never in Iran?"

"Not that I heard. Why do you ask?"

"No reason. Who knew about it?"

"Don't know. I was stationed in London at the time, and it was common knowledge among those of us in the trenches."

"Huh."

Looking over his glass, Fischer kept his gaze on Joseph. After a sip, he said, "Not what you expected?"

"Actually, if true, it answers a number of questions."

"Such as?"

"Keeping his personal life quiet and out of the public eye. The British take mental health seriously, but in the Secret Intelligence Service, it's a different story."

"What do you mean?"

"How does the CIA view it?"

"A one-way ticket out the front door."

"That's the way the SIS views it as well. Too much opportunity for blackmail." He paused for a moment. "I'm surprised Jonathan rose to the top position with an episode like that in his background."

"Maybe it is, after all, a rumor."

"Unless…"

"Unless what, Joseph?"

The National Security Advisor stood and placed two twenty-dollar bills on the table. "Have another pint on me." He hurried to the front door of the pub.

Chapter Nineteen

SOUTHWEST MISSOURI

One Week Later

The distinguished gentleman who emerged from the early morning flight from Atlanta walked through the concourse of the Springfield-Branson National Airport toward the car rental kiosks. He traveled light, pulling a small suitcase behind him. After securing a midsize SUV, he drove south through the airport exit, his destination a buff brick building in a multiuse commercial development on the city's southwest side.

His passport proclaimed him to be an American named Danny Wade from Ohio. His real name lay hidden in the myriad of false identities gathered during his tenure with MI6. As an ex-member of the United Kingdom's SAS forces, he knew the man he searched for. A specific sergeant major who might have disappeared into Australia's outback. Wade's current employer suspected the vanishing act to be a ruse. He also told Wade a computer hacker, who worked out of the buff brick building, may have forged the documents used by the sergeant major to make it appear he traveled to the southern continent.

His sole purpose for being in the Springfield area would be to determine, if in fact, Ian McGill traveled to Australia.

Patience generally solved many problems. Danny Wade possessed more patience than most.

Michael Wolfe parked his Jeep Grand Cherokee in front of JR's business in one of the slanted parking slots designated for visitors. Always cognizant of his surroundings, he noticed a middle-aged well-dressed man standing in front of the attorney's office paying way too much attention to his arrival. Sitting in the Jeep, he used the remote control to move his side mirror for a better view of the man. Pretending to check his cell phone, he waited two minutes to see what the man would do. As he suspected, the man continued to keep his attention on the Jeep.

Finally, he opened the door and stepped out. He looked straight at the man, who quickly walked toward the east. Wolfe kept an eye on him until he entered a Mexican restaurant a half block away.

Hurrying inside and up to the second floor, Wolfe walked up to JR's cubicle and asked, "Do you have any surveillance cameras on the front of this building?"

JR pushed his glasses up his nose. "Four, why?"

"Someone seemed way too interested in me after I parked the Jeep a few minutes ago. I'd like to have a closer look at him."

"Huh." JR's fingers danced on the keyboard, and the middle monitor suddenly showed four different views. "How far back do you want to go?"

"Thirty minutes."

"Done."

On the monitor appeared four separate views of the front of JR's building. One to the east, one to the west, and two concentrated on the middle. One of the middle views came from above the entrance to the building, and the other captured a wide-angle view of across the street.

On the view from across the street, Wolfe pointed to the man. "He was there thirty minutes ago. Can you back it up until he enters the scene?"

More rapid typing, and the time stamp on the video showed the time an hour and a half in the past. Wolfe said, "He's not there. Fast forward in chunks of fifteen minutes."

An image of the man appeared exactly thirty minutes later.

JR said, "That particular camera is a hi-def camera. I can blow up the image quite a bit."

"Let's get a closer look at him."

The other three images disappeared as the image of the man grew until it concentrated on his face. JR said, "Huh."

"What?"

"That's the same guy who stood there a day ago when I helped Mia unload coffee she bought for the office."

Wolfe asked, "You sure?"

"Positive. Same suit."

"Can you run his face through facial recognition?"

"Already started when I recognized him."

Five seconds later, the man's image appeared on the monitor. "Well, he isn't in the FBI or US military database."

"Can you access British records?"

The computer hacker nodded. One minute later, an image appeared on the left monitor.

Wolfe leaned down and inspected the picture of a younger version of the man.

"Isn't that interesting." He paused for a moment. "According to his British SAS file, he died in Afghanistan in 2009."

JR studied the image and pursed his lips. "I wonder." His fingers once again hammered the keyboard. When he finished, he leaned back and folded his arms. "Well, what do you know. He's a ghost."

Straightening, Wolfe placed his hands on his hips. "Mossad has been known to do the same thing. Claim someone died in military action and make them an undercover agent." He paused and studied the younger image of the man. "Does Chapman know about you, JR?"

"I don't see how."

"Would Joseph have mentioned anything to Chapman about your activities?"

The computer hacker glanced at the screen and then back up at Wolfe. "I don't know. I wouldn't think so, but…"

"Yeah, but. Time to call him."

JR and Wolfe each took a seat in the conference room. Hooking up his laptop to the Polycom conference call phone, JR initiated a call to a private number given to him years prior. Twelve seconds later he heard, "Good, afternoon, JR."

"Not sure it is, Joseph."

Only silence could be heard from the phone. After a few heartbeats, Joseph asked, "Want to explain?"

"How much does Jonathan Chapman know about me?"

"Uh…"

Wolfe said, "Joseph, we have a potential problem. An individual the British SAS claims to have died in Afghanistan during 2009 has JR's office under surveillance. And he's not being very subtle about it, either."

No response came from the speakerphone.

JR started to say something, but Wolfe held up his hand and shook his head.

Finally, after a long pause, Joseph said, "Unfortunately, I mentioned your abilities during a conversation, several years ago, about phone security. While I didn't mention your last name, he probably guessed your location and found you."

JR frowned. After taking a deep breath and blowing it out, he said, "He's searching for McGill. Our ruse about Australia apparently didn't work."

"Has McGill been there recently?"

"No."

"Good. Keep him away."

Wolfe said, "That's our plan."

"Chapman has implicated you in his fantasy as well, Michael."

"So, you've mentioned."

"What name is your visitor using?"

"Haven't had the pleasure of asking him yet."

"Wrong question. Since you know he was in the SAS, who is he?"

JR said, "File indicates his name is Logan Dillon. He was a staff sergeant."

"How old?"

"The file says he was thirty when he died in 2009."

"That would make him over forty-two, now. About the right age."

Wolfe folded his arms. "Right age for what?"

"Serving under Chapman when he was a major in the SAS."

"Huh."

"Gentlemen, my guess would be, he would know McGill on sight."

"Thus, why he's hanging out in front of JR's office building, hoping to catch a glimpse of McGill."

"Michael?"

"Yeah."

"Do you think you need to have a word with him?"

"Great idea."

The man with the passport claiming him to be Danny Wade sat near a plate glass window at the front of the Mexican restaurant with a clear view of JR's building a half a block away. The Jeep Grand Cherokee he'd observed park an hour previous remained in the slot. As he pushed his lunch plate away, he felt the food could scarcely be called Mexican or even Tex-Mex. Keeping his eyes on the comings and goings of the business, he sipped a glass of iced tea.

With his back against a wall, he also possessed a clear view of the establishment's front door. He sensed, rather than saw, a man approach his table. As the person passed, he suddenly reversed direction and sat across from him in the booth.

Wolfe said, "Don't bother to leave, Dillon. I found your rental car. Did you know you have a flat tire? Hope the rental company has an account with AAA."

With a Midwestern American accent, the ex-SAS sergeant said, "You have me at a disadvantage, sir. Who do you believe I am?"

"Don't know what you're calling yourself today, but your real name is Logan Dillon, a former staff sergeant in the SAS who seems to have died in 2009."

"Well, there you go. I couldn't be this Dillon character, now, could I?"

Wolfe showed him the picture from his SAS file now displayed on his cell phone. "You're a little older than when this was taken, but it's you."

Dillon's eyes widened briefly and then he regained his indifference. "Haven't got a clue who that is."

Wolfe leaned forward. "Cut the BS, Dillon. You're working for Jonathan Chapman. You were assigned to find Ian McGill, or am I jumping to conclusions?"

The mention he worked for Chapman caught Dillon off guard. He continued to stare at Wolfe. Finally, he said, "Uh —you've got me mixed up with someone else, partner."

"Hate to tell you, partner, but McGill's in Australia. You're wasting your time here." Wolfe stood and walked out of the restaurant.

Instead of walking back to his Jeep, Wolfe circled the building and stood out of sight in an alcove to keep an eye on Dillon's rental. His wait did not last more than three minutes before the man approached the rented SUV. When he saw the flat tire, he kicked it and pulled out a cell phone.

Wolfe pulled his own phone out and texted a message. *On the phone now.* He lowered the device and returned to keeping an eye on Dillon. As he watched, the former SAS soldier pressed his phone to his ear with a shoulder and prepared to change his tire. Five minutes later, Wolfe felt the receipt of a new text message. JR had responded with one of his own, *Got him.*

Chapter Twenty

LONDON

The hustle and bustle of the small pub in the east London Borough of Newham catered to the local immigrants from former British colonies. The Irish family that ran the place held anti-Crown sentiments and condoned hushed conversations in darkened corners of the establishment.

Into this atmosphere, Noah Anderson sat and waited for his contact to appear. At exactly ten minutes past the appointed time, a dark-haired figure walked through the front door and strolled up to the bar and ordered a beer. After receiving his order, the man sipped it and casually surveyed the room. Taking his time, he meandered over to where Anderson sat.

"Did you find McGill?"

Anderson shook his head. "No. We were told he went to Australia, but confirmation on his whereabouts cannot be obtained. But we did locate Wolfe."

"McGill is the one he wants, not Wolfe."

"We believe Wolfe will lead you to McGill."

"Why?"

"Because McGill left Scotland and went straight to where Wolfe lives."

"Hmmm." The man took a sip of his beer. "Where is that?"

"A place called Missouri in the United States."

"I have never heard of this place called Missouri. Where in the US is it?"

"The middle."

"It is a big country. You will have to be more specific."

"Do you know where Dallas is?"

"Yes."

"It is 670 kilometers northwest of Dallas."

"That tells me nothing, Anderson."

Chapman's assistant's hand covered a flash drive, which he slid over the tabletop. He raised his hand slightly revealing the object and said, "Details are on this."

With a nod, the dark-haired man accepted the object, and it disappeared into his pants pocket. "Does Chapman suspect anything?"

"No, he thinks Al-Qaedi is a double agent."

"For a man of such importance, he is a fool."

"People tend to believe what they want to believe."

"Make sure he continues to believe that." The dark-haired man stood. "Do you wish your compensation handled the same as usual?"

"Yes."

Without a response, the man walked out of the pub.

Anderson kept his gaze on the nearly empty pint of beer in front of him. He held the glass with one hand and twisted it clockwise then counterclockwise. He said in a low voice, "Chapman's not a fool, just a little overoptimistic."

The dark-haired man left the pub and walked east. Two blocks later, a Vauxhall Corsa pulled to the curb. The pedestrian slipped into the passenger seat and the vehicle sped away.

The driver turned to his new passenger. "Did you get his location?"

Holding up the flash drive, Amir Zamani said, "The details are on this. Someplace called Missouri. But the Americans claim McGill is in Australia."

The driver kept his attention on the road, not offering a comment. Finally, after several minutes, he said, "Who is in America?"

"Wolfe."

"That may be where you need to start."

"Maybe. We have brothers in Australia, correct?"

"Correct. Why?"

"I think we need to confirm if McGill is there before we send a team."

"Al-Qaedi will not be pleased. He wanted this done by now."

"It will be done when Allah wishes it done."

The driver frowned. "Do not let him hear you say that."

"I answer to Allah, and Allah only."

"Yes, but Al-Qaedi pays us."

Zamani remained quiet as the driver navigated the crowded streets of London. After ten minutes of silence, he said, "I will leave for America tomorrow. Let our brothers in the United States know I am coming."

"Very well."

"Tell them I will fly to Detroit."

"May I suggest Toronto and meeting our brothers there? They know how to get you into America without creating a record of your arrival."

"Wise. Make it so."

Langley, Virginia

Mandy Foster did not consider herself to be part of the generation classified as millennials, she felt more like a Gen Xer. With a birthdate in 1981, she fell into the early years of this generation. Independent, single, highly educated, and multilingual, she enjoyed her job with the CIA as a signal analysist and prided herself on her ability to connect seemingly unrelated dots.

Today was one of those days. Random intercepted cell phone calls and text messages merged into a pattern she had seen before. Storm clouds were gathering in the Northeastern United States. She texted her supervisor to come to her cubicle.

Ellen Hayes, ten years her senior, arrived ten minutes later. "What've you got, Mandy?"

Pointing to a map with a collection of dots surrounding Buffalo, New York, Mandy said, "See this cluster?"

"Yeah."

"Ninety percent originate from three separate cell phones. They are composed of text messages and a few voice ones. They're all in Farsi, and all mention a pending visitor."

"What kind of visitor?"

Mandy looked up at Ellen Hayes. "A high-ranking one. Not religious in nature because the visitor is never referred to as an imam but as a sheik."

Ellen frowned. "Where is this sheik supposedly arriving from?"

"London."

With this news, Hayes pursed her lips. "That's a bit unusual. Write it up with your references and get it to me ASAP."

"Yes, ma'am."

The email appeared in Carla Webb's inbox twenty-four hours after Mandy Foster told her supervisor about the arrival of the sheik. She scanned it, flagged it, and went on to the next email. A minute later, she came back to the flagged message and read it more carefully. After her second reading, she frowned and sent a text message to a number with the simple words, *Call Me.*

Ten minutes later, her cell phone rang. She heard, "What's up, Carla?"

"You know that place we met last time?"

"Yeah."

"Be there in an hour."

"Got it."

The call ended, and she read the email one more time. "Damn."

Jerry Griggs entered the tavern at four in the afternoon. Despite having met numerous contacts in dingy bars during his career with the CIA, he could never get used to how dark the interior of a building could be during the middle of the afternoon. After his eyes adjusted, he spotted Carla in a far corner and hurried toward her booth.

When he sat, he said, "You never ask me out."

She slid the printout of the email over to him. After he read it, he returned his attention to her. "When?"

"Just before I called you."

"You think it's related?"

Rolling her eyes, she tapped the sheet of paper and then leaned forward. "Read it more carefully. This sheik person is coming from London. He is traveling to Canada. The communications are in Farsi. They plan to sneak him into the US. Their target is in the middle of the United States." She paused for effect. "Just how many scenarios does that fit, Jerry?"

"Only one I can think of."

"Exactly."

"Could this be a coincidence?"

She rolled her eyes a second time. "What's happened to you? Did your brain suddenly turn to oatmeal working at the White House? Of course, it's not a coincidence, dumbass."

"Okay, I need to get this to Joseph."

"Duh."

"Glad to see you haven't lost your cuddly disposition, Carla."

"I told you before, I like Michael and Nadia Wolfe. I don't want anything to happen to them."

"Who's this Mandy Foster?"

"I've met her. She's good at her job and 99 percent of the time correct in her assessments."

"Can you get in touch with her?"

"How do you think I got the email?"

"I won't ask."

"Probably best."

"Joseph will want more details."

She sighed. "Jerry, you don't give Joseph enough credit."

She pointed to the email. "He is one of the best at putting small pieces of a puzzle together and seeing the big picture. You need to let Michael know immediately."

"I understand that, Carla. Can you ask Mandy to tell us when all of this will start?"

Closing her eyes, Carla took a deep breath and then glared at Griggs. "Did you suddenly develop an advanced case of dementia?"

Griggs remained silent as he read the email again.

"Jerry, it's happening now."

Chapter Twenty-One

SOUTHWEST MISSOURI

Wolfe listened as Joseph and Jerry Griggs summarized what they knew. When they finished, he turned to Nadia. "What do you think?"

"Are they searching for Ian or you or both?"

Returning his attention to the laptop, Wolfe said, "Nadia raises a valid point. Are they looking for Ian or me?"

The disembodied voice of Joseph spoke from the laptop. "Does it matter, Michael?"

"Probably not. But if they are trying to find Ian, they won't."

"Can you get a message to him?"

"Possibly. What is it?"

"There is chatter on the Internet about a search going on in Australia for him."

"I'm not sure getting in touch with him would be a good idea if they are searching there."

"See what you can do."

"Is that all?"

"Are you going to take precautions?"

"I appreciate the warning, Joseph. But I'm not going to wait for them to come to me."

"Be careful, Michael. The police might not appreciate a shootout in downtown Ozark."

"Not what I had in mind."

"Okay. Is there anything we can help you with?"

"Not that I can think of." Wolfe hit the end call icon and said to Nadia, "I've seen that look before. Want to tell me?"

"I am not rebuilding this house again, Michael."

"I would prefer not to as well."

"We go on the offense."

The caravan of three cars traveled southwest on US Route 24 cutting across the northwest corner of Ohio into Indiana. At Fort Wayne, they went south on Interstate 69 until they reached Indianapolis where the six men stopped at a motel owned by a fellow Iranian on the city's south side. The owner's father immigrated to the US right after the overthrow of the Iranian shah in February 1979. The father, having passed away over a decade ago, left the motel to his son. A son who did not share his enthusiasm for western culture.

It was not the young man's first time to offer safe haven to travelers from his native country. Amir Zamani met with him after his team checked into the hotel.

After they shook hands, Zamani said, "Salaam, my brother."

George Falah placed his hand over his heart and gave Zamani a slight bow. "It is my honor to welcome you, Sheik, to my humble house of rest."

After giving his host a nod of the head, Zamani continued, "I am told you have helped a number of our brothers in need of safe sanctuary. For that, I thank you."

"It has been my honor."

"Why do you stay in this country?"

With a shrug, Falah said, "It is the only country I know. My father and mother left Iran when I was just six months old. I tried to learn Persian, but alas, few speak the language around here. Besides, my family is here, so I stay."

"A good reason. I am told you know how to, uh, provide certain supplies and equipment."

Falah nodded in response.

"If I gave you a list and money, can you secure these supplies?"

"Yes."

"Here is the list." Zamani offered the piece of paper to the innkeeper. "How much money will you need?"

After scanning the list, Falah returned his attention to his guest. "The first six items are common and can be purchased easily. The last item is rare and more subject to scrutiny. It can be located. However, it could be expensive."

"How much?"

"I take it you do not want these items to be traceable?"

"Correct."

Checking the list again, Falah said, "Fifteen thousand American dollars."

"And your cut?"

"I am a middleman. My fees are subject to how much the individual buying the product will require."

"How much?"

With a shrug, Falah remained quiet.

"Very well. When can you deliver?"

"There is a gun show this weekend in Columbus. I can

have all but the final item on your list delivered by nightfall Saturday."

"When can the last one be delivered?"

With a slight smile, Falah said, "That one, my brother, will be delivered separately. Probably Saturday afternoon. I will personally bring it to you."

Sunday Morning

With the delivered weapons and supplies packed and concealed within the three cars, each took a different route to their destination in Southwest Missouri. The car carrying Amir Zamani took the most direct route following Interstate 70 and then Interstate 44. They would arrive several hours prior to the other two and secure a storage unit to secure their purchased equipment. They would then sequester themselves in a motel several miles outside of the large city and plan their assault.

Late Sunday night, Zamani asked the man who drove the car to join him for a walk. As they circled a park near their hotel, Zamani said, "Abbas, there is a building we must keep under surveillance. We need someone to keep an eye on it during the day, but that person will have to be discreet."

Abbas remained quiet.

"You have the paperwork to get a job in this country, correct?"

"Yes, Sheik."

"There is a restaurant a short distance from this building seeking new employees. I need you to get hired there and be our eyes and ears."

The man locked eyes with the sheik and dipped his head slightly.

"I hope your ordeal will not be lengthy. We need to find someone." He handed Abbas a picture. "This is the man. We do not know what name he will use, but we believe he will visit the building at some point."

"What if he comes while I am working? I could miss him."

"Yes, that is why we will have others keeping their eyes on the building. But you will be there constantly."

"I will go tomorrow."

Zamani placed his hand on Abbas' shoulder. "I promise it will not be a long wait, my brother."

"Allah willing."

The sheik nodded. "Yes, Allah willing."

Wednesday

JR Diminski, in the early years of running his business, seldom ate lunch. During those days, if he ate at all, he would run home and grab something. As the business grew, and more of his daily responsibilities were handled by others, he started to treat himself to a meal at the Mexican restaurant a block from his building three or four times a month. He knew the owner and most of the serving staff.

Today, the owner greeted him at the table he normally occupied. "Good to see you today, JR."

"Good to be here, George. What did Jorge come up with today?"

George sat across from him and beamed. "You're in

luck. He's been experimenting with street tacos. The ones he is making today are filled with shrimp or carnitas."

JR thought about his choices for a moment. "Shrimp sounds good."

"I'll hook you up."

As George stood, JR asked, "New waiter?" He was pointing to a man taking a customer's order three tables away.

Following the direction of JR's hand, the owner said, "Yeah, we lucked out. He's got experience. I don't have to train him."

"I'm glad for you."

"I'll tell Jorge the tacos are for you."

Before the owner could walk away, JR asked, "When did your new guy start?"

"Hired him Monday. He started yesterday. Why?"

"Just curious. Have you ever seen him around before?"

"No. He just moved to the area over the weekend."

"Lucky him."

JR watched the man for several moments and then opened his cell phone and reread an email. When George passed his booth, JR stopped him and said, "Hey, can I get them to go? Something came up at the office."

"Sure, I'll get it taken care of."

The shrimp street tacos, sitting on his desk in a sack, were forgotten as he conferred with Alexia Gibbs. "Can you take the security camera images for the past several weeks and see if there are any young men with dark curly hair that resemble soccer players?"

She looked up at him and frowned. "What do you mean, resemble soccer players?"

"I'm trying not to be racist here, but there's a new waiter at the restaurant down the street who just started this week. He appears to be from the Middle East."

"So?"

"Did you see the email from Jerry Griggs about the Internet chatter concerning an Iranian hit team who might be trying to find McGill?"

She tightened her lips. With a curt nod, she returned her attention to the computer. JR returned to his cubicle and considered the sack containing the shrimp tacos. With his appetite squelched, he tossed them into the wastebasket next to the coffee service station.

Thirty minutes later, Alexia, laptop in hand, appeared at his desk and motioned for him to follow her into the soundproof conference room. When he shut the door he asked, "What'd you find?"

"Over the past two days, there have been a total of four men matching the general description of young and from the middle east, loitering in various spots around the area. Going back four weeks, there is nothing out of the ordinary, until Monday of this week. That's when they appeared." She opened her laptop and pressed the space bar. A picture appeared of a young man leaning against the side of the building across the street. "For instance." She then hit the enter key. Another picture of a different but similarly appearing male could be seen on the screen. "This guy's been somewhere on the street each day."

JR adjusted his glasses and bent over to study the image. "He resembles the new waiter I saw today."

"These are just two of the images I found since

Monday. Nothing like this appears before then going back four weeks."

"Did you run them through the facial recognition software?"

She nodded.

"Let me guess, no matches."

"None, whatsoever."

"Okay, send the images to the drop box we use for Joseph. I'll call him and see what he wants us to do."

"Should we warn Michael and Ian not to come by the office?"

"Probably should Ian. He knows to stay away, but it wouldn't hurt to remind him. If we tell Michael, he'll want to take care of it himself. Not sure that's a good idea right now."

Chapter Twenty-Two

SOUTHWEST MISSOURI

Ian McGill surveyed the southern slope of the land he now owned. He felt at peace with himself for the first time in decades. Lori stood next to him, holding his hand.

She said, "It is beautiful, Ian."

"Aye, it is." He paused for a few moments as he checked his wristwatch. "Drillers will be here today and tell us where they can place the well. Then we can determine where to lay out the house."

"Kind of exciting, isn't it?"

"Starting to be." His cell phone vibrated, announcing a new text message. He read it in silence and put the phone back in his pocket.

Lori asked. "Who was that?"

"Spam."

"It kept your attention too long for it to be spam."

"Aye."

"Then what was it?"

"Nothing for you to worry about."

She folded her arms and raised an eyebrow. "Is that how

it's going to be, Ian? Don't worry your pretty blonde self about things. It's a man's problem."

He remained quiet.

She continued, "If you don't trust me enough to share bad news, then this relationship is on shaky ground."

With a deep breath, he said, "Aye. I've lived by myself too long. I'm not used to sharing everything with someone. You'll have to be patient with me."

Her stern glare softened. "Okay, I can do that. What's happened?"

"Message from JR. It appears me past is catching up. Apparently, there are several young men hanging around JR's building who appear to be from the Arab world. He warned me to stay away in case they are searching for me. I can confirm that's what they are doing."

"Why you?"

"Because, Mohammed Al-Qaedi will not rest until he is spitting on my corpse."

This announcement brought silence to the conversation as the two stood on the rise overlooking the southern slope of the property. Lori drew closer to McGill as they concentrated on the land in front of them. She wrapped her arms around his waist, and he draped his arm over her shoulder. "Ian, maybe it's time to have JR move forward with helping you change your name."

"I've thought about it, but I'm proud of who I am. Changing my identity isn't the answer."

"Then, what is the answer?"

With a grim smile, he said, "Spitting on Al-Qaedi's corpse."

A Jeep Grand Cherokee parked behind their vehicle near the entrance to the property. Ian said, "Didn't know Michael was stopping by."

"Actually, it's probably just Nadia. She's taking me to meet with the contractor who built their house. He has a few different floorplans he wants you and me to consider."

Pointing toward the vehicle, McGill said, "Then why is Michael driving?"

Lori watched as Wolfe and Nadia stepped out of the Jeep at the same time. "Don't know. Hope everything is okay."

McGill disengaged from their embrace and headed down the slope with Lori close behind.

JR finished sending the text message to McGill and then returned his attention to the security videos. Once Alexia discovered numerous men keeping JR's building under surveillance, they knew what to search for. She detected four distinct individuals, all male, at various times loitering around keeping tabs on their front entrance.

Reviewing the security videos, he decided it was time to involve Michael Wolfe. He made a VoIP call to the man's cell phone.

"Wolfe."

"Michael, it's JR."

"Ah, it's you. I take it you're not in Utah."

"No. I've got some bad news."

Wolfe remained quiet.

"There appear to be at least five different men keeping my building under scrutiny. All are Middle Eastern in appearance."

"Since when?"

"Monday of this week."

"How did you know?"

"Alexia discovered it."

"Any guesses as to what they're doing?"

"After your encounter with Logan Dillon, I am sure he passed on the information to Chapman. If I had to guess, I'd say they are looking for Ian."

"I would, too. Nadia and I just arrived at his property. I'll tell him to stay away from your building."

"I sent him a text, but I'm glad you can explain it to him in more detail."

"I'll get back to you."

Wolfe and McGill met halfway up the southern slope of the land. Wolfe said, "JR said he sent you a text."

"Aye."

"Can you think of a reason why, all of a sudden, everyone has their hair on fire about you?"

McGill did not answer right away as he watched Lori and Nadia heading back to the Jeep. Finally, he said, "I can't unless it has to do with our time in Iran."

"Which brings up the question, how many individuals knew we were in Iran? It's not like we strolled down the streets of Tehran every night."

"Maybe it's time we find out."

Wolfe gave his friend a sly smile. "What've you got in mind?"

"Before I closed on this property, I spent a few days wandering around the place. Guess what I found about a klick from here?"

"Wouldn't have a clue."

"Something you Americans call a sinkhole."

"Yeah, they're pretty common around here." Wolfe's eyebrows rose. "How deep is it?"

"Deep enough I didn't hear the rock I tossed in hit bottom."

Using security photos of the four men keeping tabs on JR's building, Wolfe spotted one on the street across from JR's. An hour later, he followed the man to a parking lot behind a five-story building several blocks away.

As the man got into a car, a white Ford Transit Van screeched to a halt directly behind it. The black-haired man with a full beard stared at the rearview mirror and then stepped out of the small Kia rental. As he walked toward the van blocking his exit, Wolfe came up from behind and pressed the barrel of his Walther PPK into the guy's back. In Farsi, Wolfe growled, "Get in the van, or prepare to meet Allah."

Once inside the vehicle, the Iranian alternated his glare between Wolfe and the driver. After repeating this process several times, he pulled his legs to his chest, encircled them with his arms, and placed his forehead on the knees.

Keeping the Walther pointed at the man, Wolfe said in Persian, "What is your name?"

The man did not answer.

"We can do this the easy way or the hard way, your choice. What's your name?"

The man did not respond, keeping his face hidden.

With a move so swift the Iranian did not have time to react, Wolfe grabbed him behind the neck and rammed his face into the floor of the van. With his cheek pressed against the cold metal floor, Wolfe secured both hands behind the man's back with a zip tie. He then secured his ankles together with another one. Pressing his knee into the guy's back, Wolfe nuzzled the gun hard against the nape of his neck. He repeated his question. "What's your name?"

The man said in English, "Fuck you."

Wolfe said to McGill, "Our guest isn't being cooperative."

"That's too bad."

Forty-five minutes later, the Ford Transit van, driven by McGill, turned west onto a narrow gravel road. After following the increasingly narrow lane for a mile, he stopped where the path ended.

Wolfe pulled the Iranian into a sitting position and placed a strip of duct tape across his eyes and, just as he started to protest, another one over his mouth. After McGill opened the side door, Wolfe cut the zip tie securing the man's legs and forced him out of the van. They grasped him by the arms and duckwalked him forward.

Neither spoke as they neared the spot where McGill found the sinkhole. Once they were standing next to the location, Wolfe secured the man's legs together with another zip tie. After this was done, he ripped off the tape covering the man's eyes.

The prisoner flinched. The retired Marine then peeled off the tape covering his mouth.

He saw the gaping hole in front of him and with wide eyes alternated his attention from the hole to both McGill and Wolfe. After repeating this several times, his attention focused on the hole.

McGill growled, "What's your name, laddie?"

The man remained quiet.

Wolfe stepped over to the hole and dropped a large rock into it. When he failed to hear the sound of the rock hit anything, he turned back to the bound man. "What's your name?"

With pleading eyes, the scared man said, "My name is Mostafa Abbas."

"What are you doing in the United States, Mostafa?"

"I was minding my own business until you kidnapped me."

"Actually, both of us will testify you volunteered to get in the van and then attacked us."

"My government will file a protest."

"What government might that be, Mostafa?"

Realizing he had revealed too much, the Iranian said, "I am a diplomat. My country will file a formal protest about you abducting me."

"Would that country be Iran, Mostafa?"

The man did not answer.

McGill stepped closer to the man and growled. "Because Iran does not have diplomatic relationships with the United States, and I suspect the US government does not even know you are in this country. Would I be right?"

The quiet of the woodland setting returned.

Grabbing the man under his arms, Wolfe and McGill inched him closer to the edge of the opening in the earth.

Wolfe said, "You probably aren't familiar with the geology of this part of the United States, are you, Mostafa?"

The Iranian kept his eyes on the hole but said nothing.

"I didn't think you would be. Let's put it this way—most of the bedrock under the soil in this part of the world is made up of limestone. Water has a way of dissolving it and creating large caves. They can be up to thirty or forty meters deep. If you survive us throwing you into the pit, no one lives out here, so no one will hear your screams for help. Are you getting the picture now?"

The man nodded.

"Plus, when it rains, which is forecasted for tonight, water will gush into the hole and, if you are still alive, you'll drown."

"You wouldn't. That would be murder."

McGill glared at the Iranian. "Think about it for a second, laddie. You're in this country illegally, and you probably don't have your real identification on you. Even if you do, we'll take it before we throw you in. The chances of you ever being found are slim. If, for some reason, your body is found, no one will know who you are and probably won't care."

Mostafa's eyes widened as they locked on McGill.

Leaning forward toward the bound man, the Scotsman said, "I wonder what you will be thinking if you survive the fall. It takes about ten days for a body to die of thirst. If, for some reason, you have water to drink, it can take up to seventy days for the body to shut down without food. That's a long time to contemplate your poor decision of not talking to us."

More silence from the Iranian.

Wolfe said, "My friend and I are not with the police. So, we don't follow any rules about dealing with terrorists. And, Mostafa, my young friend, we consider you a terrorist."

After a nervous gulp, Mostafa said, "What do you want to know?"

"Kind of what I thought. Are you planning to tell me the truth?"

The Iranian nodded with enthusiasm.

"We can check on your truthfulness. If you lie, well..."

"I will not lie. I want sanctuary."

"Why are you in the United States?"

Chapter Twenty-Three

SOUTHWEST MISSOURI

That Same Day

Across the street and one building west of JR's building sat a three-story unit built during the same time period as the surrounding structures. Over the two decades since its completion, the building hosted a variety of businesses, none of which found lasting success. Then, in 2015, a savvy investor bought the underutilized location and changed it into a multiuse facility. On the ground floor, attracted by a reduced per-square-foot lease agreement, a highly successful law firm moved in. In the renovated two floors above the attorney offices, contemporary loft units were constructed. Within two months after renovations were completed, the building started returning a positive ROI for the investor.

Of the ten apartment units, two were designated as short-term luxury lease locations for in-transit executives. Furnished and commanding a higher monthly rate than the unfurnished versions, the man with the passport claiming his name to be Danny Wade scrutinized the building across the street. He also witnessed the successful abduction of Mostafa Abbas.

Using binoculars to witness the kidnapping closer, he recognized the driver of the van as it screeched to a halt behind the hapless Abbas' vehicle.

As with all things, patience rewards those who practice it. Logan Dillon confirmed the fact Ian McGill did not move to the Australian outback.

Christian County
Two Days Later

Wolfe folded his arms as he watched Joseph clean the gas grill on the back deck of his home in a rural part of Christian County. As he scrubbed the iron grates, Joseph said, "From what I was told, your friend Mostafa Abbas has developed a serious case of diarrhea of the mouth."

"He's not my friend."

"Figure of speech, Michael." Joseph closed the lid and lit the grill. When he finished, he faced Wolfe. "There were five of them. The leader's name was Amir Zamani, a known associate of Mohammed Al-Qaedi."

"JR said the minute Abbas disappeared, so did the others. The guy working at the restaurant took his apron off and walked out in the middle of lunch rush. Any idea of who the rest were?"

"Apparently, Zamani was the only name the others were told. CIA believes they have all been living in the US for a few years under assumed names. Mostafa revealed he had been in the US for five years, living under the name Oliver Garcia in Chicago. They infiltrated Zamani into the country somewhere in the Detroit area.

"Which tells me there are others still out there we don't know about."

"That's Dwight King's assessment as well. While you and McGill won't get official credit for this, the FBI and Homeland Security are singing your praises."

"I don't need the praise."

"I know. I've tried to keep it quiet."

"What about McGill? What's his status?"

"State Department is keeping a lid on this, but he is now protected under a presidential executive order. He will be awarded citizenship papers on an expedited basis."

"Good." Wolfe sipped the beer he held. "What about Chapman? Does he know?"

"Not unless we have a leak somewhere."

Wolfe tilted his head. "Don't discount the possibility." He paused for a moment. "You know the guy. I don't know him at all, but Ian is really puzzled by Chapman's involvement. What's your opinion?"

"I have to agree with Ian. It is out of character for Jonathan. However, I did learn something he has been able to sweep under the rug."

"What's that?"

"He had a brief nervous breakdown, which seems to correspond with his disappearance during Operation Desert Storm."

"He wasn't in Iran?"

"No."

After several moments of silence, Wolfe said, "Kind of blows up the theory he met Al-Qaedi in Iran, doesn't it?"

"Very much so."

"Could someone else be feeding him this crap about Ian?"

Joseph placed the grill brush on the shelf next to the cooking area. "I'm leaning in that direction myself."

"Nadia and I want to take the offensive to Al-Qaedi. Send us to England."

Joseph picked up his crystal tumbler of scotch and took a sip. He kept his gaze on Wolfe. After a lengthy silence, he asked, "Why?"

"Several reasons. First, he's not going to give up his quest to kill McGill. Second, maybe we can discover who's feeding Chapman misinformation."

Joseph smiled. "There's a third reason, isn't there?"

"Maybe."

"You still want payback on Al-Qaedi, right?"

Wolfe shrugged.

"You can't go as US Marshals."

"Why not?"

"You two will need deeper covers."

"Not following you, Joseph."

"Chapman is aware of your and Nadia's nom-de-guerre. Plus, you really don't have a legitimate reason to be there as US Marshals."

"Okay, I get that. You apparently have a plan, or you wouldn't have brought it up."

Joseph sipped his scotch and said, "Maybe."

"A maybe from you, Joseph, is another way of saying you have a plan."

"As a matter of fact, I do."

"I see his point, Michael."

"As do I." Wolfe continued to pack his small duffel bag as Nadia laid out what she would take. "Apparently, Joseph anticipated our need for new covers some time ago. We are to fly to Joint Base Andrews, where Jerry will meet us with our new IDs and passports."

"And then what?"

"We jump on a flight to London."

She chuckled. "I know that, silly. What happens when we get to London?"

"We meet up with Carla Webb."

Nadia stopped what she was doing. "You're kidding."

"Nope, she's been in London for several weeks getting ready for us to arrive."

"Michael, how…"

Wolfe shrugged. "You and I both know Joseph is always three or four steps ahead of the rest of us. How he does it, I haven't a clue."

"Did he mention what our covers would be?"

"He didn't tell me. Apparently, arrangements were still being made."

"That's a little surprising."

Wolfe hoisted his duffel bag to his shoulder. "Not sure if he actually didn't know or didn't want to tell me yet. You ready?"

"Yes, all I have to do is set the security system."

Wolfe exited the Beechcraft and shook Jerry Griggs' hand on the tarmac of Joint Base Andrews. Griggs said, "I've arranged for the Baron to be hangered, courtesy of Uncle Sam."

"Thanks, Jerry."

Nadia circled the plane and walked up next to her husband. She nodded at Griggs.

"Morning, Nadia." He returned his attention to Wolfe. "A Gulfstream will pick us up in thirty minutes."

"Us?"

"Yeah, I'm going, as are two others."

"Not part of the deal, Jerry. Nadia and I work alone."

"All we will be doing is providing logistics and support."

Wolfe folded his arms and shook his head. "Then, Nadia and I are done. We'll fly back home, and you guys can figure it out on your own."

"Those are my orders, Michael."

As he leaned closer to Griggs, Wolfe spoke in a growl. "You guys never learn, do you?"

Taken aback by the attitude, Griggs folded his arms. "Learn what?"

"The more people involved in an operation multiplies the probability of things getting screwed up. Nothing against your team, but I prefer to rely on Nadia and myself."

"Michael, this could be our first good chance of capturing Mohammed Al-Qaedi in years."

Wolfe narrowed his eyes. "Why do you say that?"

"New intel indicates he's going to be in London for a while."

"Carla?"

Griggs nodded.

Taking a deep breath, Wolfe asked Nadia, "What do you say?"

She studied Griggs for a moment. "As long as you and the others stay out of Michael's and my way, I say we go."

Before agreeing, Wolfe felt his cell phone vibrate with an incoming text message. The unexpected interruption allowed him additional time to determine his response. He read the message and stood silent for several seconds before he said to Nadia, "JR needs us to call him immediately."

Nadia's eyebrows rose, and she started to say something but stopped as Wolfe dialed the computer hacker's number.

"Where are you two?" JR spoke with a concerned tone.

"Tarmac at Joint Base Andrews. Why?"

"Get back as quickly as you can. Ian and Lori were injured in a car accident."

After several silent moments, Wolfe said, "How bad?"

"Both are in critical condition."

"Shit."

Nadia frowned as she listened to the one-sided conversation.

Wolfe said, "Do you know what happened?"

"Police don't know, but Lori's Audi Q8 went down a ravine near their property. The wreck wasn't discovered for six hours."

Walking back to the Baron, Wolfe said, "We'll head back. Thanks for the call, JR."

The line went dead as he put his phone back in his pocket. "We have to get back. Ian and Lori were in a car accident."

Her eyes widened. "Are they alive?"

"Yes, but both are in critical condition and need our help." Wolfe returned his attention to Griggs. "Sorry, Jerry. Our little excursion to England needs to be put on hold for the moment."

"Understood. Keep me posted on their condition."

Southwest Missouri

Sitting in a chair next to his friend's hospital bed, Wolfe mindlessly watched the vital signs monitor. From his years in the military, he understood McGill's condition to be stable. The fact the man remained unconscious concerned him.

"What ya staring at, laddie?" The voice sounded weak and raspy.

Shifting his eyes to the Scotsman, Wolfe said, "Waiting for all those lines to go flat."

"Not today."

Wolfe stood and moved closer to the bed. He studied McGill's face. Both eyes were swollen, with a large purple bruise next to the right one. A white bandage encircled his forehead and covered his right ear. "What happened, Ian?"

"Not sure. Is Lori, okay?"

"Yes, Nadia's with her. She fared better than you did."

"Good."

"What do you remember?"

"Not much. We finished signing papers at our bank and were headed back to the property to meet the contractor. I remember Lori staring at the rearview mirror and commenting on a truck following too close. Then I woke up here with you perched in that chair."

"I was told the only reason you two are still alive is because of the Audi SUV you were in."

"Damn Germans always were good engineers."

Silence filled the room except for the beeping of the monitor. It remained that way as McGill closed his eyes. Wolfe glanced at the machine and observed the blood pressure measurement rise.

"You still with me, Ian?"

"Aye."

"I think it's time for Ian McGill to be declared dead. JR has a new identity ready for you."

The ex-SAS sergeant slowly shook his head. "No."

"Why?"

"I want to marry Lori under my name, not some made-up one."

Wolfe grinned. "Understandable. Did you know you are now an American citizen?"

McGill opened one eye. "Since when?"

Checking his wristwatch, Wolfe returned his attention to his friend. "As of noon today. That was about six hours ago."

"How?"

"You have friends in high places."

"Joseph?"

"Yeah. He hand-walked the paperwork through, and the president signed the declaration yesterday." He paused for a few heartbeats. "Our little road trip with Abbas has produced a treasure trove of intel for the FBI. All of Abbas' buddies, except their leader, have been apprehended. Plus, those individuals helped the agency to uncover ten additional sleeper agents."

"Glad to have helped. Who was their leader?"

"An Iranian named Zamani. He disappeared." He paused. "Did I mention Uncle Sam is picking up your and Lori's hospital bill?"

McGill opened his left eye again.

"Who arranged that?"

"Let's just say I can be very persuasive at times."

With a chuckle, McGill said, "Aye, that you can."

Folding his arms, Wolfe's expression hardened. "I'm serious here, Ian. We need to make sure Al-Qaedi thinks you're dead."

"You'll get no argument from me."

"Good. JR will handle the details of getting the information on the Internet. You and Lori will need to find someplace quiet to heal until Nadia and I return."

"Don't like someone else settling me debts."

"You're not. I owe Al-Qaedi payback, myself."

"Michael?"

"Yes."

"Does this mean I get to keep my real name?"

"As long as I find Al-Qaedi, it does."

McGill closed his eyes again. "I'm good with that."

Chapter Twenty-Four

LONDON

Jonathan Chapman scanned the intelligence brief, occasionally stopping to scrutinize a topic. On the final page of the report, he paused and read the third item from the bottom again. He leaned back in his chair, placed his elbows on the arms and made a steeple with his fingers. Staring at the computer screen again, he muttered, "That was what I tried to prevent, my old friend. Sorry I failed you."

He closed his eyes, recited a prayer from his youth, and then picked up the phone. Not caring about the time, he dialed a cell phone number he knew by heart.

"Good morning, Jonathan."

"Sorry for the early call, Joseph, but I just read something concerning."

"What might that be?"

"The death of Ian McGill."

"Yes, I just learned about it myself."

"Do you have any details?"

"Not really. All I know is the car he was riding in left the road and plunged down an embankment."

"Not the way a brave soldier should go out."

"No. I would agree with you." Joseph paused for a moment. "Were you aware five Iranians infiltrated the US to find him?"

"No, but it was a concern of mine. One of the reasons I wanted him back in England. I could have protected him. Do you think one of them caused the accident?"

"It's possible. I don't have any details."

"That's unlike you, Joseph."

"Jonathan, you weren't exactly truthful with me on why you wanted him back in the UK."

"I had my reasons."

"I'm sure you did. But if you had been more truthful about it, he might have considered returning."

Chapman remained quiet for a considerable length of time. "What's being done with the body?"

"His fiancée is handling the arrangements."

"Fiancée? When did this happen?"

"There was a lot you didn't know about Ian. He sold his ancestral home in Scotland before he came to the US. He was making a clean break from his past."

"Apparently." More silence.

"Jonathan, as soon as I know more about what happened, I will get you the details."

"Thank you, Joseph."

Chapman ended the call and focused on his computer screen. "Damn."

The funeral for Ian McGill occurred on a Wednesday at a small funeral home in Christian County. Few were in attendance except Lori Shepard, Michael and Nadia

Wolfe, JR and Mia Diminski, Joseph Kincaid, and Jerry Griggs. The funeral home director, being a friend of Joseph's and a former Marine, went along with the charade.

The celebration of life and obituary were announced in the local paper and also on the funeral home's website. Since the body had been cremated, there would be no interment. The whole thing lasted thirty minutes. Lori collected the urn and left in the company of Michael and Nadia.

Across the street, in a small café, a man kept tabs on the arrivals and departures of the funeral participants. He took pictures of Lori walking out of the funeral home carrying an urn and getting into Wolfe's Jeep Grand Cherokee. He paid for his meal with a credit card proclaiming him to be Danny Wade and exited the diner.

Once the fictious Danny Wade sat in his rental car, he sent the picture to an email address based in London. He then drove to the airport and, two hours later, boarded a plane to Chicago.

Rural Christian County

Joseph handed Wolfe and Nadia the passports they would use to travel to London the following day. He said, "Your covers will be state department interpreters. Since both of you are multilingual, we thought it would give you some credibility. Plus, there is an international business conference in a week, which will give you additional cover. You need to stop by the American embassy in London as soon as you arrive. Jerry will be there and will introduce you to the CIA Chief of Station. He will be the only one at the embassy who knows your real assignment. Dwight King briefed him personally."

Wolfe narrowed his eyes. "How many people know what Nadia and I are really there for?"

"Besides Jerry and I, Dwight King, the Chief of Station, and, of course, the president."

"That's almost too many."

"I would normally agree with you Michael, but it can't be helped." Joseph handed them a packet.

After checking the contents, Wolfe frowned. "What's this?"

"Credit cards and cash. There's ten thousand pounds in paper currency. Plus, an HSBC debit card you can use to withdraw additional cash you might need to, uh—obtain information."

"Where do we meet Carla?"

"She'll be picking you two up at Heathrow."

"Thought we were flying in on a government plane?"

"Change of plans. Less visibility. I've been told Chapman gets a report of every foreign government plane that lands in the UK, concerning who's on board and their reason for being in the UK. We don't need any additional scrutiny about your trip. Particularly if he or someone on his staff are the backchannel to Al-Qaedi."

"I take it you're not convinced Chapman is the leak."

"I didn't say that. But I'm finding it difficult to believe he is.

Nadia frowned. "Why is Al-Qaedi still in London?"

"That's a good question, Nadia."

"Is he there to disrupt the conference?"

Silence filled Joseph's living room as he determined just what to say to her. Finally, he said, "That's what the CIA believes and is telling the president."

Folding his arms, Wolfe glared at Joseph. "And just when was this information going to be shared with us?"

"I just did." He paused. "Besides, the president believes you and Nadia can have this matter settled before the sessions start."

"So, we have a week?"

"By the time you get there, six days, Michael."

Wolfe's jaw muscles tightened. "When we're done with this little chore, remind me to retire."

The sly smile on Joseph's face betrayed his words. "Of course, Michael. I'll be happy to."

The Next Day

London Heathrow, during a normal year, handles over eighty million international passengers. To say it is a busy airport is an understatement. Wolfe and Nadia arrived in London on a Delta flight connecting through Atlanta at 10:47 a.m. After spending eleven hours and thirty minutes on a plane and navigating their way through customs, they exited the airport a few minutes past noon chauffeured by the diminutive Carla Webb.

Carla glanced at Nadia in the front passenger seat and asked, "How was the flight?"

Nadia exploded with a variety of French expletives and then said, "Wonderful, if you like sitting next to a mother with a crying child for the seven hours it takes to fly over the Atlantic Ocean."

Wolfe, while trying to hide his smile, said, "Nadia hasn't been on a commercial flight for a very long time."

Carla said, "I take it you didn't fly business class."

With a huff, Nadia said, "No, and I will be upgrading my seat on the return flight."

Everyone remained quiet as the driver navigated the busy streets in the heart of London. After ten minutes, Carla said, "We're heading to the American embassy. Jerry should already be there waiting. He didn't think you'd be there more than an hour. I'll wait with the car."

"Thanks, Carla." Wolfe turned his attention to the passenger window. "I'm not real comfortable with the Chief of Station knowing we're here. I don't normally operate that way."

"He's a good guy, Michael. He's not the normal Chief of Station. He used to be a case officer here in London and throughout Europe. I've worked with him a few times. He's a former Marine, just like you."

Nadia said to her husband, "Is that good?"

"Don't know. I'm still not comfortable with it." He paused and said, "Carla, what have you learned about Al-Qaedi?"

"Latest intel places him in the Borough of Newham. It has the second highest Muslim populations in London and one of the highest poverty levels in the municipality. There are several mosques considered off-limits to London constables. Scotland Yard has them under surveillance but is unable to determine if Al-Qaedi is staying in one. Last sighting of him was in the city of London. But they lost his trail five minutes after they spotted him."

"Great. Do you think he's still here?"

"Oh yeah. He's here. In my opinion, the international business conference is too rich of a target next week for him to ignore."

"Carla, once Nadia and I meet with the Chief of Station, we need to disappear."

The diminutive CIA agent said, "Cool. We can make that happen."

Chapter Twenty-Five

LONDON BOROUGH OF NEWHAM

To Mohammed Al-Qaedi, the differences between Shia and Sunni beliefs were immaterial. Born in Iran during the waning years of the monarchy of Mohammed Reza Pahlavi, he grew up adhering to the Shia brand of Islam. Curious and constantly questioning authority, he found the arguments between the two sects illogical and counterproductive.

Politically active as a young teenager, he became a foot soldier during the 1979 Islamic Revolution. Then on November 4, 1979, he participated in the student movement that seized the US Embassy in Tehran. For 444 days, over fifty Americans were held hostage and occasionally paraded before the public and international news crews. Several of the more famous pictures from this era show Al-Qaedi in the background. This movement helped topple the Pahlavi monarchy, sending the Shah into exile in Egypt. During this period, he discovered his love of anarchy. Equally comfortable with both his Shia and Sunni brethren, he traveled the world not advocating for the unity of Islam but advancing the cause of bringing Western civilizations to their knees.

His current location, a mosque in the London Borough of Newham, provided a secure location to visit with local radical clerics and their followers.

After pouring tea, Al-Qaedi sat on a floor pillow and said as he handed his guest the glass, "Tell me about the funeral."

Amir Zamani took a sip of the dark liquid. "I did not actually see it, but the man Dillon showed me pictures taken before and after the service. Afterward, the woman carried an urn as she exited the funeral home."

"But no one saw the body?"

"No. One of my men attempted to break into the funeral home, but they have an all-night attendant and a dog roaming the building at night."

"Most unfortunate."

"I followed the truck that forced them off the road. It would have been difficult for McGill to survive."

"The woman did."

"True, but the SUV hit a tree on the passenger side where McGill sat. I climbed down the embankment to see the results."

"You did not confirm it by putting a bullet through his skull?"

"That would have been foolish. The authorities would have then known he was assassinated which would have led to an investigation and additional scrutiny. This way, he died in an accident. Everyone mourns but soon forgets."

"Hmmm." Al-Qaedi paused as he sipped tea. "Have you made contact with Anderson recently?"

"No."

"Maybe it is time. If McGill is truly dead, Chapman would know."

"Good idea. What about Wolfe?"

"What about him?"

"He may try to avenge McGill's death."

"Maybe. But Chapman has knowledge of all foreign agents being sent to British soil. Another reason to contact Anderson. See if his boss has heard anything about Wolfe traveling to the UK."

Zamani stood. "Yes, my Sheik."

Wolfe shook the hand of the London CIA Chief of Station, Nick Soto. Soto tilted his head and said, "You look vaguely familiar. Have we met before?"

"Can't say that we have."

Soto folded his arms and brought a hand to his chin. "Now I remember. In those days, I was a Blackhawk pilot with the Marines. I pulled you and your spotter out of Kuwait a few days before Desert Storm started. I'll never forget him telling everyone about the shot you made." He paused. "I noticed you didn't say anything about it. All you did was close your eyes."

Wolfe kept his expression neutral. "Rick liked to talk. I think it helped calm his nerves."

"I didn't run into you again after we landed."

"Sorry, I don't remember much about the flight. Thanks for pulling us out."

"My pleasure." He moved his attention to Nadia and shook her hand. "A pleasure to meet you, Ms. Picard."

"I go by Nadia Wolfe now."

"Ahh, yes. Dwight mentioned you two were married. You used to work for the Mossad, correct?"

She nodded, keeping her eyes on him.

The Chief of Station then said to Wolfe, "So, I've been told you're searching for Mohammed Al-Qaedi."

"Yes."

"Any idea where he might be?"

"Newham."

Soto's eyebrows rose. "How's your Farsi and Arabic?"

"Fluent."

"You'll need it there. The Queen's English is rarely spoken on those mean streets."

"That's our understanding as well."

"The British don't like big guns used in their city, Michael. May I call you Michael?"

Wolfe shrugged, curious about the direction the conversation might be headed.

"If you do decide to use one, I would recommend the use of a suppressor. And I might even know of a warehouse where you might find a Barrett M82A1 sniper rifle with a factory suppressor attached. I believe that particular model is your preferred tool of the trade. But then, I'm being presumptuous?"

Barely suppressing a smile, Wolfe said, "No, you are not being presumptuous."

"You will also find a Ford Focus there for your use. It will keep you from having to rent one and having your names recorded. I'm told the car has been tuned by an excellent mechanic." Soto handed Wolfe a black object with a key attached.

As he pocketed the key fob, Wolfe said, "Nadia and I are familiar with London. Your hospitality is appreciated."

"I might add," the CIA man paused for a second, "Scotland Yard is aware of Al-Qaedi's presence but do not have the resources in place to tell them where he is."

"What about MI5?"

"Same problem. Both would be more than pleased to find his dead body in an alley one morning. I doubt there would be much of a fuss or even an investigation."

"Do they know I'm here?"

"No. Let's try to keep it that way."

"They won't hear it from me."

Soto gave Wolfe a slight grin. "I didn't think they would." He paused for a moment. "What else can we do to assist you?"

Nadia said, "I can't think of anything, can you, Michael?"

"Just the warehouse address."

"Carla knows where it is. She can take you."

Wolfe asked, "I thought Jerry Griggs was supposed to be here?"

"Unfortunately, MI5 detained him for a short period at the airport. Something about Chapman monitoring all government flights from the US. He'll be here shortly."

"Glad we came in commercially."

"Yes. Chapman can be so predictable at times."

Offering his hand, Wolfe said, "I hope we don't have to see each other again."

As they shook, Soto said, "Probably a good idea, but if you determine you need anything, don't hesitate to call."

"So, where is this warehouse Soto referred to, Carla?"

"Near the River Thames in Thurrock, about forty-eight

kilometers from here. With traffic, it'll take about an hour. Do you want to go now or wait until dark?"

"Now's fine. Tonight, I want to get a feel for Newham."

"Are you sure, Michael? Statistically, Newham has the second-highest rate of crime in London."

"At least it's not the highest."

She checked his reflection in the rearview mirror. "Sorry, I sometimes forget who you are."

Ignoring the comment, he said, "Canfield used to hang out in a pub east of Canary Wharf on the north side of the River Thames. I met him there a couple of times. Not sure if the clientele has changed, but I thought Nadia and I would start there."

"That's west of Newham."

"I know. Jeffrey used the place to keep his finger on the pulse of what was going on in Tower Hamlets and Newham. The Borough of Newham has the largest non-European population in the country. Geoffrey told me more than 60 percent of its residents are descendants of Middle-Eastern or South Asian immigrants. He always knew more about the politics within the local Muslim community than anyone in MI5."

Carla remained quiet for a moment. "So, you're going to this pub to see if you can find out where Al-Qaedi is hiding?"

"More or less."

"Michael, that's crazy. How long's it been, ten years since you were there?"

"Probably."

"No one will remember Geoffrey."

"On the contrary, I called the place, and the bartender remembers him. He wants me to stop by and fill him in on what happened."

The response from Carla was only silence.

The Copper Lamp tavern and grill contained a mixture of day laborers and college students from nearby University of the West of Scotland, London Campus. Wolfe and Nadia arrived as dusk settled over the city.

When Wolfe entered the pub, he casually scrutinized the customers. "Clientele's a bit different. There weren't as many young couples in those days."

Nadia also checked their surroundings. "So much for Muslims not drinking alcohol. Half the patrons in here appear to be from the Middle East."

Wolfe chuckled. He then pointed to the bar. "That's the bartender. He hasn't changed at all since I last saw him. Let's see if he recognizes me."

They found two empty seats together at the far end of the bar. It took a few moments, but finally the bartender sauntered toward them and started wiping the counter in front of them with a towel. "Haven't seen you in here for a while, mate."

"It's been a few years."

"Who's your friend?"

"My wife."

The man nodded in Nadia's direction. "What can I get ya?"

"Couple of pints."

"Guinness?"

"Please."

The man wandered back to the middle of the bar, speaking to several customers as he walked. He filled two glasses in the proper way for the dark ale and returned to

Wolfe and Nadia. After placing the Irish stout in front of them, the bartender said, "Sorry to hear about Canfield."

"Yeah, so was I."

"I've got a couple of drinks to pour. I'll be right back."

When he was gone, Nadia asked, "What's his name?"

"Duncan. Not sure if it's his first or last one."

When the man returned, he asked, "Where'd Canfield disappear to for all those years?"

"Grand Caymans. He and his lady doctor friend."

Duncan nodded again. "Good for him." After a short pause, he continued. "He always told me if he disappeared, he'd be someplace warm."

"How many years did he come in here, Duncan?"

"Maybe a decade, or more. I've been here since 2001, and he was a customer before that."

"I understand he had his finger on the pulse of the Muslim community back then?"

"He did."

"Know how he did it?"

"He'd come in here and pay attention to all the conversations in the room." The man pointed to the spot where Wolfe sat. "He'd sit right there and just listen."

Duncan moved away to service another customer at the bar. Wolfe and Nadia waited. When he returned, he said, "There's a reason you're here, isn't there, mate?"

"Yes."

"Want to tell me?"

"Ever hear about visiting Muslims who don't have the best interests of London at heart?"

"Funny way of putting it, but occasionally I do."

"Are there any rumors right now?"

"Maybe."

Wolfe remained quiet as he sipped his Guinness and kept his attention on Duncan.

"Since you're a friend of Canfield's, would ya by chance be in a position to do something about it?"

"Maybe."

Duncan chuckled. "Visit the pub again tomorrow night about eight. I'll keep those two seats open for ya. It's where Canfield used to sit."

"Yeah, I remember."

"You'll need to keep your ears open, mate."

Chapter Twenty-Six

EAST LONDON

The Next Day

By eight p.m., Wolfe and Nadia once again occupied the two barstools recommended by Duncan the previous evening. They nursed the two dark stouts sitting in front of them. Not knowing what to expect or how long it would take, he ordered fish and chips for him and Nadia to share.

At exactly eight-eleven, a bearded man entered the pub and headed toward an isolated table just behind where the husband and wife sat munching on their meal. Wolfe caught Duncan's eye. The bartender just nodded.

He nudged Nadia's leg with his and whispered, "Behind us."

She acknowledged him with a blink. Five minutes later, another bearded man, this one older than the first, entered the pub and joined the original occupant of the table.

Remaining quiet, the couple from America kept their eyes on a TV above the bar where an English football match between minor league teams could be seen. The men behind them spoke in Farsi and kept their voices low enough Wolfe only caught parts of the conversation. What he did hear increased his concentration.

"Thank you, my friend, for meeting me. The sheik is getting anxious about recruits."

"The sheik should not be worried. He will have his volunteers."

"I wish he shared your confidence. But he is not hearing good news about your recruiting methods."

A goal by one of the teams on television created a roar, and Wolfe missed pieces of the conversation. He searched for a mirror with their reflection, with the hope that watching their lips might help to understand their words. Finding none, he settled on listening in between cheers from the bar crowd.

"The sheik is not from this area. How would he know if our recruiting methods are falling short?"

"Lower your voice. He has his sources."

"Well, whoever they are, they are wrong."

"Not likely, the source is well placed."

"Who is it?"

"Anderson."

"How would Anderson know?"

"He is—" A shot on goal skipped off the crossbar, and the rest of the sentence disappeared in the groans from the bar crowd.

Wolfe heard a chair scraping on the floor.

"Sit down. You are drawing attention to yourself."

"I am leaving."

Out of the corner of his eye, Wolfe saw the older man walk out of the pub. Tapping Nadia on the hand, he motioned with his eyes toward the door. He stood and said to Duncan with a slight cockney accent, "We square on the bill, mate?"

Duncan waved, and Wolfe and Nadia walked out of the pub. Across the street, in the shadows of an alley, they waited for the younger man to exit. Their wait lasted ten minutes.

When the man emerged, his head turned left and then right. He crossed the street and walked toward the west.

Wolfe said, "Get the car and I'll follow him for a while. Maybe I can get a license number. It'd be helpful to know who this guy is."

"Keep your cell phone handy." She hurried away.

He waited until his presence would seem normal behind the bearded man. Two blocks from the pub, the man stopped and unlocked a car. Wolfe kept a steady pace and, just before the car exited the parking space, he memorized the license plate.

Two minutes later, he slipped into the passenger seat, and Nadia sped toward their hotel. While she drove, Wolfe sent a text message with a time.

At the precise moment mentioned in his electronic note, Nadia received a VoIP call on her laptop. Wolfe stood behind her at the desk as she accepted the call.

"What's up?"

She said, "Thanks for calling, JR. Can you run license numbers from England?"

"Sure. What do you need? The owner, addresses, or something else?"

"Name and address."

"Okay, shoot."

Nadia gave him the license plate number of the car driven by the man from the pub.

"Give me a moment."

The only sound they heard were JR's fingers typing on the keyboard. Then, "Hmmm."

"What?"

"The car is registered to a mosque in Newham. Does that make sense?"

"Maybe. What's the address of the mosque?"

JR gave it to them.

Nadia entered it into Google Maps, which displayed the location.

Wolfe said, "It's a start, JR. Thanks for the help."

"Want me to do some snooping on the place?"

"Anything you can tell us would be valuable."

"All part of the service."

The call ended.

Touching his wife on the shoulder, Wolfe said, "Let's take a drive to Newham. I've got an idea."

As they drove toward the address given to them by the computer hacker, Wolfe asked Nadia, "How much of the conversation did you hear?"

"Not much. The noise from the TV and the reaction from the crowd drowned out most of what they were saying."

"I only caught a little of the conversation myself. It sounded like they have something planned but don't have the volunteers needed at this time."

Nadia turned in her seat to face her husband. "That's what I heard also."

"I'll drive by the mosque. We may need Carla to secure a few listening devices for us."

"How long do you think we have?"

"If they are having difficulty recruiting, at least a few days. We can learn a lot in that length of time."

The mosque appeared on their left. As he steered the small Ford by the property, Wolfe observed a buff brick two-story structure on a corner lot. What appeared to be Muslim-owned shops surrounded the location. While he did not notice anyone on the outside, he detected security cameras strategically placed on every corner of the building.

He said, "What did you see?"

"On first pass, not much. How about you?"

"Security cameras everywhere."

"Not good."

"No, and it appears the neighbors would not be receptive to us hanging around the place. Let's drive by again in thirty minutes. I want to confirm something else I thought I saw."

On their second pass, Wolfe confirmed what he only glimpsed on the first drive-by. "We need to talk to Carla."

Next Morning

Carla Webb sipped her tea as she listened to Wolfe describe what he needed. She nodded occasionally but did not comment until he finished. "I can get most of what you need. Jerry might be able to secure the large item."

"We need them ASAP, Carla. Something big is in the

works and I don't think we have a lot of time to figure out what it might be."

"I can have the listening devices here this afternoon."

"That's a start."

"As far as the voice-activated recorders, not sure. The ones you need are pretty sophisticated. Our cousins here in England might not approve of planting them in a mosque."

Wolfe tapped his lips with a finger. "I understand. But they've got security cameras all over the building. I doubt I'd be able to plant any on the outside without being seen. Best I go in for prayers and plant them while I'm inside."

The diminutive woman tilted her head. "Your beard will pass. Most of the Muslims here in London keep theirs trimmed because of their jobs."

Nadia chuckled. "At least it doesn't tickle me anymore."

Carla glanced at her friend, frowned, but did not respond.

Wolfe said, "I just need to pass as a visiting Muslim. I'll attend a few sessions and then determine where to plant the bugs."

"Be careful. If they are planning something there, they'll be scrutinizing strangers."

"That's why I will attend a few times before I decide to plant the devices. Can you get in touch with Jerry for us?"

"Yes."

"Good. Then I'll go in for Dhuhr today."

With a surprised look, Carla said, "You know about that kind of stuff?"

"Not my first time in a mosque."

Nadia stood. "Let's go, Michael. We have plans to make."

Nadia dropped her husband off two blocks from his destination. She would pick him up in a different predetermined location an hour later. Walking toward the mosque, he trailed behind a group of other men into the male entrance. Once inside, he followed edict by removing his shoes and then washing before prayers.

So far, no one paid much attention to him other than a slight bow with their hand over their heart. He positioned himself toward the back of the room as other men lined up for prayers.

During this time, he scanned the room for security cameras or spots offering a hidden one. He found four likely locations. After prayers, he stood and retrieved his shoes. Just before he departed the building, a man in a white thobe and kufi approached and said, "Assalamu Alaykom, my brother."

Wolfe bowed slightly and replied, "Wa Alaykom as Salam, Imam."

"I have not seen you before. Are you new to the area?"

Responding in the same Arabic dialect, Wolfe said, "My employer has requested I assist several of my co-workers for a few weeks here in Newham. I am from Manchester."

"Ah, then you are welcome to join us. What is it you do?"

"Electrical contractor."

"Where are you working?"

Suddenly recognizing the man, Wolfe smiled. "We are going over the upcoming renovation of an apartment building a few blocks from here."

The imam placed his hand over his heart and said, "Welcome to our humble mosque, my brother."

He walked away leaving Wolfe to casually exit the building.

Nadia slowed to a stop at an intersection agreed on prior to letting him out. Wolfe opened the passenger door and slid into the seat. After closing the door, he said, "We've got a problem."

Accelerating away from the pickup spot, she glanced at her husband. "What do you mean?"

"Remember the man from the pub whose car license we asked JR to check on last night?"

"Yeah."

"He's the imam. We've got to talk to Jerry."

Chapter Twenty-Seven

WASHINGTON, DC

Joseph Kincaid accepted the call at a little after nine a.m. Eastern time. "Good afternoon, Jerry. I hope all is well."

"We've had a setback. Does the name Anderson mean anything to you?"

The National Security Advisor remained silent for several moments. "Maybe. What setback?"

"I just had a meeting with Michael. He believes he's been compromised in his surveillances of the mosque."

"Most unfortunate."

"What about the name Anderson?"

Silence prevailed again on the call. Finally, after about fifteen seconds, Joseph said, "The only person I can think of might be Jonathan Chapman's assistant, Noah Anderson."

"Shit."

"Want to explain?"

"The name came up during a conversation Wolfe overheard between two men. Both spoke Arabic and one is the imam of the mosque where we suspect Al-Qaedi is staying."

"Hmmm."

"Joseph, if Anderson is the leak, that would explain a lot."

"Yes. Jonathan relies heavily on him."

"So, what do we do now, boss?"

"Does Michael need you in London?"

"Not really, as you know, he and Nadia like to operate by themselves."

"Yes, I know. Why don't you head back? I may need to speak to Jonathan in person and will need you here to cover for me."

"Got it. I'll be there by morning."

The call ended, and Joseph swiveled in his chair to view the open window behind him. After several minutes of silence, he faced his computer again. He sent an encrypted email and started making plans for an unannounced trip to London.

As Jerry Griggs packed his duffel bag for his return to the States, he said to Wolfe, "Joseph believes Chapman's assistant might be the Anderson you heard mentioned in the pub."

"That makes sense. It could also explain why Chapman seems to be the leak. It's not him, it's his assistant." He paused for a few seconds. "Which makes talking to Chapman problematic. His assistant will find out and relay the information."

"Not if Joseph handles it correctly."

Tilting his head, Wolfe said, "Explain."

"He and Chapman go back a long way. While both have heavy responsibilities, both men know if a leak is suspected anywhere near them, discretion will be essential. Joseph will know how to explain it to Chapman."

"If I trust anyone to handle it discreetly, it would be Joseph."

Griggs looked at Wolfe. "You need anything before I head to the airport?"

"Yes. Nadia and I will not be going back to the pub, or I to prayers at the mosque. Too many opportunities to alert Al-Qaedi. We need to tap into all the cell phone calls originating inside the mosque."

With a smile, Griggs said, "The CIA has some wonderful toys that do that sort of thing."

"That's why I'm asking you. If I ask Carla, they'll know who it's for. I would prefer not to ask Soto, either. If you, uh, could appropriate the right equipment, no one will be the wiser."

"Can JR help?"

Wolfe shrugged.

"In other words, don't ask. Right?"

"Probably best not to."

The Next Day

Joseph Kincaid shook the hand of Jonathan Chapman. They stood in front of the MI6 director's desk in his office at Vauxhall Cross. The National Security Advisor said, "Thank you for seeing me on such short notice, Jonathan."

"What brings you to London?"

"I need to discuss a sensitive matter with you."

"Oh."

"Is there somewhere else we could discuss this?"

Tilting his head slightly, Chapman crossed his arms. "That's not like you, Joseph. This must be serious."

"I'm afraid it is extremely serious."

"We have a secure room downstairs. Would that work?"

"I would prefer to be offsite."

"What about my assistant, Noah?"

"Just you and me, Jonathan."

"Oh dear." Raising one eyebrow, Chapman picked up the handset on his desk phone and waited a second. "Amanda, please have the car pick me and my guest up at the front entrance." He paused. "No, it will just be the two of us." Another pause. "That will work, thank you."

He replaced the handset. "Five minutes. Let's head that way."

As they took the elevator to the ground floor, Joseph said, "I was sorry to hear about Ian."

"Thank you. Not a very noble way for a soldier to go out." He kept his eyes glued to the floor indicator display as the numbers counted down. "Do you have details about the accident?"

"Yes."

"Can you tell me?"

"As soon as we are in a secure environment."

"I say…" He held the door as Joseph walked into the lobby.

At the front entrance, a black BMW 750i with blacked-out windows stood idling. Chapman pointed to it and the two men slipped into the back seat. As the car pulled away from the curb, the director of MI6 held his hand up. Joseph remained silent.

"Where to, sir?"

"My apartment."

"Very good, sir."

Chapman did not speak during the ride nor did Joseph. When they pulled up in front of a row of dark-brick row homes less than ten blocks from Vauxhall Cross, the driver stopped the car. Chapman exited, followed by Joseph. Once inside the four-story house, Jonathan said, "I have a secure room downstairs. They installed it when I became number two. It should be satisfactory."

Joseph asked, "Is anyone home?"

"No, my wife is in the country, visiting our son. We will have the place to ourselves. Can I offer you tea?"

"Let's talk. Then you can make a decision on what to do next."

Raising his eyebrows, Chapman nodded and showed Joseph the stairs leading to the basement.

When they reached the bottom, Joseph observed a normal-size room with a fireplace, a sofa, and two leather wingback chairs.

Once in the room, Chapman closed the door and flipped two switches. He said, "This is the most secure room in London to have a discussion. What's on your mind, Joseph?"

"How well do you know Noah Anderson?"

Wolfe followed the progress of a Gulfstream G500 as it taxied to a stop in front of the building where he stood. The building, located on RAF Mildenhall Air Force in Mildenhall, stood in a remote part of the base. After a distinguished period serving RAF Bomber Command in World War II, it transitioned to the home of the USAF 110th Refueling Wing, servicing military planes traveling on to Europe or the Middle East.

The engines of the plane did not spool down as an airman, dressed in a tan Nomex flight suit, hurried down the air stairs and walked toward his position. The man carried a black backpack over one of his shoulders. When he stood in front of the retired Marine, he yelled over the din of jet engines in the background.

"You Wolfe?"

"Yeah."

He offered the backpack. "Compliments of Jerry Griggs."

The man wore no insignias or rank on his flight suit. Realizing he was not talking to an USAF pilot, he said, "I appreciate you dropping this off."

"You know how to use that thing?"

Wolfe nodded.

"That's what Griggs said." He offered his hand. As they shook, he said, "You take care of yourself."

"I will."

The man did an abrupt about-face and jogged back to the Gulfstream.

Chapman's reaction to the question was a raised eyebrow. "He's been my assistant for some years. Why do you ask?"

"I didn't ask how long he's been your assistant. I asked how well do you know him? There's a difference."

"How well do you know anybody who works for you? I know he has a wife and two kids. I say, where is this line of questioning going, Joseph?"

Producing a piece of paper from his inside navy blazer pocket, he unfolded it and laid it in front of Chapman.

"This was taken yesterday in Victoria Park." He tapped the image of Anderson. "That's Noah, isn't it?"

"Yes."

"Recognize the chap walking beside him?"

"Oh dear. I do."

"Everything you have told Noah is being fed directly to Mohammad Al-Qaedi via that man."

"When did you say this picture was taken?"

"Yesterday."

"What time?"

"Noon."

"Bloody hell. He left for a few hours about that time. How long have you known about him?"

"Day before. His name was mentioned in an overheard conversation. Since the CIA had no reason to suspect him before that, he was off their radar. One of their operators followed him yesterday. He took a circuitous route from your office to the park. However, it really wasn't that hard to follow him."

Chapman held the picture and studied at it for a while. "Damn."

"Sorry, Jonathan."

"Better to know now than later."

"What do you know about the man he's talking to?"

The director of MI6 stared at a spot above Joseph's shoulder. "He used to be in the SAS, where his name was Logan Dillon. Supposedly he died in 2009. Since then, as you can imagine, we didn't pay too much attention. A year ago, we heard rumors he wasn't dead but working under the name Danny Wade." Returning his attention to the picture, he rubbed his forehead and asked, "How do you know he's working for Al-Qaedi?"

"TSA video of him leaving the Springfield-Branson

National Airport right after McGill's accident. There is speculation he might have been involved with it."

"That doesn't directly tie him to the accident."

"No, but this does." Joseph unfolded another picture and placed it in front of Chapman. It showed Wade next to Amir Zamani.

"Where was this taken?"

"After finding Wade in the picture at the Springfield airport, they did a search and found a shot of him in the security line at DFW three days earlier. We were surprised to find Zamani standing next to him."

"Joseph, that does not prove they were together."

"None of these pictures prove anything, Jonathan. But, in our line of work, we sometimes don't deal in proof. The mere suggestion of collusion is all we need."

"Damn."

"What are you going to do about Anderson?"

Chapman pursed his lips. "Bloody take him to the country for a long talk."

Chapter Twenty-Eight

LONDON

Nadia turned her attention to her husband. "Can you identify the imam's voice if you hear it again?"

"I believe I can." Wolfe followed with fascination the process his wife used to set up the receiver and laptop for the cell phone eavesdropping device. "The only concern I have right now is how do we get the device close enough without creating suspicion. The area is busy with pedestrian and vehicle traffic all day. Plus, the imam knows me by sight. I don't think it's the best neighborhood for parking a car occupied by two non-Muslims for any length of time."

"No. I agree with you. How close do we need to be?"

"Last time I used one of these, it needed to be within a hundred meters."

"For how long?"

"As long as possible."

She shook her head slightly. "Michael, how much time?"

"A minimum of twenty-four hours."

"I don't believe we have that much."

"I know. My guess would be there will be little activity around the mosque after Isha."

"Sunset until twelve a.m. might be our best bet. I found some crime statistics for the area, and it gets fairly active after midnight."

He paused and rubbed his chin. "This time of year, that gives us about six hours. How do we hide in plain sight for that length of time?"

She stood and patted his chest. "I have no idea, but I am sure you'll think of something."

"Let's make a drive-by."

By late morning, Wolfe, wearing a ball cap pulled low over his eyebrows, drove slowly around the neighborhood adjacent to the mosque. After two passes, spaced thirty minutes apart, he said, "I think I just found a possibility."

"Where?"

"East side of the mosque. It appeared to be an abandoned shed behind a house. Definitely less than a hundred meters from the mosque." Wolfe paused. "Let's come back after dark. I can check it out without being seen."

"Do you think this is smart?"

"No, but it's all I've got at the moment."

At fifteen minutes before ten in the evening, Wolfe entered the ancient shed. Dressed all in black, jeans, long-sleeved T-shirt, utility vest, New Balance athletic shoes, and a balaclava, he transitioned the streets without raising alarms. A pair of night-vision goggles he found in the backpack helped him explore the shed once inside.

With the NVGs down, Wolfe viewed the shed's interior in the greenish hue of the device. A rusty potbelly stove dominated the center of the littered space. Roughhewed wood workbenches lay against one wall with assorted junk piled against the opposite one. As he searched for a spot to place the receiving device, he ran into cobwebs running from the stove to the ceiling. Swiping them aside, he looked up and found the perfect location. Heavy beam rafters supported the roof and provided a spot to prevent the small device from being seen by anyone entering the shed.

After standing on one of the workbenches, he placed the cigarette-pack-size unit on top of a rafter near the wall closest to the mosque. Before he could jump down, he heard voices approaching the structure speaking Arabic.

"The sheik insisted someone check out the shed."

"Why?"

"He claims someone in dark clothes possibly entered the shed."

"I did not see anything."

"Nor I. But we must grant him his wishes, for now."

The voices were drawing nearer. Searching the small space, Wolfe found an alcove on the back wall and jumped down. Moving silently, he reached the space and tried to make himself as small as possible.

Standing deep in the shadows, Wolfe kept a close eye on a flashlight beam as it swept the darkness of the shed. It passed over his position and then moved on. Finally, he heard, "I did not see anything, did you?"

"No, and we will report we did not see anyone."

Wolfe heard the flick of a lighter and the unmistakable sound of someone inhaling deeply. As the individual blew out the smoke, he said, "The sheik grows restless with the lack of progress on finding recruits. Do you think he will demand some of us sacrifice ourselves for this folly he has envisioned?"

Silence prevailed until another click of a cigarette lighter broke the stillness. The scent of a newly burning cigarette permeated the small interior space. "We must be careful about what we say. I plan to stay out of his way. What he proposes is madness and will bring Scotland Yard down hard on our community."

The two men stood inside the shed silently for a few moments. "He has the imam wrapped around his finger. When this mess is over, I will be changing mosques. I no longer trust the imam to act in the best interest of our congregation."

"I agree, but we must keep our thoughts to ourselves, otherwise we might be chosen."

"If I am, I will disappear. Nothing good can come from what this crazy sheik has proposed."

Wolfe heard steps and the voices recede into the distance. When silence returned to the interior of the shed, he remained in the shadows for another ten minutes. Finally, he emerged from the darkness and rushed toward the rendezvous location with Nadia.

The black BMW 750i stopped in front of a small MI6-owned cottage deep in the English countryside seventy-five kilometers from London. Jonathan Chapman sat next to Noah Anderson without a word being exchanged between them since leaving Vauxhall Crossing. Any attempt by the assistant to the MI6 Director to initiate a conversation had been met with total silence during the hour-long journey.

Glancing at the man who would soon be his ex-assistant, Chapman noted a trickle of sweat rolling down the side of his head next to his ear. As soon as the car stopped, he exited the passenger door just as an identical Black BMW 750i parked behind his car. Two large men in suits exited this vehicle. Chapman motioned toward the other side of his automobile, and the two men intercepted Anderson as he stepped out.

Noah's eyes widened. "What's this all about, Director?"

Without giving a response, Chapman headed to the front door of the cottage. The two men from the other BMW insisted Anderson follow.

Once inside, with the front door closed. Chapman pointed to one of the chairs surrounding a round table in the kitchen area. "Sit down."

"Why am I here, sir?"

"I believe you know."

"No, I don't, why am I here?"

Chapman placed a picture retrieved from his suit coat pocket and placed it in front of the suspect. "Recognize these two chaps?"

Anderson, wide-eyed, took in the photo. After twenty seconds, he slid it back toward the director. "This picture's been photoshopped."

Chapman shook his head. "You know it's real."

Returning his eyes to the picture, Anderson took a deep breath and then let it out slowly. "Yes."

"Good. I'm glad you decided to acknowledge it." Taking another picture from his suit coat pocket, he laid it down next to the other. "Want to explain this one?"

The former assistant gasped but then shook his head.

"Noah, I am sure you are aware the penalty for treason under the Crime and Disorder Act of 1998 is life imprisonment?"

The suspect did not answer.

"How much were you paid?"

Still no answer.

"We've impounded your bank account. I must say, for a man making your salary, you have quite the savings account. Probably not the smartest thing you've ever done, keeping it in your bank."

The suspect continued to stare at the two photographs.

"You probably need to know that two female MI6 agents are at your home discussing your activities with your wife."

Anderson's eyes narrowed, and his attention fixed on Chapman. "She has nothing to do with this. Leave her alone."

"We only have your word for that. She could get fourteen years in prison for espionage, and where would that leave your children?" He paused for a moment. "Probably in an orphanage until they are sixteen and declared independent. I believe you have a fifteen-year-old daughter, don't you? If she is placed in an orphanage, the odds of her continuing her education are slim to none. And I don't even want to mention what could happen to her once the relative safety of the orphanage is removed."

Anderson's glare intensified. "You're a bloody bastard."

"At least I'm not a treasonous bastard."

Lowering his head, Anderson shut his eyes and said, "What do you want to know?"

"First, I would like to know why, and second, I want to know just what the hell you've told them."

Chapter Twenty-Nine

BOROUGH OF NEWHAM, ENGLAND

Mohammad Al-Qaedi screamed at the two men standing in front of him, "You found no one in the building?"

The shorter one said, "No one, Sheik, the shed was empty."

"You doubt that I saw someone enter?"

"No, Sheik. Maybe it was an animal you observed."

Al-Qaedi's nostrils flared as his eyes darted from one man to the other. Finally, after thirty seconds, the sheik took a deep breath and let it out slowly. His eyes narrowed, and he said, "Both of you are dismissed."

When the men were gone, Al-Qaedi asked Amir Zamani, "What do you think?"

"I think you and I need to search the shed. It is close enough to the mosque someone might have placed an electronic eavesdropping device. They could have left before those two fools arrived."

Checking the time, Al-Qaedi said, "Yes, at least we would know what to look for. Make sure you take your phone. If we find someone has planted a listening device, we will need to secure other accommodations."

"Do you believe someone has discovered you are in London?"

"It is inevitable. As we have done in the past, my friend, we must be one step ahead of those who oppose us."

"If we are to abandon this mosque, it will set your plans back at least a month."

With a shrug, Al-Qaedi hoisted a backpack to his shoulder. "I suggest you prepare to leave. If we find nothing in the shed, we can return, and no one will be the wiser. If we do find something, well, better to be prepared."

"Yes, my Sheik."

Thirty minutes later, the two men stood inside the shed, moving the beams of their flashlights around the dark interior. After several complete sweeps, Zamani clicked his flashlight off. He turned his attention to Al-Qaedi who continued to sweep his light around the exposed roof beams of the building. "I cannot find anything."

No answer came from the aging terrorist, his attention now drawn to a particular beam. "Place your flashlight on this spot, Amir."

Clicking the light back on, Zamari placed it on the spot indicated by his friend. "What are you seeing?"

"Something we have seen before, my brother."

Zamari climbed onto a workbench below the wooden beam indicated by Al-Qaedi. Using his flashlight, he examined the area closer. "Yes, my friend. We have seen this type of device before. It is identical to the one we found in Turkey, two years ago."

"So, the CIA knows I am here."

"Or, they suspect you are. This could be an attempt to find you."

"No, they know I'm here. We will—"

Al-Qaedi's words were interrupted by the sound of tires screeching to a stop. "Shut off your flashlight, Amir, hurry."

Through a dirty window, Al-Qaedi witnessed heavily armed men leaping out of vans and an armored vehicle. The front door to the mosque flew open as two men swung a battering ram against it. Ten tactically dressed and heavily armed men rushed into the building.

"There is no way this device could have provided information to the police. We have not made any cell phone calls."

The sheik kept his attention on the activities across the street. Finally, he said, "You are correct, Amir. Something else has occurred. Let us fade into the night and get as far away as possible."

The Next Morning

Wolfe pressed the cell phone against his ear as he listened to Joseph relay the information about the previous night's raid on the mosque.

"Apparently, Chapman had a long talk with Noah Anderson, after which, MI5 agents raided the mosque. No Al-Qaedi. But they did get confirmation the man had been there. The imam is keeping quiet, but two men volunteered information. It seems Al-Qaedi saw someone entering an abandoned building near the mosque last night and sent those individuals to check it out. When they told him no one was in the shed, he flipped out. Know anything about an empty building next to the mosque?"

"How would I know anything like that, Joseph?"

"I didn't think you would, but I had to ask."

"So, Al-Qaedi has disappeared?"

"Afraid so."

"Do you think the leaks all came from Anderson?"

"That's the working theory within MI6. My faith in Jonathan has been restored."

"I'm glad to hear it."

"What do you plan to do, Michael?"

"We didn't have a clue where he was when Nadia and I first got here. We'll stay a few more days and see if we can pick up his scent. If not, we'll head back to the States."

"There's someone Jonathan wants you to meet with."

"Does he know Nadia and I are here in the UK?"

"I told him you two would be there sometime today. No need for him to know otherwise."

"Who is it?"

"His name is Grayson Cooke. He's an expert on Middle East radicalism and has been studying Mohammed Al-Qaedi for over a decade."

"Great, an academic."

"Also, an ex-colleague of Ian McGill."

"SAS?"

"He suffered a paralyzing spinal injury and is confined to a wheelchair. While he's an academic, he's also a highly decorated soldier. You'll have to determine if he can help you find Al-Qaedi."

"Okay, I look forward to meeting him. When and where?"

"Jonathan said he would be in contact with you."

Grayson Cooke offered his hand to Wolfe. "It is an honor to finally meet you, Michael. Ian McGill spoke highly of you the last time he and I met. I was sorry to hear of his death."

Cooke still maintained the posture of a member of Her Royal Majesty's Special Air Service, ramrod straight. Wolfe guessed he would have been six foot tall before the accident. His rusty-blond hair remained regiment short, and he sported a bushy mustache. The man's green eyes kept their gaze locked on Wolfe's.

"You from Ireland?"

"Aye."

Wolfe surveyed the office where he and Nadia had been escorted to inside the Vauxhall Crossing complex. "I understand you are an expert on Mohammed Al-Qaedi?"

The man sitting in the wheelchair gave Wolfe a half grin. "He is a complicated man. Do I know a few things about him? Yes. Am I an expert on him? The answer would be no. My friend McGill had a past with Al-Qaedi, as do you, if my intel is correct?"

Wolfe nodded.

"Is that past going to cause a problem in our search for him?"

"It was a long time ago. What do you mean by our search?"

"I'm your partner moving forward."

"My wife and I work alone."

"Not if you want to catch him in the UK."

"Is that Chapman's idea of cooperation?"

"No, it's the Prime Minister's."

"Ah, in other words, we have no choice."

Cooke just smiled.

Returning the gesture, Wolfe said, "Okay, where is he?"

"Unfortunately, he has managed to elude our efforts to take him off the streets. However, we might have a lead."

"Indulge me."

"On the night of MI5's ill-timed raid, Al-Qaedi and his lieutenant, Amir Zamani were not on the premises. Where, we don't know. They were spotted by several CCTV cameras near Big Ben and the House of Parliament around three in the morning. They were picked up by a beige Kia Sportage with the license plates obscured. Scotland Yard managed to trace the Kia via CCTV to the East End of London, where it vanished. They think it's parked in a garage somewhere and the lad's changed cars."

"Thought you had a lead?"

Smiling, Cooke said, "We do, but it is Internet chatter." When Wolfe did not respond, the man continued. "Facebook and Twitter activity increased threefold in the Borough of Tower Hamlets. That particular borough has one of the highest percentages of Muslims in London."

"What about cell phone activity?"

"Also up. GCHQ is monitoring the calls."

"So, he seems to be in another heavily Muslim-populated section of London, but no one knows for sure. Am I understanding you correctly?"

"You are."

"That's not a lead, that's an assumption."

"True. London is a large and diverse city. Knowing the area helps us determine what to do next."

"And what might that be?"

"Simple, old chap. When we find him, you do what you do best."

Wolfe folded his arms. "You'll need to find him soon."

"And why is that?"

"I overheard a conversation the other night about his plans."

"Oh?"

"The two individuals having the discussion felt the plan was audacious. They also indicated Al-Qaedi seemed to be having trouble recruiting for the project."

"I say, did they mention the target?"

"No, but the fact they were seen at three a.m. near the House of Parliament and Big Ben tells me something."

"Oh dear. You don't think that's his target, do you?"

"Think about it for a moment. There has to be a reason they were there."

Chapter Thirty

LONDON

Grayson Cooke remained quiet as he alternated his gaze between Wolfe and Nadia. Finally, he said, "A bit disquieting, isn't it?"

Nadia spoke for the first time during the meeting. "The House of Parliament is on the River Thames, correct?"

"Practically in the water, Ms. Wolfe."

"You also indicated his last known location put him in the Borough of Tower Hamlets?"

With a nod, the retired SAS operative said, "Yes."

"What would prevent someone from loading explosives on a barge on the Thames from there and navigating toward the House of Parliament late at night? It's not that far, correct?"

Cooke grew quiet for several seconds and then faced his desk. He picked up a phone handset, pressed a button, and said, "I need to speak with the director immediately."

Ten minutes later, Wolfe and Nadia were escorted by Grayson Cooke into the office of Jonathan Chapman. The director stood and offered his hand to Wolfe. "Someday you'll have to tell me why McGill moved to the States."

"Someday, maybe I can."

The director drew his attention to Nadia. "I understand you have a theory of what Al-Qaedi may have planned."

The ex-Mossad agent gave Chapman a slight smile and said, "As you just mentioned, it's just a theory. Al-Qaedi loves to blow things up, the bus where Michael's young wife died and the Madrid train bombings in 2004. Since then, he's been orchestrating numerous terrorist attacks across the world, all of which have included the use of bombs."

"You have my attention, Ms. Wolfe, go on."

"From July of 2016 through the end of 2018, there were roadside bombings or grenade attacks monthly in Israel. I was still with the Mossad at the time, and the majority of those attacks could be traced back to the activities of Al-Qaedi."

"Why didn't Israel do something about him?"

"They tried, but he had an informant within the Mossad and knew when there would be an operation launched to catch him. He would simply return to Iran and wait."

"Asa Gerlis?"

"We may never know. Gerlis died before anyone could question him. But he was a suspect."

Sitting behind his desk, Chapman nodded. "So just because Al-Qaedi loves to blow things up and he is now in Tower Hamlets which has a loading dock on the Thames, you think he will try to blow up The House of Parliament."

Nadia narrowed her eyes and crossed her arms. "Yes."

Chapman's gaze went to Wolfe and then trained on Cooke. Neither man contradicted Nadia's assessment. The director then said, "You've sold me. Now what can we do about it?"

Wolfe wandered over to the window in Chapman's office and looked out over the River Thames. On his right, the view stretched toward the north. Big Ben and the House of Parliament could be clearly seen. "How hard would it be to put all the docks in Tower Hamlets under surveillance?"

Cooke said, "It'd be difficult. There are six hundred and eighty areas along the Thames considered to be docks. Some are active, some retired. We would be hard-pressed to cover all of them."

Wolfe returned his attention to the room. "How many are privately owned?"

Chapman said, "I say, old boy, you might have something there. They would need a warehouse to stage the explosives and then a way to load them onto a barge." He focused on Cooke. "Grayson, it shouldn't be too much of a bother to determine the number of privately held warehouses on the Thames, would it?"

"I wouldn't think so." He spun his wheelchair toward the door and exited the room.

When the door closed, Wolfe said to Chapman, "How much do you know about Ian's accident?"

"Not much, I'm afraid, only what Joseph told me."

With a smile, Wolfe continued. "It was a ruse. Ian was hurt but is very much alive. We felt it necessary to protect him from Al-Qaedi. Several other attempts were made on his life before the accident. Ian felt there had to be a leak in your office and partially suspected you. Now that we know it was Anderson, I believe you should know the truth that he's alive."

The Director of MI6 stared hard at Wolfe and then slowly closed his eyes. "Thank you for telling me. The last time I spoke to Ian, we did not depart on the best of terms. I regret some of the words I said." Chapman paused. "Why did he decide to move to the United States?"

"He's never admitted it, but I believe he felt both the service and his country turned their back on him. He's found a little peace in Missouri."

"His country and service did not turn their back on him. I believe it was I who may have betrayed his trust."

Wolfe tilted his head but remained quiet.

"You see, Michael, I was livid with him after you and he returned from Iran."

"Why?"

"For not communicating with us."

"Uh, that would have been difficult."

"Why? You had various options for getting the word out to us."

"Not really."

"You are like Ian. We did not receive even so much as a briefing. Nor did we receive an explanation for your three-month silence."

"The silence was necessary."

"Why?"

"You'll have to ask Ian."

Chapman glared at Wolfe, his face growing crimson. Finally, he relaxed and took a breath. "That bad?"

Wolfe said, "The Iranians murdered women and children in an attempt to get people to turn us in. The individuals they killed did not know where we were and were never involved. I still have nightmares about it."

Nadia walked over to him and put her arms around his waist. She said to Chapman, "Michael has never said anything about their experiences. Until now." She paused, looked at her husband, and then back to Chapman. "I believe we need to change the subject back to Al-Qaedi."

The only reaction Chapman gave was a slow nod of his head.

Grayson Cooke returned to Chapman's office and closed the door before he spoke. "I requested a survey of all privately held warehouses on the Thames. There are actually quite a few. However, once we narrowed our search to warehouses owned by a foreign entity, it is a different story."

Chapman raised an eyebrow. "From your tone, I take it they found something."

"Actually, they did. There is a block of buildings on the north side of the River Thames owned by a local businessman. His parents immigrated from Iran just before the fall of the Shah in 1979."

Wolfe asked, "What's his name?"

"Arman Hamadi."

Frowning, Chapman said, "Why is that name familiar, Grayson?"

"*The Sun* has proclaimed him to be the second richest man in England."

The Director raised his eyebrows. "Now I remember. He is also a fervent supporter of the current mayor of London."

Crossing his arms, Wolfe said, "Grayson, why did it show up as being owned by a foreign entity?"

"While Arman Hamadi is a naturalized citizen of the UK, he owns several companies registered in Switzerland and the Middle East."

Chapman remained quiet for a few moments. "We have

no reason to believe he would provide warehouse space for Al-Qaedi. Just because his parents are from Iran, is no reason…"

Wolfe remained silent, keeping his arms folded. Nadia stood beside him, staring at Chapman who now studied the top of his desk.

The director lifted his gaze and focused on Wolfe. "What is your cover story?"

"Nadia and I are posing as interpreters for an upcoming UN summit."

Sitting down, Chapman drummed his fingers on his desk. "Grayson, you will provide any and all support for Michael and Nadia. We need to know if Hamadi is providing assistance to Al-Qaedi." Returning his attention to Wolfe, Chapman said, "You two keep me posted through Joseph. Hopefully, we can keep a lid on what you're really doing here."

Wolfe steered the small Ford past the block of warehouses owned by Arman Hamadi. None of which bore the name of the owner. The only signage on the outside simply stated an address and dock number. Many appeared abandoned or seldom used.

Nadia said, "Not a very prosperous part of London?"

Driving slowly, Wolfe swiveled his head as he surveyed the area. "Like all major cities, London has its seedy side. I wonder what JR could discover about these buildings."

"Wouldn't hurt to ask him."

Wolfe kept their speed low on the access road until they passed the last building. He said, "What stood out about the area?"

"Other than being depressing, not much. Why?"

"No activity at all. None. I would think there should be something going on, unless this has been planned for a long time and access to the buildings is from the river only."

"We're making a lot of assumptions, Michael. None of which could be correct."

"I agree. But there is something off about this area. Almost like it's been abandoned for a reason." He paused as he accelerated away from the area. "Let's get back to the hotel. I've got a few phone calls to make."

Chapter Thirty-One

WASHINGTON, DC

Joseph read a text message from an old friend. Not wishing to reply to the request while at his desk in the White House, he closed down his computer and gathered a few items he would need at his townhouse.

After exiting the White House grounds, he pressed the send icon on his cell phone. The individual he called picked up on the second ring.

"What the hell has Michael gotten himself into this time?"

"Good evening to you, JR."

"Whatever. So, what is he doing?"

"Trying to find Mohammad Al-Qaedi."

"I know that." JR paused for a few moments. "He called and asked me to check out someone in London. I'm supposed to relay the info to you."

"Did you discover something unusual?"

"Downright scary."

"Okay, stop right there, JR. Don't say anything until I can get to my place."

"Wasn't going to, call me as soon as possible."

It took thirty minutes for Joseph to navigate DC traffic. After he arrived at his townhouse, he made the call using his computer.

When JR answered, Joseph asked, "What's so scary?"

"Were you aware of the individual Wolfe asked me to check out?"

"Not really. Why?"

"He needs information on a guy named Arman Hamadi. I'd personally never heard of him. But he should be on everybody's radar."

"Care to enlighten me?"

"He's one of the richest persons in Europe and probably one of the more dangerous ones as well."

Joseph did not respond.

"He's well connected within the London social scene and supports a variety of charities and local London politicians. Plus, he owns a considerable amount of property up and down the River Thames. Most of which he uses as a tax write-off. His real wealth comes from weapons smuggling."

"Excuse me?"

"That's the exact reaction I had at first. Then I dug a little deeper. Michael was right to suspect this guy. He has ties all over the Middle East particularly in Syria, Iran, Turkey, and Pakistan. One corporation he owns, through a complex series of shell companies, is one of the largest arms brokers in the world. They sell everything from knock-off automatic pistols to state-of-the-art fighter jets. The jets are generally of Russian design."

"I'm not going to like where this is going, am I?"

"Probably not. I'm not easily scared, but this guy scares me."

"Okay. What else?"

"One of the subsidiaries he owns sells chemicals. Most of these chemicals are benign by themselves, but, when combined with other seemingly inert compounds, can produce very powerful explosives. I've been able to trace the shipment of some of these chemicals to a warehouse on the Thames. This particular warehouse is owned by a subsidiary of a Hamadi's shell company."

"JR, can you determine if any of these shipments have been delivered?"

"One has. The other is still at sea."

"Place of origin?"

"The delivered one came from Syria, the one enroute shipped out of the Port of Mogadishu in Somalia."

Joseph did not respond immediately. Finally, he said, "Wouldn't the British authorities question the ports of origin?"

"One would think so, but they haven't so far. Apparently, these types of shipments have been happening for about a year. My guess is the operation has been in the planning stage for some time."

"Where is the warehouse located?"

"In the Borough of Tower Hamlets, not far from the Tower of London."

"Michael and Nadia suspected somewhere around that area."

"I'm aware of that. Most of the buildings he asked about are currently unused by Hamadi's corporation and have been for some time."

"When is the shipment out of Somalia due?"

"About a week, give or take a few days."

"Do you know the name of the ship?"

"Yes."

"Send it to me, and I'll alert Chapman." He paused. "Thanks, JR."

"All part of the service."

The call ended, and Joseph checked the time displayed on the lower right corner of his computer screen. He called Chapman.

"Oh dear. This gets worse every time I talk to you."

"Sorry, Jonathan, but at least half of the explosive mixture is still at sea. I would have your Navy intercept the ship once it reaches the English Channel."

"Can you send me proof?"

"Yes."

"Good. Does Michael have the tools of his trade with him?"

"If he doesn't, I can make arrangements."

"I might need to utilize his skills if we can't stop the ship."

"Understood."

The call ended, and Chapman pressed his palms against his weary eyes. After several minutes, he shut off his computer, stood and left his office.

Grayson Cooke looked up from his desk as Chapman entered his office and shut the door. "This can't be good."

"I'm afraid it isn't, Grayson."

"What's happened?"

"Wolfe and his wife may have stumbled upon a terrorist attack aimed at the very heart of our democracy." He paused for a sccond and told the ex-SAS member the details of his phone call with the American advisor to the US president.

After he finished, Cooke pursed his lips and kept his gaze on Chapman. Finally, he said, "How hard will it be for the Royal Navy to find the ship?"

"Not hard, but I still think we need to have Wolfe strategically placed across from the warehouse."

"It's quite wide in the area you are referring to, sir. It would challenge any sharpshooter."

"I'm aware of that."

Cooke tilted his head slightly to the left. "I see. Keep him from interfering with the action we need to be taking?"

Chapman nodded. "Exactly."

The Next Day

Wolfe peered through the scope on his suppressed Barrett M82A1 sniper rifle from his position high atop the south tower of Tower Bridge. The marina below him held one of the empty buildings owned by Arman Hamadi. From his observations of the area, he noted numerous restaurants, apartments, offices, and a four-star hotel adjacent to the marina. Constant pedestrian and automobile traffic occurred around the site, unlike the buildings he and Nadia drove by the previous day.

Secure communications with his wife were accomplished via encrypted military-grade handheld radios courtesy of Grayson Cooke. His wireless earpiece remained quiet as he waited.

Time passed slowly as the sun reached its zenith and

moved toward the western horizon. At two p.m., he heard Nadia say, "There's a black Jaguar pulling up to the front of the building. Windows deeply tinted."

"Hamadi?"

"Don't know. Stand by."

He waited silently. After two minutes, he heard, "Bingo, Michael."

"Who is it?"

"Amir Zamani and an unidentified male who appears to be of Western European descent."

"Tall, with short dark hair and a hawk nose?"

"That's him."

"Logan Dillon."

"Michael, this must be the right place."

"It would appear so, Nadia." He lowered the scope. "Activity in the marina. A boat is approaching the building's docking berth." Putting the scope back on the vessel, he said, "It's a small touring vessel, contents are obscured by a tarp. Have you heard if they intercepted the Somali ship yet?"

"Grayson has not said anything about it."

"Okay. I'll keep an eye on this. What is the status of Dillon and Zamani?"

"Standing outside the car. Dillon is smoking."

Wolfe put the scope back on the boat and waited. Once it nudged against the dock, a man appeared and jumped down to secure a line. Centering his crosshairs on the man's face, he did not recognize him.

The man surveyed the area around the marina and then disappeared beneath the canvas covering. Thirty seconds later, he reappeared and offered assistance to a man who refused the help and jumped to the wood of the pier. An opportunity to get a clear view of the man's face did not present itself as he kept the hood of a jacket pulled low over his head. He walked briskly toward a door and quickly disappeared inside.

"Nadia, a man just got off the boat and entered the warehouse. I couldn't ID him. This might be Al-Qaedi. Take as many pictures as possible if he comes out."

"Someone just did. He's heading toward the Jaguar."

Wolfe heard the rapid clicking of a digital camera capturing images of the scene Nadia witnessed. After three minutes, she said, "The man got into the car, and they drove away. I got a clear shot of the license plate."

"Good. Get the number to Grayson Clark. Maybe we can learn who the car is registered to. Meanwhile, I'll keep an eye on the boat."

Chapter Thirty-Two

LONDON

Al-Qaedi sat in the back of the Jaguar and pulled the hood back. "The second ship is ahead of schedule and should enter the English Channel today. Amir, have you heard anything?"

"No, my Sheik."

"What about you, Dillon?"

"Not a thing."

Silence filled the automobile as Dillon drove the luxury car out of the marina and north on Thomas More Street. No one dared interrupt Al-Qaedi as he stared out the passenger window in the back seat.

Finally, as Logan maneuvered the Jaguar XE through the heavy London traffic, the terrorist asked, "Who is guarding the chemicals we already possess?"

Logan concentrated on driving. Zamani did not answer immediately. Finally, he said, "It is safe."

"I did not ask that, Amir. I asked who is protecting it."

"Uh, my Sheik, no one at the moment."

The muscles in Al-Qaedi's neck tightened as his face

grew crimson. Closing his eyes, he took a deep breath. Through clenched teeth, he said, "No one is keeping it secure? Is that what I heard?"

"Yes, my Sheik."

"And why not?"

"Few of our Muslim brothers in London share our exuberance for your plans. We only have a few volunteers."

"What has happened to our movement, Amir?"

"Unfortunately, my Sheik, immigration laws have severely limited the number of young immigrants into Europe. Most Muslims, particularly in England, are first, second, or even third generations born inside Britain. They are far less likely to agree with what must be done to establish a European caliphate."

"What about our brethren in Belgium? Can't they travel to Britain without a visa?"

"At one time, yes. But since Brexit, if they have any criminal charges on their record, getting a visa to work in the UK is impossible."

Al-Qaedi returned to staring out the passenger window as they headed northeast on the A11.

Brody Rees, a three-year-veteran constable with the London police force checked the license plate on the black Jaguar XE he followed against the bulletin just received on his computer. They matched.

He keyed his radio, identified himself, and said, "I have an ID on the subject car referred to in bulletin 555 of this date. Over."

The response came back immediately. "State location."

"Heading northeast on the A12, approaching the first Bushwood exit."

"Keep following. We will direct backup to your location."

"Roger."

Logan Dillon noticed the yellow-and-blue checkered police car behind him. He slowed to see if the constable would pass. The brightly colored car slowed to match his speed. Logan said, "We have a London bobby following us."

Al-Qaedi twisted in his seat to get a better view of the car behind them. "Best to get off this road and see what happens."

"Got it."

Logan exited the A12 at the Green Man Interchange and followed it to the A114 entrance heading northwest. The police car followed.

Frowning, Al-Qaedi said, "Pull over and let him pass."

Logan slowed the car and came to a stop on the side of the road. The police car pulled in behind him.

The passenger in the backseat mumbled an Arabic curse as Logan prepared to confront the constable.

Wolfe rose from his pronc position inside the south tower on Tower Bridge. Two hours had passed since the black Jaguar disappeared with Al-Qaedi inside. He rubbed the back of his neck as his patience waned. He keyed his mike. "Nadia, what the hell is going on? We're wasting our time here."

"I have not heard anything for an hour, Michael. Do you think it's time to leave?"

"Isn't it amazing how we identify Al-Qaedi and, all of a sudden, we're out of the loop? I'm coming down. Pick me up where you dropped me off this morning."

"I'll be there in ten minutes. Will you have time to disassemble your equipment by then?"

"Definitely."

Eight minutes later, Wolfe placed his gun case on the back floorboard and then slipped into the passenger seat. Nadia pulled away from the curb and said, "What now?"

"Back to our hotel. This whole deal has been jacked up since Chapman got involved. I think it's time you and I head back to the States and let the British deal with Al-Qaedi."

"Fine with me."

On the way to the hotel, Wolfe's cell phone vibrated with an incoming text message. *Call when you can be secure.*

Wolfe raised an eyebrow. "JR must have something. He wants us to call."

Back in the hotel room, Nadia set up her laptop and made the VoIP call to JR. He answered, "You two can sure stir up trouble."

Wolfe frowned. "Not sure what you're referring to, JR. We just got back from our surveillance."

"London has a dead cop. Plus, Arman Hamadi reported a stolen car, which the police found burned in an industrial yard on the east side."

"Huh."

"That's kind of an understatement, isn't it, Michael?"

"Well, since Nadia and I were basically sidelined by Chapman, I'm not surprised the whole thing went sideways on them. How'd the cop get killed?"

"From what I've been able to piece together from police radio traffic, he stopped the car you two identified at the marina."

Wolfe said, "That was a dumb move. Who authorized him stopping it?"

"A BOLO went out, and the cop spotted the car almost immediately. The police had backup heading his way, but the Jaguar stopped, and the cop checked it out. End of cop."

"Have you told Joseph?"

"Not yet. I wanted to check with you two before I did."

"Yeah, call and tell him Nadia and I are done. Chapman pulled an end run on us and stuck us where we would be out of the way. I'm booking two seats on the first flight out of here."

"Don't book them yet. I'll have Joseph arrange for your ride. It will be interesting to see what Chapman tells him."

Joseph ended the call from JR and drummed his fingers on his desk. He then pressed a button on his phone and, five seconds later, Jerry Griggs walked into his office. "What's up, boss?"

"I know you just got back from the UK a few days ago, but I need you to go back."

Griggs raised one eyebrow. "Are Michael and Nadia, okay?"

"Yes, but there's been a development."

"Oh?"

"Chapman took charge of Michael and Nadia's activities to get them out of the way. Now a London cop is dead, and Al-Qaedi knows he's being watched."

"That's not good."

"I haven't talked to Jonathan yet. But I imagine he's not happy about how this incident went sideways on him."

"The question is, does this screw up Al-Qaedi's plans to blow up Big Ben?"

"We don't know for sure that was the target, but I would guess the answer is yes. Half of his explosives were intercepted by the British Navy, and the other half has been located and confiscated in an empty warehouse on St. Katrina's Marina."

"Couldn't happen to a nicer guy."

"Right now, we need Michael to stay in England, but he believes Chapman took him out of the game and he is not happy about it."

"Did he?"

"I have no idea. I need to talk to Jonathan." He paused and checked the clock on his desk. "It's almost ten p.m. there. Get your flight arranged, and make sure you have room for Michael and Nadia on the return flight."

"Got it."

After Griggs shut the office door, Joseph dialed the number to Chapman's private line. He answered on the second ring.

"I was wondering how long it would take you to call."

"How bad is it?"

"Excuse the vulgarity, it's a bloody royal clusterfuck."

"What happened?"

"I made the wrong decision keeping Michael and Nadia on the sidelines. They did their job, but, once it was in our court, we mucked it up."

"Not following you, Jonathan."

"Your chap JR discovered a building on St. Katharine's Marina owned by Hamadi. I asked Michael and Nadia to put it under surveillance. They observed Al-Qaedi get in a car and drive away. Instead of having them follow it, I gave the license plate number to the bloody London police department. They jumped the gun and stopped the car. Now they have a dead constable, and I am being asked questions on why I didn't tell them the occupants of the car were dangerous."

"Did you explain you just wanted the car followed?"

"Yes, but they chose to ignore those instructions."

"What can I do to help?"

"Do not recall Michael and Nadia back to the US. They seem to be the only two individuals in this city who understand how dangerous Al-Qaedi can be."

"What about the explosives?"

"That is the only bit of good news we have. The British Navy intercepted the ship out of Somalia. Plus, MI5 raided the building on the marina. The two components of Al-Qaedi's bomb are now in our possession."

"Then the threat level has subsided."

"For the moment."

Chapter Thirty-Three

BOROUGH OF TOWER HAMLETS

The cellar under the home in central Tower Hamlets smelled of mildew and earth. Pacing in the middle of the small area, Mohammad Al-Qaedi kept his hands behind his back as he moved from one wall to the next.

Amir Zamani watched him intently. Having been around the man for a decade, he knew the signs of contemplation. During these reflective times, Zamani knew not to disturb Al-Qaedi with trivial matters.

Suddenly, the terrorist stopped and glared at Zamani. "Have you contacted Anderson in the past few days?"

"No, my Sheik. He is not responding to my messages."

"We must conclude he has been compromised."

"Maybe he is being cautious."

"He would know our shipments were intercepted. His duty would be to contact you. He has not. We must proceed as if he is under arrest."

"Yes, my Sheik."

"This leaves us blind to the activities of the British authorities."

"Do you wish me to contact him again?"

Al-Qaedi did not respond immediately. He started pacing again. After several minutes, he stopped and said, "Yes. Only, this time, do not meet. Give him a location and then observe the area around him. If he is being followed, we will know he is no longer of use to us."

"If he is not, should I meet with him?"

"No. We cannot take the chance. If you believe him to be alone, send him a message that you were unexpectedly delayed." Al-Qaedi took a deep breath and let it out slowly. He continued, "We will need to leave this country very soon. I fear we will be, once again, unsuccessful with our plans, my brother."

Zamani nodded and walked up the staircase.

The Next Morning

"Jerry, I don't care what Joseph wants. Nadia and I are going home."

Griggs stood with his hands behind his back as Wolfe and his wife packed their duffel bags. "I understand your frustration, Michael. Chapman admitted he sidelined you both on purpose. We don't know why, but my guess is he didn't want you two getting credit for stopping Al-Qaedi. People like Chapman can be territorial at times."

Shaking his head slowly, Wolf kept his attention on his packing. "I've had to deal with his type before. As a rule, it screws up a mission. If they had left it alone, Al-Qaedi would have returned to the marina, I'd had him in my sights, and the problem would be over. Now a cop is dead, leaving behind a wife and a one-year-old daughter."

"Not your fault."

"I'm very much aware it isn't our fault. But that doesn't change the fact a police officer died needlessly."

"Joseph wants you to stay. Apparently, Chapman wants to set a trap for Al-Qaedi. Your skills will come in handy."

Wolfe stopped what he was doing and turned his attention to Griggs. "How? His explosives have been seized, his mole within MI6 is under arrest and, from what I heard in the shed, his recruiting efforts are not producing any volunteers willing to blow themselves up." He paused for a few seconds. "We think Al-Qaedi has outlived his movement. He's old news to the local Muslims."

"Why do you say that?"

"Terrorist attacks by radical Islamists have declined since 2014. Particularly in the EU. There are still attacks, but they are fewer in number, and deaths have fallen by half."

"I saw those statistics."

"Good, you're paying attention." Wolfe paused and returned to packing his duffel bag. "Al-Qaedi has been doing this for over twenty years. He's caused a lot of collateral damage during those two decades and burned a lot of bridges in the Arab world. I'm surprised someone hasn't already taken steps to get rid of him. But so far, they haven't."

"Are you saying we need to let him go?"

Narrowing his eyes, Wolfe shook his head. "No." He took a slow breath. "What I'm saying is Nadia and I believe he is trying to become relevant again. He's trying to create one last big event while he still has some support."

"You mean Arman Hamadi?"

"Yes. Which raises the question, why is he supporting Al-Qaedi? The guy is rich and part of the London social scene. It doesn't make—" Wolfe stopped suddenly and focused on Nadia for a few moments. He returned his attention to Griggs. "I just figured out the relationship."

Nadia walked over to her husband. "What is it, Michael?"

Wolfe said, "My guess would be Hamadi's business is down. His bottom-line feeds on unrest and chaos in the world."

With a chuckle, Griggs folded his arms. "It's always about money, isn't it?"

"Yes, Jerry, it normally is. Okay, we'll postpone our departure because Nadia and I need to have a one-on-one discussion with Hamadi."

Nadia concentrated on her laptop. "He is all over social media, Michael."

"Do any of his posts give us information about his whereabouts?"

"Yes." She pointed to a picture display on the screen. "He has a townhouse in London, heavily guarded by a private security firm. He also mentions an estate near Alton in Hampshire County."

"How far from here?"

"Eighty-eight kilometers. His country home is south of Alton."

"How often does he go there?"

"From his Facebook page, it appears he goes there every weekend. He has hunting parties on the land as well."

Wolfe walked over and considered the laptop screen. "Why do people make it so easy for others to find them? Particularly this guy."

"Michael, to the public, he is a philanthropist and a celebrity. What better way to shield your true intentions? With his social media platform, he can direct the narrative. If any negative publicity comes out, all he has to do is point to all the good things he does and the bad news goes away."

"Never thought of it that way." A grin slowly appeared on Wolfe's lips. "Let's check out of the hotel. I think it's time we determine how well guarded Mr. Hamadi's estate is in the country."

The first Corbyn Park House in Hampshire County near the small town of Alton was originally a square building built in the mid-1700s. Over the decades, it grew to over 900 square meters, which by American measurements equaled almost 10,000 square feet. Each successive owner added to the estate until it met a sad fate during World War II. A German V-1 flying bomb went off course on its flight toward London and crashed into the structure. The owner and his family perished in the resulting explosion. The property sat vacant until Arman Hamadi's father bought it in the late 1950s.

The elder Hamadi started construction on a two-story stone mansion to rival the original structure. Completion occurred in 1969 on the same day the Beatles performed their last live concert on the roof of the Apple studios in London.

The mansion stood on one end of a six-hundred-acre forest containing a species of red-tail deer whose lineage dated back to the late 15th century. Twice a year, the Hamadi family sponsored a hunting trip that required the attending hunters to purchase a deer tag for ten thousand pounds sterling. Proceeds were forwarded to a local charity in Alton after Hamadi extracted his 70 percent processing fees. A fact the general public never knew.

Wolfe and Nadia drove by the manor thirty minutes before dusk. A large paved circle drive led to the massive front entrance. Off to the left, they noticed workers loading their equipment onto trucks after constructing a huge five-point pole marquee.

Wolfe said, "I wonder what that's all about?"

As Nadia thumbed a Google search on her phone, she said, "Don't know." She grew quiet for a few moments as they drove the access road around the estate. Finally, she smiled. "One of Hamadi's semi-annual deer hunts is this weekend. From the size of the tent, it must be a big deal."

"Interesting." He concentrated on his driving as the entrance to the country home receded in the rearview mirror. "Are you up for a midnight hike?"

"I am, if you are."

"Let's find a place to get a few hours' sleep."

By one a.m., Wolfe and Nadia were within a hundred meters of Hamadi's country home. Both wore night-vision goggles and black clothing. Looking through his NVGs, Wolfe said, "Not sure being in the forest on Saturday is a good idea with all those hunters with questionable skills wandering around."

"I was thinking the same thing. Any thoughts?"

"A few, all bad." He grew still as they surveyed the mansion. "The tent is set up next to the hedge maze on the western side of the house. I wonder if running the maze is part of the weekend festivities."

"Don't know, but it would make sense."

After a few moments, Wolfe said, "I wonder how much it would cost to get added to the guest list?"

"What do you have in mind?"

"Trying to grab Hamadi from outside the festivities would be challenging. We wouldn't have any forewarning of his location at any given time. We would need to be guests to pull it off."

"Are you thinking out loud, or do you have a plan?"

"What if we have JR hack into the guest list and add our names? While we are attending, we can follow Hamadi. There might be an opportunity to sneak him out through the hedge maze or during the hunt."

"What if he doesn't attend?"

"Why go to the bother if you aren't going to schmooze with all the social elites at one of these things?"

"We'll need a cover, Michael."

"I wonder." Wolfe remained quiet for a few minutes. "If there are any international businessmen attending, JR can register us as interpreters. I would think that would give us access to anywhere on the property."

"Lots of ifs and buts."

"I didn't say the plan was perfect, but if we go as guests, we'll be unknown and under more scrutiny. As interpreters, we'll already be vetted."

Chapter Thirty-Four

HAMPSHIRE COUNTY, UK

"Are you two insane?" JR's words came through the laptop speaker.

With a smile, Wolfe said, "No, JR. But the situation forces us to take a risk. We need to get to Arman Hamadi and isolate him for a while. It would be practically impossible in London. He's too heavily guarded. At his villa, he'll be less cautious because he will be among friends and business associates. We can't go as guests. Nobody would know us. As interpreters, we will be free to mingle."

"What if he doesn't have interpreters scheduled for the party?"

"JR, you forget I posed as an international business consultant for years. No one in Hamadi's business throws a big party for international guests without having a few interpreters on staff."

"Huh." After a few moments of silence, JR said, "Makes sense. Okay, let me see what I can find. Call you back when I know more."

"Thanks, JR."

Nadia shut down the laptop. "Think it will work?"

With a shrug, Wolfe said, "It could be a little dicey. We'll need a contingency plan in case someone grows suspicious."

"You mean, shoot our way out?" Her grin told him she was kidding.

"No, I mean, head for the hedge maze and disappear."

"What about through the forest behind his house?"

"Depends on when the hunt is scheduled."

"Michael, deer only move during early morning or late evening. If we have to bug out, as long as it isn't during those hours, there shouldn't be any hunters in the woods."

"Good point. We'll have to play it by ear if we come under suspicion. Through the hedge maze would be a shorter distance off the property. Through the forest would be about a kilometer or more."

"Should we have Carla or Jerry on standby? We won't know where to stash our car."

"My dear, you are brilliant."

"But of course. I am French."

Noon: The Next Day

"You two got lucky. Hamadi requested four interpreters from a service. I've managed to get you two assigned."

"Through the service? They won't know who we are."

"Michael, are you forgetting something?"

"Ah, that."

"You two have been on retainer with the service for two years. Once this is over, your records will suddenly disappear, and no one will know the difference. All you need to do is use the IDs Soto gave you."

"Got it."

"You are scheduled to be there by three p.m. on Friday. There's a reception with cocktails at six."

"What about dress?"

"Professional attire. Since I booked you as a husband-and-wife team, navy suit for you and a navy pantsuit for Nadia. You have an appointment at Harrods in London for a fitting this afternoon at four. They have been given the specifics of what you will need. I gave them a credit card number which Harrods now has on file."

"Who does it belong to?"

"Who do you think?"

"Arman Hamadi?"

"You guessed it. While you're there, pick up anything else you might need."

"Seems you have thought of everything, JR."

"Almost forgot. You will need to ask for a woman named Sophia Price. She is a professional shopping assistant and will help you both." He paused. "Do you have weapons?"

"Always."

"Good. Let me know if you need anything else."

The call ended, and Michael checked his wristwatch. "We need to head back to London for a suit fitting."

"Where?"

"Harrods."

The only response he received back was a beaming smile.

They arrived back at the hotel a little after nine p.m. With a free day on Thursday, they planned on exploring more of the land surrounding Corbyn Park House.

Nadia took her shower after Michael got into bed. He heard her singing in her native language. She had failed to follow her normal routine for several weeks, so her return to it comforted him. He lay with his hands behind his head as he determined which part of the estate they would need to become familiar with.

When the door to the bathroom opened, she wore a sheer gown he had never seen before. When she slipped into bed beside him, he said, "Is that new?"

"Very. You like it?"

"Better than the pantsuit. And I thought you looked fabulous in it."

They fell asleep in each other's arms an hour later.

Trudging around the northern edge of the Corbyn Park House property, Nadia recorded GPS locations pointed out to her by her husband.

"Michael, what are you searching for?"

"A place where we can bring Hamadi, stay hidden until we're done talking to him, and then let him loose. I'd like to keep it on his land, but I haven't seen the right spot yet."

"Do you mean a cave?"

"Not sure. We need somewhere we can stay hidden for a few hours."

She consulted her cell phone and then placed a few numbers into the GPS unit. "Michael, there is a formation of rocks about half a kilometer to the west. Do you want to explore them?"

"Might as well. I haven't found anything useful here."

Twenty minutes later, Wolfe stood at the top of a crag, looking down into a shallow ravine. While Nadia explored routes into the small canyon, he examined the area from above.

"Michael, I think I found something."

He hustled in the direction of her voice and found her in an area under an outcrop approximately the height of a man and seven feet deep. Wolfe said, "This isn't visible from the top. I believe it will work."

Nadia pointed to the south. "It's at least a kilometer back to the house. Can we drag him that far?"

"Not sure we have a choice." He surveyed the surrounding area. "How far to the nearest access road?"

She consulted Google Earth on her phone and moved the view with her finger. She gestured toward the west. "Not that far, maybe three hundred meters."

"If they have dogs, we're screwed. Unless—" He brought his cell phone out of his jeans pocket and pressed an icon. When Griggs answered, Wolfe said, "How fast can you find a compact delivery van?"

"Pretty fast, why?"

"We've got a job for you."

"Good. I was getting bored."

Corbyn Park House
Friday

By five p.m., Nadia and Wolfe were signed in, briefed, and given their badges identifying them as certified interpreters. Wolfe's badge identified him as fluent in Arabic, Farsi, and German. He chose not to tell them he also understood Pashto. Nadia's badge indicated she could translate French, Spanish, and Hebrew. She also failed to tell them of her knowledge of Arabic. Their wardrobe from Harrods allowed both to stand out as professionals. Two of the female organizers quietly appraised their suits when they first arrived, nodded to each other, and never questioned their credentials.

Guests started arriving a few minutes before six. Thirty minutes later, both Nadia and Wolfe caught their first glimpse of the host, Arman Hamadi.

As the evening drew on, Wolfe found himself shadowing a gentleman from the United Arab Emirates who spoke English with such a thick accent, he finally asked Michael to translate his Arabic for him.

To Wolfe's surprise, Hamadi approached the UAE attendee and asked in Arabic if his interpreter was doing a good job. The man flattered Wolfe's work and thanked his host for having the service available for him.

Hamadi bowed and said, "My pleasure, Assad." He turned to Wolfe. "Would you be willing to accompany my good friend here on the hunt tomorrow morning?"

With a slight bow, Wolfe said in perfect Arabic, "My pleasure. Although I did not bring suitable hunting clothes with me."

"Not a problem. What are you about 180 centimeters, ninety-one kilos?"

"Yes."

"I will make sure you are well equipped in the morning." Hamadi smiled at his guest and said, "Fear not about tomorrow. You will be accompanied by our friend, here."

The couple arrived back at their hotel room after ten p.m. Per a request from her husband, who had remained silent during the entire drive from the estate, she set up their laptop for a VoIP phone call with Joseph.

When he answered, Wolfe asked, "Any updates on Arman Hamadi?"

"Yes, JR uncovered evidence he had his fingers in a 2019 bombing in Lyon, France. I forwarded this info to Chapman, who has sent it on to the French GDSE. Because of it, Interpol will be issuing an Arrest on Sight warrant Monday."

"How solid is their information?"

"Pretty damn solid."

"That's all I needed to know."

Wolfe ended the call. He took a deep breath and trained his attention on his wife. "An opportunity has presented itself to rid the world of Arman Hamadi. Change in plans. If it works out, the party may not have need for our services tomorrow afternoon."

She tilted her head. "Want to explain yourself?"

He told her his plan.

Chapter Thirty-Five

CORBYN PARK HOUSE

5:00 a.m. GMT Saturday

"Good morning, gentlemen. My name is Nigel Hughes. I am a professional deer stalker with Gunderson Field Sports. I will be managing this morning's hunt. With me is my associate, Henry Stevens. As you have already been told, we have two exciting days of stalking lined up for you this weekend."

Wolfe listened and scanned the room. There were two groups of would-be hunters. Six per group. Hamadi sat in the same group as Assad al-Safar. Wolfe's duties were to accompany al-Safar for the morning hunt. Sitting slightly behind the man, he whispered the instructions into the ear of the Arab as the deer stalker explained the day's events.

Hughes continued. "The day will be conducted in time-honored tradition. If your stalk results in a successful kill, the stag will be carried back to the Corbyn Park House by pony for preparation. If you wish to donate the meat from your hunt, a venison dealer will be on site to make the proper preparation. If you wish to keep the proceeds, the dealer will assist with the appropriate arrangements.

"Upon commencement of our hunt this morning, you will be accompanied at all times by either myself or Mr. Stevens. We know where to locate several herds and will properly guide you to them depending on wind direction and prevailing conditions. Are there any questions, so far?"

Hughes stood in front of the group, ramrod straight, with his hands behind his back. Wolfe remained silent until al-Safar said in Arabic, "How long will the hunt last?"

Wolfe raised his hand and asked the deer stalker the question.

"Ah, yes," said Hughes. "Our hunt will commence at exactly six a.m. and conclude at precisely eight-thirty a.m. Any other questions?" When there were none, Hughes stepped toward the group. "When we locate the herds, you will see they can consist of as few as ten or as many as forty red-tail deer. At this point, myself or Mr. Stevens will select the stags that, in our opinion, are suitable for you hunters to cull." He returned to his parade-rest posture. "After all, must keep the herd properly managed, don't you know."

All the hunters except for al-Safar nodded in agreement. He tilted his head toward Wolfe and asked, "What does that mean?"

"I will explain it later, sir."

The Arab returned his attention to Hughes.

After Hughes finished discussing gun safety, he called for both groups of hunters to follow him to their transportation. During the walk to the two Range Rovers, Wolfe followed al-Safar internally debating if his plan would work, or if they needed to go back to the original abduction scenario. As the hunters secured their weapons in the back of the SUV, Hughes motioned for Wolfe to join him.

"You're not one of these characters, are you?"

"No, sir. Interpreter for al-Safar."

"Yank?"

Wolfe nodded slightly.

"You have a look about you. Military?"

"Retired Marine."

Hughes offered his hand. "Thought so. Royal Marine myself." As they shook, Hughes asked, "What's this al-Safar chap like?"

"Nice enough, but doesn't understand the reasons for all the gun safety or the concerns about the deer population's health. I'm a little worried about him being here."

"Typical Arab. I don't mind saying, that's one of the downsides to this job. I have to deal with rich Arabs who think their shit don't stink. Gotta go. Keep an eye on al-Safar for me."

"Will do."

As Wolfe followed Hughes' progress back to the Range Rover, his confidence in the revised plan started to grow.

An hour into the hunt, the members of Hughes' hunting party were spread out side by side, separated by thirty meters each. The underbrush and tree cover were less dense than when they first started their stalk. Wolfe noted that Hamadi occupied the middle position of the group, with al-Safar on the far left. One hunter, a man from Germany, separated them.

As they approached more open ground, al-Safar started complaining about how heavy his rifle had become. Wolfe made his decision.

When the two men reached an area with thick underbrush, Wolfe offered to take the rifle so al-Safar could maneuver easier. Calculating the distance and angle to Hamadi, the retired Marine sniper made his move. With al-Safar slightly behind the rest of the five men, Wolfe tripped him and shoved his head against a tree. At the same time, he aimed the 30.06 Remington 700 at Hamadi from waist height and pulled the trigger.

A Hampshire County constable listened to Wolfe describe the circumstance of the hunting accident that claimed the life of the Corbyn Park House owner. When he finished, she asked, "So, you don't think Mr. al-Safar did this on purpose?"

"I don't see how. He appeared uncomfortable handling the rifle. I noticed several times how careless he seemed to be with the weapon as we moved through the wooded area."

"Why didn't you say something to Nigel Hughes about him?"

"I had planned to when we stopped, but the accident happened before I had an opportunity to speak with him."

"Tell me again what happened."

"I was trailing behind him, trying to keep from tripping myself. He stumbled, hit his head on a tree, and the gun went off."

"So, an unfortunate mishap."

"Yes, unfortunate for Mr. Hamadi."

She made a few more notes and then looked up from the pad. "Thank you, Mr. Lyon. You've been a big help. If you don't mind, please stay on the property for a while longer. We would appreciate it."

"I'll stay as long as you need me."

After she moved on to talk to some of the other hunters, Hughes walked up to Wolfe and said, "You called it, Yank. The Arab shouldn't have been on the hunt."

"He did pay for the deer tag. Not sure Hamadi could have kept him from it."

"Guess our host won't be making that mistake again."

"Probably not."

By noon, Nadia and Wolfe were in the delivery van Griggs had secured and heading back toward London. Wolfe said, "Jerry, I think it's time Nadia and I returned to the States."

"Already have it planned. You two will be in the air by midafternoon. Soto already has someone securing the Ford from the hotel parking area and is quietly erasing all traces of your visit to the UK."

"Thank you."

Glancing at Wolfe's image in the rearview mirror, he said, "There will be a major story about Hamadi in the *Times* tomorrow."

"Guess Nadia and I will miss it."

"Yeah, guess so."

Nadia sat in the passenger seat next to Griggs. "What's it going to say?"

"Hamadi's entire operations will be exposed. There are going to be more than a few very embarrassed British socialites tomorrow."

Wolfe stayed quiet for a few moments. "What about his financial holdings?"

"Ceased by MI6. When Chapman learned of his activities, he went to the Bank of England and had them put a hold on all of Hamadi's assets. Interpol helped out with some of the other banks in the EU. I'm told they got almost 95 percent of his known holdings. They also shut down the arms-trading side of his business."

"So, Al-Qaedi no longer has a major donor for his activities?"

"According to Chapman, that's correct."

"Good."

"Michael?"

"Yeah?"

"Chapman sends his thanks. He is sorry he sidelined you."

Wolfe's mouth twitched, but he kept his thoughts to himself.

Borough of Tower Hamlets

A blood vessel on Mohammad Al-Qaedi's temple pulsed. His teeth were clenched and his face crimson as he glared at Amir Zamani. "What do you mean, Arman Hamadi is dead?"

"My Sheik, it is all over the newspapers. He was killed in a hunting accident."

"What about our money?"

"I do not know, but there is also a report Interpol issued a Red Notice on him."

Al-Qaedi emitted a sound similar to a trapped animal. "If we no longer have access to his money, you and I need to leave England immediately."

"Yes, my Sheik. I am told Scotland Yard is on the lookout for you."

Maintaining his glare at Zamani, the elder terrorist took a deep breath. "Someone is responsible for these constant blockades."

"Yes, my Sheik."

Al-Qaedi growled, "Do you not know anything else to say besides yes, my Sheik?"

Zamani shook his head.

Silence filled the room as Al-Qaedi started to pace. After several minutes, he stopped. "Has anyone heard from Noah Anderson?"

"No, Dillon believes he is under arrest."

"How did everything unravel so fast?"

"I do not know, my Sheik. But you need to see this copy of the *Times*."

Al-Qaedi accepted the newspaper being handed to him. "What?"

"It is a picture published with the story of how Arman Hamadi died in a hunting accident. Notice the man in the background with the circle drawn around him."

The Iranian terrorist studied the slightly out-of-focus picture for a long time. He said, "Why does this man look familiar, Amir?"

"Because that man is Michael Wolfe."

Returning his attention to the newspaper, Al-Qaedi narrowed his eyes. "Now that you mention it, this is Wolfe." Silence filled the room as he studied the picture. "Let us return to Iran and determine what must be done about this meddlesome American."

Part III

Chapter Thirty-Six

WASHINGTON, DC

Two Months Later

Jerry Griggs rapped on the office doorframe of Joseph Kincaid. Looking up, Joseph said, "Come in, Jerry."

"You've got a call on line one."

"You could have just buzzed me."

"I know, boss. It's Chapman."

"Come in and close the door."

Joseph placed the call on speaker and said, "Good afternoon, Jonathan."

"It is afternoon, but not sure how good."

"Oh, want to explain?"

"Noah Anderson has reached a plea deal with the government."

"I see. I take it you are not agreeable with this arrangement."

"Not really. Noah knows too many, uh, facts that do not need to be shared."

"Are you in trouble, Jonathan?"

"Me, no. Our friends Michael Wolfe and Ian McGill could be."

Raising his eyebrows, Joseph glanced at Griggs who frowned.

Chapman continued. "While McGill never officially filed an after-action report, Noah was privy to the few communications that occurred while our two men were in Iran."

"I don't see—"

"That's the point, Joseph. No one knows exactly what happened over there, and Anderson could just start making stuff up."

"So, what do you want me to do?"

"Get a bloody after-action report from them."

"Have you told anyone else about McGill's situation?"

"No, everyone here believes he died in an accident. All of this will fall on Wolfe's head."

"I see."

"If they believe Anderson, Downing Street might ask for Wolfe's extradition. At that point, you might never get him back."

"That would be unfortunate, Jonathan. Remember, we had this type of conversation earlier in the year."

"I know, but this time, the PM is involved."

"I can say something to my boss, if that might help."

"It could, one of the reasons I called."

"What was the other reason?"

Chapman paused for a second. "Lots of Internet chatter about Al-Qaedi rattling his sword again."

"Do your cousins at Langley know anything?"

"You and your boss might want to have a chat with Dwight King."

"Appreciate the heads-up, Jonathan. I will keep you appraised."

The call ended and Joseph said, "See what you can find out. I would prefer to know more about this before I take it to the president."

Standing, Griggs headed back toward the door. "You got it, boss." Before he opened the door, he turned. "Am I dismissed for the day?"

"You are."

"Jerry, I am going to stop meeting you if you don't upgrade the bars we go to." Carla Webb glanced around the dark tavern on the northern edge of Washington, DC's Columbia Heights district. "My shoes stuck to the floor when I walked in."

"Ambiance, Carla, ambiance."

"At least the beer is drinkable."

Griggs raised his bottle. "Hard to screw up a bottle of beer."

"So, what do you need this time?"

"Al-Qaedi. My boss is hearing about rumors concerning his activities."

Carla took a sip of her beer and lowered it to the table in a long, drawn-out stall. "I was afraid you would ask about that."

"Why?"

"Seventh floor is screaming at all the department heads about needing more information before King has to inform the DNI and the president."

"Why would that make everybody nervous?"

"Because Al-Qaedi supposedly slipped into Canada last

week and may already be in the United States. No one, and I mean no one, saw that coming."

Griggs took a swig of his beer and remained silent, keeping his eyes on the diminutive CIA agent. "But they're not sure, right?"

"No one's sure where Al-Qaedi is right now. It seems the sources we supposedly have in Iran missed it and even the Israelis missed it. They normally keep the guy under a microscope."

"Did the Israelis know he was in England two months ago?"

"Of course, they knew."

"And they didn't tell us about it?"

Carla shrugged. "I know. Shocking, isn't it?"

"Does anyone know why he's in the US?"

"Nary a clue. Even the FBI got caught flatfooted."

"Why has no one told the president?"

"Think about it—self-preservation, mainly. Plus, they really don't have any hard data telling them he's here. The only thing they have are a few cell phone intercepts and that's it. It's a complete conundrum."

Griggs stood. "Thanks, Carla."

"Want me to walk you to your car?"

"Why would I want you to do that?"

"You know, you working in the White House, getting all soft and lazy."

He flipped her the bird as he walked out.

Newly installed Director of National Intelligence Christina Dixon sat to the president's right with CIA Director Dwight King next to her. FBI Director Ryan Clark sat across from

King and next to the president's national security advisor, Joseph Kincaid. The NSA always placed himself to the left of President Roy Griffin who sat at the head of the conference table in the Situation Room.

Griffin said, "According to today's PDB, there is no hard evidence this Al-Qaedi person is in the US, but you disagree, is that correct, Dwight?"

"That is correct, sir."

"What is your opinion, Ryan?"

"On the side of caution, I believe we have to assume he is."

"What about you, Christina?"

"From the information Dwight gave me, I would tend to agree."

Leaning back in his chair, Griffin placed his elbows on the arms of the chair and made a steeple with his fingers. He then proceeded to tap his lips. "What are we going to do about it?"

Dixson put her pen down and took off her glasses. She then surveyed everyone at the table. "I apologize for not being quite up to speed on this Al-Qaedi individual, but why is he so worrisome?"

Griffin's attention went to Joseph. "You have the most experience with him. Care to enlighten all of us?"

Leaning forward, the NSA clasped his hands together on the table and said, "He has a long history of utilizing bombs to cause havoc and death. While most terrorists of his ilk have short careers, hc has survived for over two decades. He is considered one of the masterminds of the Madrid train bombings in 2004. Since 2010, it is believed he assisted or contributed to numerous terrorist bombings in Saudi Arabia, Iraq, and Turkey.

"Two months ago, his plot to detonate a massive bomb

on the River Thames next to Big Ben and the House of Parliament was thwarted. It is believed he escaped to Iran and has been silent since."

Dixon frowned. "I did not hear anything about a plot on the House of Parliament."

"That's because the Brits kept it quiet."

Clark spoke next. "Joseph, do the Brits have any idea why he would be in the US?"

The president answered. "I do."

The attendees directed their attention to the president. He said, "I believe he is seeking revenge on the man who stopped the bombing in England."

Dixon asked, "Who's that?"

Dwight King hid a smile with his hand, and Ryan Clark intently studied his notes. Joseph said, "Someone who works for the president."

The DNI stiffened. "Why is this the first time I've heard about someone like that?"

The president said, "As you said before, Ms. Dixon, you are new to your position, and there has been no need for you to know until now."

She remained silent.

Joseph said, "His name is Michael Wolfe. He's a retired Marine sniper and works for the president when needed."

"As Director of National Intelligence, shouldn't he answer to me?"

Griffin shook his head. "No."

Her face grew crimson. "Excuse me, sir. I am tasked with keeping tabs on everything related to our nation's security. I should know about what this man is involved with."

"Normally, I would agree with you, Ms. Dixon. But Michael Wolfe has served this country with honor in more ways than any of us at this table ever will. Unlike us, the public will never be aware of his service. He will continue to answer to me, and only me. Is that understood?"

Her glare remained on the president. After a few moments, it softened and she nodded.

"Now that we have that settled, Attorney General Delgado received a request from Her Majesty's attorney general to have Wolfe extradited to England to answer questions concerning his involvement with a mission to Iran earlier this year." The president surveyed the faces at the table. He noted Dixon kept her eyes down. Everyone else kept their gaze on him. "I am instructing the attorney general to deny this request."

King asked, "What instigated the request, Mr. President?"

Griffin motioned for Joseph to respond. The NSA said, "They uncovered a mole in MI6. It was Chapman's assistant, Noah Anderson. Apparently, he is claiming misdeeds conducted by Wolfe and his companion during their mission to Iran. What deeds they are accused of perpetrating are currently unknown."

"Do we know the details of their mission, Joseph?"

The president answered, "Michael and an ex-British SAS sergeant major were tasked with destroying the remaining supply of Iran's bioweapons. They were successful."

The CIA director added, "This was the same bioweapon smuggled into the US last year in an aborted attempt to attack the president."

"That is why I am providing a blanket pardon for both Wolfe and McGill. They will not be extradited to Britain."

Dixon raised her head. "McGill is in the US?"

The president nodded. "Yes."

The discussion moved to other matters and concluded

ten minutes later. As everyone rose to leave, Griffin said, "Ms. Dixon, please remain."

She remained seated. When they were alone, Griffin said, "I appreciate your desire to perform your duties as DNI at the highest level."

"Thank you."

"However, when it comes to individuals like Michael Wolfe, I will make the decisions. Is that clear?"

She stiffened and said, "Yes, sir, very clear."

"Thank you, Christina. You will make an excellent DNI."

Chapter Thirty-Seven

SOUTHWEST MISSOURI

Wolfe parked his Jeep behind the pristine 2006 Ford F-150. As he stepped out of the Grand Cherokee, the sound of a chainsaw stopped. He glanced up the gentle slope to see McGill wave. Returning the greeting, he trudged up the incline toward his friend.

"I see you got the truck repainted."

"Aye, laddie. Thanks for the recommendation. It looks new."

As the two men shook, Wolfe swept his gaze around the property. "You've gotten a lot done over the last couple of days."

McGill, dressed in a sleeveless sweatshirt, faded jeans, and leather work gloves put the chainsaw down. "Aye, I had to. They start preparing for thc foundation on Monday." He paused and appraised his friend. "But you knew that. You're not dressed to help, so why the visit?"

"Want to return from the dead?"

"What's happened, mate?"

"It seems our friend Al-Qaedi has evaded the authorities

and slipped into the US. I got a warning about him this morning from Joseph."

McGill narrowed his eyes. "He'll be after you, Michael. As you just said, I'm supposed to be dead."

With a chuckle, Wolfe said, "I keep forgetting. You appear so alive."

McGill said, "How good is their intel?"

"Mostly hearsay and Internet chatter. But I believe we need to plan accordingly."

"Aye."

"One other thing, Ian."

McGill crossed his arms. "Go on."

"Like I told you when Nadia and I returned from England, Noah Anderson was the leak within MI6. Chapman didn't betray you. But Anderson is making shit up to cover his butt. He claims you and I committed an atrocity while we were in Iran earlier this year."

Placing his hands on his hips, McGill's eyes narrowed. "What did we supposedly do?"

"He won't say. The British attorney general wants me extradited to London to answer their questions."

"Get a barrister. Fight it."

"No worries. We have a friend in the White House. He put a squelch on it."

"Good."

"Back to Al-Qaedi. I don't like being hunted. I prefer to be the hunter."

"Aye, laddie. What've ya got in mind?"

With the assistance of JR, the two men were given access to the security camera feeds on JR's building. With the high-definition views and strategic location of each camera, they could keep tabs on the surrounding area without physically being in the vicinity. They each possessed an image of Logan Dillon for comparison. Located on the second floor of Wolfe's hangar, he took the day shift so Ian could continue working at his property.

On the fourth day of their vigilant watch, Wolfe spotted someone paying too much attention to JR's building. At first, it appeared to be just another pedestrian walking on the sidewalk across from the building. But on the third pass, Wolfe zeroed in on the impostor. The man's pattern, while irregular, became obvious as the day went on.

He called McGill.

"What have ya got?"

"Where are you?"

"Just left the property."

"There's a white male, thirty something, with longish brown hair, paying way too much attention to the coming and goings at JR's. Sometimes his hair's in a ponytail. Occasionally it's under a hat or hanging loose. He changes it on each pass."

"Sounds like someone we need to talk to."

"Eventually."

"Then why the call, Michael?"

"If there is one, my guess is there will be two or more, only stationary."

"I would agree with ya, laddie."

"Want to help me flush them out?"

"How?"

"The same way we got the location of the bioweapon in Iran."

"That did work well." McGill chuckled. "Think it will work here?"

"Won't hurt to try."

Wolfe sat in a rented Ford Transit Van keeping tabs on the corner, where the individual he'd identified, normally would stand for a few moments to study JR's building. As soon as the man stopped, Wolfe accelerated toward the location. Coming to a stop at the corner, he rolled down the window. "Hey, buddy. I need directions."

The man contemplated Wolfe for a few moments. "Where to?"

"Can't hear you. Come closer to the window."

The man frowned. He checked the street in both directions. Seeing nothing, he stepped off the curb and bent over. "Where're you headed?"

The Glock 21 rose to within two feet of the man's head. Wolfe growled, "Get in or die."

Without a word, the man opened the passenger door and sat. Immediately, Wolfe accelerated away from the corner. Before the man could protest, the retired Marine brought his right elbow up hard against his temple. The passenger crumpled forward as the Ford Transit turned left and sped away from the multiuse business center.

McGill concentrated on the rearview mirror of this truck parked at the curb east of JR's building. A minute passed without seeing anyone making a mad dash to follow the van. Two minutes into his wait, a white Ford Fusion roared past his position with two men inside. They ran a red light in pursuit of the van. Putting his Ford F-150 in gear, he followed.

Wearing a Kansas City Chiefs ball cap and dark sunglasses, McGill kept the Fusion in sight as he followed. As expected, they took the entrance to an east-west four-lane express around the city.

Knowing Wolfe's final destination allowed him to keep a safe distance behind the white car as they raced toward the east on the four-lane thruway.

Twenty minutes later, McGill accepted a call on his cell phone.

"Did anyone follow?"

"White Ford Fusion, six cars behind you."

Wolfe remained quiet for a second. "Got it. How many in the car?"

"Two. Both had black hair and beards. That's all I could determine as they drove by."

"Okay, we'll assume they know what they're doing."

"I would agree. How's your passenger?"

"Sleeping like a baby."

"Good. Let me know when you're in position."

"Almost ready to turn west. See you in a few."

Wolfe followed the deserted country road, five miles from his property. He parked the van sideways in the road. A steel guardrail marked the end of the lane and prevented cars from driving into a tributary of a local river. They chose this location due to the rise fifty yards from the end. The driver of the Ford would have a difficult time seeing his trap until he cleared the top of the hill. By then, McGill would be right behind him, and the snare would be closed.

After putting zip ties on the hands and feet of his passenger, Wolfe stepped out of the van and secured himself behind the engine with his Glock pointed toward the top of the hill. He pressed an icon on his phone, sending a one-word text to McGill. *Ready.*

Five seconds later, the Ford topped the hill. As the car skidded in the loose gravel of the road, Wolfe fired the Glock, shredding the front and back tires on the side of the car facing him.

Almost at the same time the Ford slid to a stop, McGill's F-150 topped the crest and bore down on the now-trapped men.

Braking to a stop, twenty feet from the disabled car, McGill scrambled out and pointed his Sig Sauer 1911 Emperor Scorpion at the car. The two men in the Ford stared at Wolfe and then at McGill. Lowering the windows, they showed their empty hands. While Wolfe ran toward the vehicle, McGill kept his aim on the two men. His partner forced them out of the car and secured them with zip ties. The incident lasted less than thirty seconds.

Wolfe said in Arabic, "Into the van, quickly."

Both men complied. After Wolfe secured them with more zip ties inside the van, he emerged to see McGill pushing the disabled car out of the way. When the car stopped next to a barbed wire fence, the Scotsman reached in and extracted two black objects from inside the car.

With all three prisoners blindfolded, they headed toward Wolfe's property, the Transit Van taking the lead and the F-150 following close.

Secured to chairs in a room on the second floor of Wolfe's hangar, the three men sat blindfolded in total darkness. Standing behind them, McGill ripped off the tape covering their eyes, one at a time. At the same moment, Wolfe turned on a blinding white light, illuminating the three prisoners. Each man squinted at the brightness.

Wolfe said in Arabic, "Who are you working for?"

No response came forth from any of the men.

McGill's 1911 automatic pistol appeared out of the darkness and pressed against the head of the man who had driven the car. "Answer him, laddie."

Eyes widened, he said, "We do not know what you are talking about."

McGill flicked off the safety on the pistol, and his thumb pulled back the weapon's hammer. "Me fingers on the trigger, asshole. Answer the man."

The dark-haired man in the middle tried to see who held the gun protruding from the darkness. He said in accented English, "You are Ian McGill. You are supposed to be dead."

"Someone lied to you, didn't they?"

Wolfe noticed a wet spot spread at the crotch of the third man, the one he'd abducted on the street corner. Getting an idea, he moved from behind the light and placed his Glock against the guy's head. "Who do you work for?"

The man shut his eyes and started reciting an Islamic prayer.

Wolfe said in English, "We don't have time for this." He returned to the light and switched it off. He followed McGill out of the room and just before closing the door, he tossed a gas canister into the darkness.

Ten minutes after closing the door on the three unconscious men, Wolfe's cell phone chirped. He checked the caller ID and then answered. "Who are they?"

"Two of them aren't in any database I have access to. But you hit a trifecta on the guy in the middle."

"Who is he?"

"Is Ian there?"

"Yeah."

"Put me on speaker, he's gonna love this one."

"He can hear you, JR. Go ahead."

"Of the twenty-nine defendants in the terrorist attack on the Madrid train bombing in 2004, eight were acquitted. The guy in the middle is one of those defendants who got off scot-free. He disappeared right after the verdict and apparently changed his name. He now goes by the name Ismail Habib. His parents were from Morocco and immigrated to Spain in 1960. Mossad has a lengthy file on the guy. However, in 2013, they lost track of him. They believe he fled to Iran and started working with Mohammad Al-Qaedi again."

McGill remained silent as he listened. Finally, he said, "Bloody hell," and walked out of the room.

"Thanks, JR. We can use this against them."

"Anytime, Michael."

Chapter Thirty-Eight

EIGHT THOUSAND FEET
ABOVE SOUTHERN MISSOURI

As the sun set on the western horizon, the 1979 Beechcraft B55 Baron climbed toward its desired cruising altitude of eight thousand feet. All three of the men were awake but still blindfolded. Wolfe sat in the pilot's position with no one sitting beside him. Ismail Habib sat next to the exit door with McGill next to him and the other two men in the back row seats.

McGill ripped off the duct tape acting as a blindfold for Habib. The ex-Spaniard grimaced but remained quiet. McGill said, "Welcome aboard, Ismail Habib."

The mention of his name by McGill caused Habib's eyes to bulge.

"That's right, Habib, we know who you are." McGill reached back and ripped the blindfolds off the two men in the back. "You guys need to see and hear this."

He returned his attention to Habib. "Not only do we know who you are, we know you were involved in the Madrid train bombings in 2004. The decision to acquit you of the charges appears to be a miscarriage of justice. My guess is since you worked for Al-Qaedi, you were one of the masterminds of the plot. Am I right?"

"You do not know what you are talking about."

"Sorry, Ismail, but I do. Your real name is Nizar Tahir, and your parents migrated from Morocco to Spain in 1960. You have been working for Mohammad Al-Qaedi on and off since 2000. How close am I?"

The Moroccan turned his head to the front and remained quiet.

"I will take the no-comment to mean I'm right." McGill directed his next statement to the two men in the back. "As you can see, we know more about you guys than you think." He returned his attention to Habib. "I will ask you this next question only once. Where is Mohammad Al-Qaedi?"

"How would I know?"

"Wrong answer, Ismail."

The last light of dusk faded as Wolfe flew a flight pattern keeping the plane over the middle of Table Rock Lake. After looking outside, McGill returned his attention to Habib again. "You might want to know that a dear friend of mine got on one of those trains at the Alcalá de Henares train station. I never saw her again."

Habib turned and smiled. "Good."

McGill heard Wolfe flip a switch. The door beside Habib slid back, exposing the interior of the plane to the night sky and wind. McGill raised his leg and shoved the man out of the plane with a foot to his chest. They felt the plane shake before the door returned to its closed position.

Returning his attention to the two men in the back, McGill said, "We are over two and a half kilometers above the ground, gentlemen. It will take you less than a minute to fall to the lake surface at 320 kilometers per hour. Now, where is Mohammad Al-Qaedi?"

The rapid-fire answers given to McGill's question told him and Wolfe exactly what they needed to know.

The Next Morning

Two US Marshals escorted the two remaining Muslims to a black Suburban parked in Wolfe's driveway. The prisoners were once again blindfolded as they were placed in the back of the vehicle.

Wolfe stood next to the remaining marshal. Once the two prisoners were secured, he offered his hand to Wolfe. "Thanks for holding these two guys for us. They keep talking about a third man. Did something happen to him?"

"Not to my knowledge, Frank. Those two are the only ones I knew about."

"Yeah, that was what we were told as well, only the two. Know who they are?"

"Yeah, an advance team for a terrorist named Mohammad Al-Qaedi. I had some dealings with him in Israel a few years back. I've been told he's on the FBI's most wanted list."

"That's our understanding as well. Any idea why they were in this area?"

"Not a clue, unless they were checking out the dams south of here."

"Hadn't thought of that. I'll mention it to my supervisor. Anyway, thanks, Michael. We'll take care of them from here."

"I appreciate it, Frank."

As the marshals drove away, McGill came out of the

house and stood by Wolfe. "Think they'll listen to those two?"

"I doubt it, I've known Frank for a while now. He has little patience for anything a prisoner tells him." Wolfe stopped watching the Suburban. "What we need to do now is draw Al-Qaedi into a trap."

"Think he'll send anyone back to watch JR's place?"

"Doesn't matter if he does. We have their cell phones. Nadia is working on who they've called over the past week. With Alexia's help, we should have an edge on setting a trap for Al-Qaedi."

Washington, DC

Jerry Griggs walked into Joseph's office without being asked and quickly closed the door.

"I take it this is not good news, Jerry."

"Depends on your point of view."

Shaking his head, Joseph clasped his hands together on his desk and waited.

"I heard from Michael."

"And?"

"He asked me to send the US Marshals to his place in Missouri to pick up a package."

"Oh! What happened to be in this package?"

"Two men from Iran who were in the country illegally. They also have ties to Mohammad Al-Qaedi."

"Is Al-Qaedi here?"

Jerry nodded. "Michael told me the two men confirmed it."

"Where is he?"

"That's the bad news. They didn't know."

"They could have been lying."

"Uh, Michael told me the circumstance surrounding their confessions. They weren't lying."

"I see. What else?"

"He would like to have the FBI involved."

After lowering his head, Joseph peered over his glasses. "Excuse me?"

Jerry continued. "He wants double pressure on Al-Qaedi. According to the two guys he caught, Al-Qaedi came in through a Canadian pipeline. First, he flew into Toronto on a private jet owned by a prince from the Emirate of Dubai and then crossed over into the US via a small boat on the St. Clair River near a place called Marine City. From there, he went to Dearborn and melted into the large Muslim population there."

"I take it no one knows where he is at this point."

"Correct. Can you talk to Director Clark about getting the FBI involved?"

With a nod, Joseph said, "I'm sure that can be arranged. What else?"

"Michael also wants you to tell the FBI he thinks Al-Qaedi is here because of his and Nadia's activities in England."

Joseph frowned. "Is Michael asking for protection?"

Griggs shook his head. "No, he just wants the FBI to know he and McGill won't be waiting for Al-Qaedi to find them."

"Oh dear."

Griggs said, "Yeah."

Southwest Missouri

Nadia pointed to a dot on the map displayed on her laptop. "That is the location of the cell phone last called by Habib."

Wolfe stood behind her and put his hands on her shoulders. "St. Louis?"

"Yes. The previous location was Chicago, twelve hours earlier."

"He's moving south, if it's the phone being used by Al-Qaedi."

"Those were my thoughts, as well, Michael. We do not know if it is Al-Qaedi or someone he is working with."

"The man always keeps his hands clean. I'm sure someone else is answering the phone for him."

"Alexia told me they are switching the phone on and off."

"Did she see a pattern?"

"No, the intervals are random."

"Okay. Are there any text messages between the two numbers?"

"None that Alexia could find. We could try to send one."

"Not yet. McGill isn't done setting up traps on his land."

"Thank you for not volunteering our place. I really don't want to rebuild this house again."

Wolfe chuckled. "Me, either."

She looked up at her husband. "Do you really think you can lure him to McGill's property?"

"Yes, once we let him know McGill is alive."

"Is that wise, Michael?"

"Not sure it's wise, but we feel it's the only way to get him on the land. Once we do, we'll be the hunters."

"What if he brings others?"

"We fully expect him to."

A ping sounded on Nadia's laptop. She clicked on an icon. "This is a local news update. A headless body washed up on the shores of Table Rock Lake this morning. It says the hands and feet were bound by constraints. Would that be Habib?"

"Probably. I felt the plane shake after Ian pushed him out. I'd better inspect the horizontal and vertical stabilizers."

Ten minutes later, Wolfe ran his hands along the leading tips of the horizontal stabilizers. There was no discoloration along the wing, but he felt a slight dent in the middle of the small right wing. He examined it for a few moments and then returned to the house.

Nadia turned in her chair as he entered the kitchen. "Did you find anything?"

"Small dent in the right rear wing. It's about the same size of a spinal column. My guess is he hit it after being ejected. Since the neck is mostly soft tissue, it didn't damage the plane much."

With a grimace, Nadia said, "The male human head weighs on average eleven pounds. It probably sank while the body eventually surfaced and washed ashore."

"Sometimes we get lucky."

Chapter Thirty-Nine

SOUTH OF LAMBERT INTERNATIONAL AIRPORT, ST. LOUIS

Mohammad Al-Qaedi paced while Amir Zamani sat quietly, sipping tea at the desk in the hotel room. The sheik said, "This is intolerable. Why has Habib not made contact for forty-eight hours?"

"I cannot answer that, my Sheik."

"Something has happened. He would have contacted me by now. He is a loyal believer in our struggle."

"Yes, he is."

With a glare in Zamani's direction, Al-Qaedi stopped pacing. "How many check-in times has he missed?"

"Three."

"Then we must assume he is either dead or captured."

"If he has been caught, he will not disclose your location. Of that, I am sure."

"No, he would not. However, the two men he is working with, I do not trust."

"Neither does Habib."

"Do you think Wolfe knows we are in this country?"

"My Sheik, I believe we should assume he does. As we

have seen in the past, the Americans are very tricky with their technology. I believe it is time we change our cell phones. If they have captured Habib, they can use his to track you."

"Make it so, Amir."

"As you wish, my Sheik."

The terrorist moved toward the window in the hotel room and threw back the curtains. The nightlights of Lambert International Airport could be seen to the north. Standing with his hands behind his back, Al-Qaedi kept his gaze on a jet taking off and heading toward the west as it gained altitude. "Amir."

"Yes."

"If I decide to go home, how difficult would it be for us to leave this country?"

"Not too difficult. Detroit is only eight hours by car. We have loyalists there who would be glad to help you get into Canada." Zamani raised his eyebrows. "Are you having second thoughts about seeking vengeance on Wolfe?"

"No, no second thoughts about him. However, I am disappointed in the lack of enthusiasm displayed by the local Muslim populations here in the US. I thought their fervor for our cause would be at a fever pitch."

"Alas, my Sheik, our American brethren do not share your passion of uniting the world under one caliphate."

"I am aware of that, but they have acted like we are unwelcome, which is un-Muslim."

"Yes, but most American Muslims see us as the enemy. They do not see how unjust we are treated throughout the world."

"The more reason to liberate them."

"My Sheik, the 911 attack only increased this mistrust. It did the exact opposite of its true intent."

"Yes, and twenty years of war."

"Which has only increased the mistrust of Muslims here. America is a huge country with the majority of its people Christian. It is also isolated by two oceans."

The sheik grew silent as he returned his gaze out the window. "I did not realize how large this country actually is." He paused for a moment as he followed the path of another jet taking off from the airport. "How far to where this Wolfe person is supposed to be?"

Zamani referred to his laptop sitting in front of him. "Four hours by car."

"Do we know where he lives?"

"No, my Sheik. That was the job of Habib."

"In the morning, try one more time to contact him. If silence is your answer, we will return to Detroit and leave this land that Allah has forsaken."

Southwest Missouri
The Next Morning

"Michael, it appears someone is trying to call Habib's phone."

Wolfe hurried into the room Nadia used for her computer work. When he walked in, she pointed at her laptop screen. "It's located at a Super 8 motel just south of Lambert Airport."

Taking his phone out, he called Jerry Griggs. "They are at a Super 8 on Saint Charles Rock Road, south of Lambert." Wolfe listened for a few moments. "Got it." He ended the call. "Griggs will get the FBI to the hotel. How long did the attempt last?"

"They let it ring six times. Then the phone shut off, and I lost the location."

"They have to be wondering what's happened to their guys. Nothing on the other phones?"

"No."

"Okay, keep monitoring them."

The two Iranians were in their rented SUV preparing to leave the parking lot when they observed three large Chevy Tahoes, emergency lights in the front grill flashing, approaching. Two screeched to a halt in front of the hotel, while the third circled around to the back and parked next to the rear entrance.

Zamani motioned for Al-Qaedi to lower himself in the seat to offer a smaller profile. As they watched, four men scrambled out of the Tahoe. Three entered the rear of the building while one man stayed at the back door and surveyed the parking lot.

"We now know that Habib is dead or under arrest. They were monitoring his phone. We must destroy the one we used, Amir."

"Already done, my Sheik."

"When you registered, did you give them vehicle information?"

"Yes, but I did not feel they needed to know the correct model or license plate number."

"Good. They will not be searching for this car."

"No."

"When the FBI agent goes inside the building, we will leave."

"A wise decision."

Thirty minutes later, the FBI vehicle parked in the rear of the hotel left with the four agents. Five minutes later, Zamani slowly drove out of the parking lot and headed southeast on St. Charles Rock Road.

With the hotel three miles in the rearview mirror, Al-Qaedi said, "Amir, how far did you say the location of Wolfe is from us?"

"Four hours south."

"Would we find any Muslim brothers who would be willing to help us?"

Zamani shot a quick glance at Al-Qaedi. Returning his attention to the road, he said, "Large populations of our Muslim brethren are concentrated in the larger cities of America. There are only three large cities in Missouri, St. Louis and Kansas City being the two largest. I would venture a guess we would not find too many in the other one."

"Why?"

"It is in what the people of this country call the Bible Belt."

"Hmm." He paused. "We are already in an area unfriendly to our beliefs. Let us find a sanctuary in Chicago or Detroit and decide what to do."

"Yes, my Sheik."

"Michael, they were there. Two of them. FBI found fingerprints of a man named Amir Zamani and multiple ones of Al-Qaedi's. They think they just missed them because the clerk indicated the two men checked out fifteen minutes before the agents arrived."

"What about their car? Did the hotel have a license plate number?"

"Yeah, but it was fake. When the agents ran the number, it didn't exist."

"So, we are right back to not knowing where they are."

"True, but this incident did one thing."

"What's that, Jerry?"

"The FBI issued a national BOLO on them. Someone lit a fire under Clark's ass, and now they're taking this as a serious threat."

"They weren't before?"

"Michael, you know how these things go. Unless someone important takes an interest, it gets swept under the rug. They now have proof a known international terrorist is in this country and are ratcheting up the heat."

"Let me guess who lit the fire. Joseph?"

"Well, actually, I think he asked his boss to do it."

"Good."

"What are you going to do?"

"I've got a meeting with JR."

JR Diminski's gaze fell on Wolfe's Beechcraft Baron. "I knew you had a plane, Michael. Didn't know it was a classic."

"The airframe is. The avionics and engines are less than four years old. I had it totally refitted by a company in Kansas."

"It's beautiful."

"Thanks, JR. Whenever you want a ride, let me know."

"I like to admire airplanes from the outside and on the

ground. But thanks anyway." He paused for a moment. "I think this is the first time I've been here."

"It is, and I appreciate you coming. I don't know if someone is still keeping tabs on your building. If they are, I think it best they waste their time."

"Not a problem. My wife says I need to get out more." JR lowered his backpack from his shoulder. "Where's your office?"

Wolfe pointed up. "Second floor. I have a desktop computer and a large-screen monitor. It displays all the views from my security cameras and keeps tabs on all the trip wires I have scattered around my property."

"Cool. Show me the way."

After Wolfe explained the security system, JR pursed his lips. "Uh—your setup is far more extensive than mine. When this crap with Al-Qaedi is over, would you revamp my office security system?"

"I would be honored."

As JR booted up his laptop, he said, "Now, tell me what you know about Mohammad Al-Qaedi?"

Wolfe summarized the current situation and where they believed the terrorist entered the US. JR studied a Google map as the retired Marine spoke.

He tapped the screen. "Michael, they probably rented a car somewhere in the Detroit area. Are you aware of any of Al-Qaedi's or Zamani's aliases?"

"No. The only one we do know about is for a man named Logan Dillon. He goes by the name Danny Wade."

Five minutes later, JR said, "Bingo."

Wolfe stood off to the side. "What'd you find?"

"A car was booked by a Danny Wade from Ohio. When they picked up the car, two additional drivers were added to the contract: Robert Farook and Mike Amasi. They're driving a white 2020 Kia Sportage."

"Can you get that information to Joseph?"

"I can do better. I'll send it directly to Ryan Clark."

Wolfe frowned.

"Relax, Michael. I've helped Ryan numerous times during his journey toward being named director of the FBI. He owes me."

Chapter Forty

DETROIT, MI

The small group welcomed Mohammad Al-Qaedi with a traditional Arab tea ceremony. As the men sat around the short table on pillows, one of the younger men, actually a teenager, poured the boiling water over the tea leaves. Al-Qaedi watched the young man and remembered the first time his father asked him to pour the water.

As the conversation moved from the weather and local happenings, the men grew more serious, and the two teenage boys exited the room. The elder of the group, a white-haired man named Aziz and the local mosque's imam, directed his attention to Al-Qaedi and spoke. "You honor us with your presence, my Sheik." He bowed his head slightly and continued. "How may we serve you?"

"I am in need of volunteers. I must avenge a slight on my honor."

Aziz spread his arms. "We are but simple men here, not soldiers."

"I was led to believe the opposite, Imam. You have

taught your flock the true meaning of Islam, and they are loyal to your wishes."

The cleric sipped his tea as he kept his eyes on Al-Qaedi. "What is this slight on your honor?"

"A man from the United States traveled to England. He killed my benefactor and disrupted an event designed to usher in a new reality to Britain."

"And what was this new reality to be, my brother?"

"To bring Islamic law to the millions of our Muslim brethren who have been forced to live there."

The imam considered Al-Qaedi for several moments. "A worthy goal." He paused. "What do you wish of us?"

"I have been patient, as the Prophet demands. I have endured many trials, and I have the courage to seek vengeance against this nonbelieving American."

The imam bowed his head slightly. "Muruwah."

"Yes."

"The question remains, what do you seek from us?"

"Young believers who wish to prove their belief in the will of Allah."

The white-haired man frowned. "Do not insult my intelligence, Mohammad Al-Qaedi. Your reputation precedes you. You do not seek disciples to spread the will of Allah. You seek men to help you kill this American. Am I right?"

The rebuke momentarily caught the Iranian terrorist by surprise. Finally, he said, "Yes, Imam. That is exactly what I seek."

"Will you offer tribute for their help?"

"Yes, Imam."

"Very well. I can arrange for men to assist you."

Amir Zamani stood to see who had knocked on his hotel door. Through the peephole, he saw the clerk from the front desk. He threw the dead bolt back and unhooked the security chain. Just as he turned the knob, four men pushed their way into the room knocking him onto the floor.

Two grabbed him and quickly turned him over, pushing his face into the carpet. With his hands behind him, another agent applied handcuffs. The remaining man closed the door and contemplated the bearded man being assisted to his feet by two agents. "Amir Zamani, FBI. We have a federal warrant for your arrest."

Zamani glared at the agent but remained quiet.

"Where is Mohammad Al-Qaedi?"

More silence from the handcuffed man.

The agent walked further into the hotel room. He then moved over to the small desk and pressed one of the keys with a pen taken from his inside suit-coat pocket. The screen lit up with a request for a pin.

The agent looked over his shoulder at Zamani. "Want to tell me the pin?"

No response came from the individual in their custody.

"I didn't think you would. Gentlemen, please escort the prisoner to our vehicle."

With the terrorist gone, Agent Phillip Goodman addressed the remaining agent in the room. "Brad, let's see what we can find."

FBI Director Ryan Clark listened to the briefing on the arrest of Amir Zamani. When the Detroit Field Office SAC finished, Clark asked, "No sign of Al-Qaedi?"

"No, sir. But there was a small suitcase in the closet our agents believe belongs to him."

"What about the computer?"

"Waiting on your instructions."

"I am sending someone to take custody of it. If you would meet him, he will bring it back to Washington."

"Yes, sir. When do you expect him to arrive?"

"He'll be flying into Selfridge Air National Guard Base. Can you have someone there with the laptop in two hours?"

"Yes, sir."

The call ended, and Clark drummed his fingers on his desk. What he planned to do next could end his brief stint as director of the FBI. But it would be the fastest way to find Mohammad Al-Qaedi.

He picked up his handset on his phone and dialed a four-digit number.

"Forensics, this is Charlie Craft."

"Charlie, it's Ryan."

Clark could almost hear the young head of the forensics lab at Quantico snap to attention. "Yes, Mr. Director."

"Charlie, I need your help."

Two men in suits escorted Amir Zamani through the hotel back exit to one of two parked black Chevy Tahoes. He did not struggle but kept his head down, staring at his feet until he vanished inside the vehicle.

Having returned from the mosque, Al-Qaedi observed the events of Zamani's arrest unfold from the front seat of their rental car parked at the opposite end of the parking lot. Used to surviving on his own in foreign countries, he took in the scene with a mental shrug. Turning his thoughts to strategic matters, he decided to change vehicles and exit Detroit as quickly as possible.

As the black SUV drove out of the parking lot, Al-Qaedi put his rental car in gear and left the area. He returned the vehicle to the Budget rental car lot, parked, left the keys, and walked away before an attendant could reach the car.

With his black backpack over his shoulder, he took a transit bus to the Detroit Metropolitan Wayne County Airport terminal, making sure as many security cameras as possible captured his image.

Once inside the terminal, he slipped into a restroom and secured himself in the stall farthest from the entrance. His backpack contained a change of clothing, grooming instruments, emergency cash, and two sets of fake IDs.

Using the small electric beard trimmer, he shaved his black beard as close to the face as it allowed, letting the shaved hair fall into the toilet. When satisfied with the results, he used gel to slick his hair back and away from his face. With the addition of a pair of black-framed glasses, he altered his appearance dramatically.

Finally, he changed his shirt. Before stepping out of the stall, he flushed the toilet, causing the black hair from his beard to disappear. Before leaving the restroom area, he checked his reflection in the mirror. He now looked nothing like the man who entered the room ten minutes earlier.

Leaving the terminal at the ground transportation exit, he found a taxi that accepted cash and took it to the Four Point Hotel by Sheraton near the airport. After paying the driver, he stood under the porte cochère until the taxi disappeared. He walked to the neighboring Baymont Inn and checked in using an American Express card issued to the name on one of his alternate IDs.

At exactly eight thirty the following morning, Enterprise delivered a Hyundai Santa Fe SUV to the Baymont Inn. Al-Qaedi signed all the paperwork using his new identification. After checking out, he drove the vehicle south on I-24. His eventual destination for the day: the area surrounding St. Louis, MO.

Chapter Forty-One

The Next Morning

Charlie Craft stepped off the small FBI Gulfstream on the tarmac near the FBO of the Springfield-Branson National Airport. He carried a black backpack over his shoulders and walked briskly to a waiting gunmetal gray Ford Mustang GT. After placing the pack in the back floorboard, he slid into the passenger seat.

When the car accelerated away from the business side of the airport, Charlie turned to the driver. "Thanks for picking me up."

"No problem."

"I take it JR is waiting for me?"

"Yeah, and I'll wait to bring you back to the airport."

The two old friends were silent for a while. Finally, Charlie asked, "Think Ryan will get into trouble for doing this?"

"He might, but Clark was always the type of person

who chose the righteous path over the safe path. He'll be fine, Charlie."

"I hope so."

Twenty minutes later, Charlie stood in the soundproof conference room on JR's second floor. His longtime mentor worked on the laptop taken from the hotel room of Al-Qaedi. "Director Clark asked me to thank you for providing the alias' Zamani and Al-Qaedi were using. They found the hotel in Detroit where they were staying."

"Glad I could help."

"Unfortunately, Al-Qaedi was not there."

JR looked up from the computer. "That was unfortunate."

"Yeah. How long to clone the drive, JR?"

"Not long. You'll be out of here in less than an hour."

"I don't want Director Clark to get in trouble."

"He won't. Where are they keeping Zamani?"

"I have no idea, but I do know the High-Value Detainee Interrogation Group took custody of him in Detroit."

"Good."

The owner of the Mustang sat at the end of the conference table sipping coffee. JR turned to him. "Are you taking Charlie back to the airport?"

"That's the plan."

"Well, finish your coffee. This is just about done."

Charlie Craft delivered the confiscated computer found in the hotel room of Amir Zamani directly to the office of Director Ryan Clark. After signing the transfer of custody form, Clark asked, "Any trouble?"

"None, sir."

"Good. How is JR?"

"His hair is thinner, but he looks and acts great." He paused. "Uh, sir?"

"Yes."

"The pilots know we detoured on our way back here."

"Yes, I'm very aware of that. Don't worry, Charlie. They volunteered for the flight. I've known them a long time, and both are discreet."

Charlie took a deep breath and let it out slowly. "That's good to know, sir."

Clark folded his arms. "When are you going to accept the promotion I offered you?"

"Well, uh, sir. I'm not sure I'm qualified to take over the department."

Clark placed his hand on Charlie Craft's shoulder. "You are more qualified than anyone in this agency."

After staring at the FBI director for several seconds, he lowered his head and said, "Then I guess it's time to accept the position."

"Great, Charlie. I'll take care of the paperwork."

Wolfe sat with his feet on his desk. His cell phone pressed to his ear. "So, what did you find on Zamani's computer, JR?"

"The best we can tell is the Iranian contacted seven mosques in Detroit before someone would accept a meeting with Al-Qaedi."

"Do you know which one?"

"Yeah, and there's the bad news. The Detroit police refer to it as a hot spot of Islamic unrest in one of Detroit's more impoverished neighborhoods."

"Sounds like he's recruiting."

"That's what the FBI thinks."

"Are they going to raid it?"

"If they are, I wasn't told."

"Raiding a mosque could cause other problems."

"Michael, if Al-Qaedi is recruiting, are they coming after you and Ian?"

"Probably." Wolfe paused for a moment. "If he is, we need to start taking a few precautions. How many men and women are in your building on a day-to-day basis?"

"Anywhere from five to over a hundred. It depends on what's going on."

"Can everyone work from home?"

"Yes. The office is actually more to help our clients feel warm and fuzzy about us."

"Send everyone home until this is over. I don't want a hostage situation."

"Uh, why would they—"

"Because it's the only place Al-Qaedi has used to try to find McGill and me. Do it now, JR."

The call ended and Wolfe laid the phone on his desk. "Damn."

Attorney Dan Morales poured himself a cup of coffee and walked back to his desk. Before sitting, he sifted through messages left by his assistant during his morning in court. His semi-retired helper, a woman close to seventy, worked six hours a day, four days a week. His practice barely needed that much time from her. But she insisted on answering the phone and handwriting all of his phone messages. Something he liked. He hated voicemail.

Trained as a trial lawyer, he realized after ten years of

practice, he did not care for the individuals he had to deal with as a defense attorney. So, he switched to real estate law and property litigation. While not as lucrative a practice, he made good money, got home at a decent hour, and never worked on weekends.

One message at the bottom of the pile caught his attention. After taking a sip of coffee and sitting, he read it more carefully. He checked the time on his cell phone and realized he had only thirty minutes until the individual who left the message would arrive at his office.

Morales loosened his tie and undid the top button of his dress shirt. He stared at the large clock on his office wall. Five minutes passed before he decided to stay and meet the individual.

Located in the center of a converted strip mall, the physical location of Morales and Associates did not exude success. His monthly lease on the place fit his budget and allowed him to pick and choose his clients. However, the individual he would meet in less than twenty minutes did not offer options on whether to take him as a client or not.

At five minutes after six p.m., a man stepped through the front door. The lawyer, who waited for his visitor in his lobby, bowed slightly and said, "Welcome to my humble office, my Sheik."

Al-Qaedi surveyed his surroundings. "I like the humbleness of this location, my friend. It does not attract attention, correct?"

"You are correct."

"Is anyone else here, Daniel?"

"No, we are alone, as you requested."

"Good. I have a most urgent request for you."

"Come, sit. My office is more comfortable."

Al-Qaedi raised his hand. "I am afraid I cannot take

advantage of your hospitality. I have more miles to travel before the day is over."

Morales bowed slightly again. "As you wish. How can I assist you?"

"I need the name of a real estate agent in Southwest Missouri?"

"Very well. Do you know what agency he is associated with?"

"No. I only know the names of their clients. And I am not sure if the person is a man or a woman."

"What are the clients' names?"

"Michael and Nadia Wolfe."

Michael Wolfe asked, "Did anyone ask you why you were closing the office for a few days?"

JR shook his head. "No, I told them we suspected a mold problem and needed to have someone inspect the building. We don't, of course, but no one will question an excuse like that." Following Wolfe up the stairs to his office above the hangar, JR continued. "After I cloned Zamani's computer, I found a network of clandestine contacts for Al-Qaedi."

Stopping in the middle of the stairwell, Wolfe looked back at JR. "How many?"

"More than a few. Actually, it's more like twenty individuals scattered around the country."

Wolfe started climbing again. "Any in the area?"

"No, closest one is in St. Louis. A lawyer."

When they reached the top of the staircase, Wolfe frowned. "A lawyer?"

"Yeah."

"Defense attorney?"

"No, that's what I would have guessed. The only notes by the name indicated he would help find safe houses anywhere in the country for those in need."

"Huh. Guess that would be convenient if you were hiding from the FBI or laying low after a terrorist attack. Did you check on who he is?"

"Not yet. I found the information just before I closed the building. Everyone left at noon, and I left right after. Where can I set up?"

Wolfe pointed to an empty desk on the far wall. "I had a spare one in a storage area. Thought you might like to camp out for a while."

"How fast is your Internet?"

"Four hundred Mbps, why?"

"That works. My office's speed is just a little faster."

While JR booted up his laptop, Wolfe asked, "The lawyer bothers me. When you're done there, can you see if we can learn a little more about him?"

"Sure, like what?"

"His name and details about his practice. I'd also like to know why he has ties to an Iranian terrorist."

"Now that you mention it, that would be interesting to find out."

An hour after Wolfe left the office to attend to some maintenance on the Baron, JR poked his head into the hangar area and said, "Found something. You need to see this."

Returning to the second floor, the computer hacker pointed to an email. "That's an email from attorney Dan Morales to the Christian County assessor's office requesting information concerning a possible lien against your property."

"I don't have any liens against this property."

"I know. He used it as an excuse to get the name of the real estate agent who negotiated the purchase. He indicated there might have been a problem with the original contract."

"There wasn't."

"I know. The assessor's office responded in kind he had faulty information."

Wolfe folded his arms. "But he did get Lori's name, didn't he?"

"I'm afraid he did."

"Shit."

Wolfe took his cell phone, pressed a number, and then hit the send icon. The call went unanswered. He typed out a text message and pressed send.

"Nadia and Lori were together today meeting with the contractor who's building Ian's house." He checked the time on his watch. "Their appointment should have been over an hour ago."

He dialed another number. It was answered on the second ring.

"Aye."

"Have you heard from Lori in the past hour?"

"Nae, why?"

"Call her and call me back."

Five minutes ticked by and then Wolfe's phone chirped. He accepted the call and, before he could say anything, McGill said, "I can't raise Lori on the phone, Michael. Something's wrong."

Chapter Forty-Two

SOUTHWEST MISSOURI

A flashing message appeared at the bottom right of JR's laptop. After skimming the context, he stood. "Michael, my office has been burglarized."

"Hold on, Ian. JR may have something." He lowered his phone. "What did you say?"

"There's been a break-in at my office. Police are on their way."

"Shit." He returned the phone to his ear. "Meet me at JR's office. The cops are heading there right now. This may be Al-Qaedi's way of leaving us a message."

The phone call ended, and Wolfe and JR descended the stairs two at a time.

By the time Wolfe and JR arrived at his office building, dusk had turned to night. The area surrounding the structure now displayed yellow crime scene tape. They drove by a tall, dark-haired man in the light of the police cars talking to an officer.

Wolfe slowed his Jeep. "I know him. What's he doing here?"

"He's a retired FBI agent. He's actually the first person on the emergency contact list for my business."

"I didn't know you knew him."

"Have for years. How do you know him?"

"He and I worked on a common problem a long time ago. I haven't seen him since. Does he live around here?"

"Across the street from me."

"Huh."

Wolfe noticed McGill's F-150 parked a block from the building. "I'll let you off here. Ian's parked up the road. Let me know when we can get into the building."

JR exited the Jeep and jogged to where the retired FBI agent and the police officer were standing.

After parking beside McGill, Wolfe slipped into the passenger seat of the pickup. "Heard anything from Lori?"

Shaking his head, McGill studied JR's building. "No, and I'm getting worried."

Taking his cell phone out again, Wolfe sent a second text message to his wife. After pressing the send icon, he anticipated a quick response. None came.

"Something is definitely wrong, Ian. I just sent a text message with a coded word. We both agreed if we got that particular word, to text back immediately. She hasn't responded."

"Lori told me she and Nadia were going to meet the contractor at his office. The appointment was at three. That was four hours ago."

"I'll call the contractor." Wolfe found the number in his

contacts list and pressed send. Fifteen seconds later, he said, "Ben, this is Michael Wolfe."

"Good to hear from you, Michael. What can I do for you?"

"Just wanted to make sure the meeting with Nadia and Lori went well."

"It went great. We got a lot of the details hammered out."

"Well, that's good to hear. I was curious and had not been able to discuss it with Nadia."

"They left at four. I think they said something about a few errands they needed to run."

Wolfe concentrated on JR's building as he listened. "I see. Well, I'm glad you had a productive meeting. Thanks for your time."

Wolfe ended the call. "They left at four."

"Now I know something is wrong."

"We need to get into JR's building. Come on, let's go."

Three Hours Earlier

Sitting in the driver's seat of her new Audi Q8, Lori Shepard read a text message on her cell phone. After Nadia buckled her seat belt, Lori said, "I just got a request to show a house to an out-of-town buyer who's at the address right now."

"You sound worried. Is this unusual?"

"As a rule, no, but I normally meet the client before I show them anything. The office said he requested me, on the recommendation of a former client. The place he wants to see is three miles east of Ozark and secluded. That makes me nervous. Would you go with me?"

"Sure. I'd love to. Let's go."

Fifteen minutes later, Lori parked the Audi in the circle drive of a multimillion-dollar mansion.

Nadia leaned over in her seat to get a better look at the house, her mouth open. "Wow, I've never been in a house this large."

"Don't get your hopes up. It's not as nice as your home. It's been on the market for almost a year. The seller has it priced way too high." She frowned as she looked around. "I don't see another car. Great, I wish these people…"

She did not finish her statement because two black-haired men approached the Audi with shotguns pointed straight at her and Nadia.

The wife of Michael Wolfe, a former agent for Israel's Mossad, calmly pulled her Glock 48 from her purse and held it with her right hand below the dash. "I don't believe they are here to see the house, Lori. When I tell you to do so, duck below the dash."

McGill's fiancée stared at her friend. "What are you going to do, Nadia?"

"I'm from Israel, Lori. Black-haired men with beards and shotguns do not intimidate me."

Wolfe and McGill approached JR standing next to the retired FBI agent. Wolfe asked, "JR, when can we get into your building?"

"Police detectives are still in there. Why?"

"Lori and Nadia seem to be MIA. Neither Ian nor

myself have been able to reach them. That's unusual for Nadia. She never turns her phone off. I have a funny feeling your break-in has something to do with their disappearance."

JR studied the two men and then returned his attention to his friend. "What do you think?"

The retired FBI agent offered his hand to Wolfe. "It's been a while, Michael."

As they shook, Wolfe said, "Yes, it has."

"I heard the problem in Madagascar took care of itself."

With a slight smile, Wolfe said, "Yeah, I heard that, too."

"Why would the break-in here at JR's place have anything to do with two women not answering their phones."

JR interrupted. "It's complicated, Sean."

The ex-agent studied JR for a few moments and then addressed the police officer. "You okay with them going in? They might see something your guys might not recognize as important."

"Good idea. Last I heard, nothing seemed disturbed except around the conference room area on the second floor."

JR frowned at Wolfe. "That's not good."

Wolfe started to say something when his cell phone chirped. Glancing at the caller ID, he pressed the accept icon on the screen and listened. He kept his attention on the pavement but remained quiet. After fifteen seconds, he ended the call and said, "Ian, we need to get back to my place."

Raising one eyebrow, McGill said, "What are we waiting for, then, laddie?"

As Wolfe and McGill scurried back to their vehicles, the retired-FBI agent asked JR, "Want to explain what that was all about?"

"Like I said, it's complicated."

Thirty minutes later, Wolfe and McGill climbed the stairs to the hangar's second floor.

McGill said, "She didn't say where they were?"

"No. The way she started the message is our code to keep quiet and listen, like she's leaving a voicemail message."

"Got it. What was the message?"

"She said, they showed a house and would be heading to our favorite bar and be home late."

"What bar would that be?"

"We don't go to bars, Ian. Do you know anybody at Lori's real estate company?"

"Aye, I know her assistant. Why?"

"Call her. We need to know where they were going. Something happened when they got there."

Five minutes later, McGill ended the call and turned his attention to Wolfe. "Someone requested for Lori to show them a high-end house east of Ozark. The person wasn't a current client and a friend had recommended Lori to them."

"Where's the place?"

McGill handed him a piece of paper. "Since I'm not from around here, the directions didn't make sense to me."

"They do to me."

A massive gun safe with a biometric lock stood next to a

gun rack. He placed his thumb on the access pad, and the perfectly balanced steel door swung open. Inside, he found the lethal weapons of his trade. He removed his Barrett and then surveyed the remaining weapons.

Wolfe owned four Heckler and Koch MP5SD with integrated silencers and flash suppressors. These were designed for special forces night missions. He pointed at one. “Ever use one of these?”

“More than a few times.”

Wolfe removed one and placed it on the table next to his Barrett. He also extracted six magazines and laid them beside the H&K.

Multiple handguns in various calibers were in their cases and carefully lined up on the top shelf. Wolfe removed a Springfield Armory 1911 .45 ACP, three magazines, and a compatible holster. He placed them on the table as well.

Next, he reached for two additional objects. He tossed one to McGill.

The Scotsman raised an eyebrow. “Night-vision goggles. I take it we’re going on a late-night hike.”

Wolfe nodded. “You might say that. We’ll take the Jeep. It has something we might need: four-wheel drive.”

Nadia opened the passenger door of the Audi and hissed for Lori to get down. As she slid out of the SUV, she stayed low, keeping the engine compartment between her and the two men. The shotguns fired simultaneously and, as the two men pumped them to insert another shell, Nadia popped up and pulled the trigger of her Glock four times. The two men, caught reloading, took two bullets each in the chest and fell backward.

She rushed to where they lay, kicked one of the dropped long guns away, and grabbed the other. She looked back at the Audi to check on Lori and saw her running toward her. Nadia pointed toward the other shotgun, which Lori picked up. They both ran toward the open front door of the house.

Chapter Forty-Three

SOUTHWEST MISSOURI

Mohammad Al-Qaedi focused his binoculars on the two men running back to their vehicles. He watched the Jeep and pickup drive away. He lowered the field glasses and studied the scene below from a fifth-floor loft apartment across from the office where all the police vehicles were parked.

He stood by himself, not trusting the men recently hired to assist him in his quest to rid the world of Ian McGill and Michael Wolfe. From his count, there were at least four police officers still inside the structure. At least he would have victims.

Reaching into his pants pocket, he pulled out a device resembling a garage door opener and pressed the button on the top.

Across the street flashes of light could be seen through the windows of the building as explosives detonated. The force of the blasts blew outward, showering any occupant of the area with shards of broken glass. The rumble of the explosions rattled the building where he hid.

Having practiced his craft for over two decades, he felt a sense of satisfaction as the center of the roof collapsed inward. This continued until only the outer walls remained.

Narrowing his eyes and taking a deep breath, he wiped the device clean of fingerprints and placed it on the windowsill. He then walked out of the apartment and down the stairs to a car parked a few blocks away. As he exited the building, he heard the faint sound of sirens in the distance.

Nadia slammed the large solid oak door shut and threw the dead bolt. Darkness surrounded where she stood, the silence broken only by Lori's heavy breathing.

Moving toward the woman, she placed her arm on her friend's shoulder. "Shhhh."

Lori whispered, "Sorry."

"We don't know if we are alone in the house or not." She paused and listened for a few moments. An eerie silence greeted her ears. "Are you hurt?"

"No. My heart is about to explode though. I'm surprised you can't hear it."

"We may have lucked out. Those two were probably the only ones, waiting for whoever showed up. I'll check the rest of the house and then we can get out of here."

"I think the shotgun blasts were aimed for the front of my Audi."

Nadia stopped. "How do you know?"

"The windshield was intact when I left the vehicle."

"In other words, they shot the radiator."

"That would be my guess."

"Then we are on our own for the moment."

"What's going on, Nadia?"

"Good question. Have you had any real estate deals go bad recently?"

"No. I hav…" She paused. "You know exactly what this is about, don't you?"

"I'm afraid I do."

"Want to tell me?"

Nadia moved toward a window facing the front of the house. "Do you know how to use a shotgun?"

"My father took me duck hunting when I was a teenager. Yes, I do."

"How big is this house?"

"Listing contract indicated it to be over eighty-five hundred square feet. This part of the country classifies it as a mansion."

The ex-Mossad agent took her phone from her jeans pocket and dialed a number. When it was answered, she said, "Hi, Michael, it's Nadia. Sorry I have to leave a message. Lori is showing a house to a new client, and I'm going with her. After we're done, we will head over to your and my favorite bar. Why don't you meet us there?" She ended the call and put the phone in her back pocket.

"Uh, Nadia, this is not really a good time to start making plans. We don't know what is going to happen." She paused. "I've never heard you mention a favorite bar or even a restaurant."

With a sly smile, Nadia said, "We don't have one. Over the course of the past few years, Michael and I have established ways for talking on a cell phone. He calls them glorified radios that anyone with a few simple pieces of equipment can listen to. I basically told him where we are and that we need help."

"Oh." She was quiet for a few moments. "Exactly what is going on, Nadia?"

"I'm afraid Ian's, Michael's, and my pasts are finally catching up with us."

"What do you mean your pasts are catching up with you?"

"It's a long story."

"Seems we have a few minutes."

Nadia took a deep breath and began to explain.

JR, the retired FBI agent, and the police sergeant were standing next to a police interceptor situated between them and JR's office building. The force of the explosion threw all three to the ground, but the large police vehicle based on a Ford Explorer SUV saved them from being seriously injured from flying glass.

By the time JR could stand, the building had collapsed, and dust swirled around the area. The police officer reached for his radio and started screaming for more assistance, ambulances, and fire trucks to the scene. When he finished the transmission, he checked the other two men. "Everybody okay?"

Nods came from both.

"JR, are you sure you didn't have any personnel in the building?"

"Positive, officer."

He returned to the radio. "Possible four officers down. Repeat, possible four officers down. We also need the crime lab."

The retired FBI agent stood next to JR and said, "This wasn't a simple burglary, JR." He folded his arms. "Now why would someone break into your office and plant a bomb?"

"It's complicated, Sean."

The tall man's eyes narrowed. "Try me."

The motel at one time bore the name Motel 6, but the switch from two-lane paved roads to four-lane interstate highways system finally caught up with it, and the chain sold it to a single proprietor. Located on an older section of the famous Route 66 in Southwestern Missouri, the renamed Roadster Inn catered to nostalgic adults who drove their restored 1960s muscle cars on yearly pilgrimages to various car shows. It also offered sanctuary, when needed, to any individual from countries east of the Mediterranean. The owner, born in a part of Palestine now occupied by the Israeli government, provided sanctuary to any and all Muslims. Amin Tarik kept several rooms in the very back of the establishment open for travelers needing to stay out of the sight of American authorities.

Into these accommodations, Mohammad Al-Qaedi sequestered the individuals hired from the imam in Detroit. He opened one of the motel room's doors at five minutes past nine p.m. Only three of the five men he hired were present. Two watched television and the other appeared to be reading.

"Where are Arman and Hadi?"

The man reading, whose name was Javad, looked up. "They have not returned. We thought they were with you."

"No, they were sent to take care of the real estate woman."

"We have not heard from them."

Al-Qaedi held his hand out and Javad offered his cell phone. When the call went unanswered, he said, "Something is wrong. We need to go to the house where they were to meet the woman."

All three men stood and followed Al-Qaedi from the room.

The land surrounding the mansion consisted of thick wooded areas to the east and west of the south-facing property. A meandering asphalt driveway stretched from the county farm road to the circle drive. Few trees occupied this section of the property. The land to the north consisted of rolling hills until it blended into a field of scrub brush and cedar trees.

From the western wooded area, Wolfe surveyed the front of the house through his NVGs. McGill stood next to him, doing the same. "What do you see, Ian?"

"Two bodies between the front door and Lori's Audi."

"Affirmative. They look to be male."

"Aye, laddie. I agree."

"My guess is Lori and Nadia are in the house."

"Aye."

Wolfe took a deep breath and shifted his eyes toward the farm road in front of the property. "One of us needs to get into the house and check on them."

McGill took off running before Wolfe could finish what he was saying. "I was going to add, I'll watch the road."

The Scotsman disappeared around the back corner of the house. Wolfe adjusted his earpiece for the radio and said, "What do you see?"

"A large deck and dozens of bushes. I haven't seen any lights inside yet."

"Nadia has not responded to any text or calls yet."

"Any ideas, mate?"

Wolfe could see a large SUV approaching the driveway with the lights off. "Ian, we've got company. A large truck is turning into the property. No lights."

"Got it, mate. I'm going in through the back door."

Wolfe kept his attention on the SUV. "Wait one, Ian. The truck stopped as soon as it entered the driveway."

"Aye, mate."

"Go in, Ian. Three bogies just exited the vehicle and are heading your way. Driver's side door did not open."

"Got it. Going in."

Chapter Forty-Four

SOUTHWEST MISSOURI

Wolfe keyed his radio. "Ian, you've got three bogies with long-guns heading toward the front door. Driver stayed in the vehicle. Do you need assistance?"

"Negative. Found them, Michael. Lori and Nadia are safe. Each acquired a shotgun."

"I'll handle the driver."

"Aye, laddie. We'll handle it here."

"Keep them safe."

"That's the plan."

Wolfe studied the SUV as he determined the best way to address the situation. Crouching low, Wolfe held his suppressed Barret in his right hand as he moved east within the tree line.

After taking a quick glance over his shoulder, he noted the three men were now at the front door. Returning his attention to the SUV, he noticed it had backed up almost to the county road. Dropping to a prone position, he flipped his NVGs up and sighted on the truck's engine block through the night-vision scope. Applying pressure to the trigger, the rifle broke, and a round struck the SUV's engine block causing steam to immediately boil out from underneath the hood.

He shifted his aim to the rear tire and sent another round toward its target. The tire exploded with enough force the entire vehicle shuddered. A third shot destroyed the front driver's side tire, and the large SUV thumped down hard onto the driveway. In the green hue of the NVGs, Wolfe noticed a figure exit the vehicle on the passenger side. Before he could get the crosshairs of the scope on target, it disappeared into the tree line on the west side of the property.

He keyed his mike. "Ian, give me a sitrep."

The only answer he received were the unmistakable sounds of shotguns and AR-15s being discharged within the house.

When McGill set foot on the large deck behind the mansion, he stopped and listened for a few moments. Field crickets and tree frogs created a background symphony the Scotsman had heard every night since arriving in the Ozarks, but the house remained silent.

With his NVGs down, he found a back door and tested the knob. Unlocked. He turned it slightly and pushed the door inward. The barrel of a shotgun appeared level with his eyes. He said, "Ah, bloody hell."

Lori jumped into his arms with the weapon now safely pointed away. As they embraced, he heard Nadia off in the darkness. "Good way to get your head blown off, Sergeant Major."

"Aye, glad to know you're both safe."

"Where's Michael?"

"Watching over us with his bloody Barrett."

McGill stepped inside the house and closed the door. His radio crackled in his ear. After finishing the conversation with Wolfe, he said, "We've got company coming. Let's be ready."

Al-Qaedi sat behind the steering wheel of the Ford Excursion as the three hired guns approach the house. The truck shuddered, and steam spewed out from under the hood. The engine ceased, and all the warning lights on the dash came on at the same time. The vehicle shuddered again and suddenly leaned toward the back.

When the front fell as well, he grabbed his backpack from the back seat and scrambled for the passenger door. He started running the second his feet touched solid ground. Half expecting a bullet to hit him in the back, he reached the tree line and took an immediate right.

Once he felt invisible within the trees, the terrorist took stock of the SUV. Steam belched out of the engine compartment and the vehicle leaned toward the east. His best means of escape was now a useless hulk of metal. From the direction of the house, he heard gunfire. At the same time, a high-powered bullet slammed into a tree ten yards to his right. Narrowing his eyes, he waited for another shot in hopes of seeing the flash. When none came, he realized that since he had not heard a rifle shot, he would also not see a muzzle flash.

The sounds of gunfire increased from the house. Realizing his plans for trapping Wolfe and McGill were once again compromised, he followed the tree line toward the county road. He needed to get as far away from the failed ambush at the vacant house as possible.

Intense gunfire from the mansion drew Wolfe's attention away from the fleeing figure. He held his Barrett in his left hand and ran toward the structure. Whoever the figure might be, they would have to wait. His need to help Nadia became a larger priority than whoever might have been in the truck. He crouched low as he ran and kept his attention on flashes reflected in the front windows. When he reached the door, he removed the Springfield Armory 1911 from his holster and burst through the entrance.

Total darkness greeted him, and he flipped his NVGs down. The room presented itself in a greenish hue. On the floor in front of a staircase, a man lay in what appeared to be a spreading pool of blood. An AR-15-style rifle lay next to him. Wolfe kicked the rifle away as he pointed the pistol at the man. With his foot, he nudged the body. It remained still.

Sounds from the back of the house drew Wolfe's attention and he moved in that direction.

With Lori now safe in the arms of McGill, Nadia ran toward a staircase off the kitchen leading to the second floor. As she ascended, she pumped the shotgun, injecting a fresh shell into the chamber. From her experience with the Mossad, she knew the gun to be a Mossberg Shockwave that held six shells. One of which had been discharged at the Audi. During her training, she'd learned how to use assault weapons like the Mossberg, although never this model.

She made her way to the front of the house via a hallway and heard the sounds of men mumbling instructions to each other in Arabic. From their whispered conversation, she knew one would be heading up toward the second floor on the front staircase.

As soon as the man started up the stairs, they creaked and moaned with his weight. She popped out from behind a wall and fired a shotgun round down the staircase and immediately returned to the safety of the wall. The response became a hail of bullets from what she recognized as an AR-15.

When the burst stopped, she emerged again and fired the shotgun toward the assailant advancing up the stairwell. She heard a muffled grunt and the sound of a body rolling down the steps.

Her internal celebrations were short-lived as more AR-15 gunfire rang out from the first floor. She sprinted down the hallway toward the back stairwell with the Mossberg at ready. She heard the distinct sound of a suppressed Heckler and Koch MP5SD on automatic spitting off several bursts. This had to be McGill using one of the guns supplied from Michael's armory.

Descending the stairs cautiously, when halfway down, she could see McGill and Lori crouched behind a large kitchen island. A dark stain marred Ian's shoulder.

She turned and scrambled back to the second floor and raced down the hall to the front stairwell. Before descending, she checked to make sure they were not occupied and then hurried down, stepping over the dead assailant now laying in the front vestibule. Once on the first floor, she hurried to position herself behind the two men attacking the kitchen.

Outside the kitchen door, both men hid against the wall, one on the left and the other on the right. Neither saw her. One man slipped into the kitchen and before the other did the same, Nadia let loose a volley from the shotgun.

The blast caught the man in mid-back, and he stumbled forward into the kitchen's interior.

Sounds of an AR-15 firing and the muffled shots from the H&K could be heard simultaneously. Then the house fell silent.

Nadia heard the front door creak open. With the shotgun at ready, she crept back toward the entrance to see if more intruders had arrived.

Through his NVGs, Wolfe recognized the figure emerging from the back of the house. "Nadia."

The image froze and then ran toward him. He grabbed her in a tight embrace. "Are you okay?"

She nodded rapidly. "Yes, but I think Ian's been hit."

"How many are left?"

"I got two. I heard shots from the kitchen and then silence."

"Stay here, I'll check it out."

"I will not. I'm going with you."

He chuckled. "Let's go."

The silence within the house grew in intensity as they approached the entrance to the kitchen. As Wolfe placed his back to the wall, he said, "Ian, it's Michael."

"It's about bloody time you showed up."

"Are we clear?"

"I've got two down in here. What about the third?"

"Down at the front door."

Wolfe walked through the entrance to the kitchen to find McGill standing behind the kitchen island, blood oozing down his arm. Lori stood next to him, trying to place a tourniquet above the wound to slow the bleeding.

Wolfe asked, "How bad?"

"It's a bloody nick," McGill grumbled. "What about the driver?"

"Got away."

"Damn."

Wolfe approached one of the dead men and rolled him over and examined him. "This guy isn't Al-Qaedi." The other man lay face up. "Neither is he."

"Think he was the driver?"

"Considering he never likes to get his hands dirty in these types of operations, I would almost guarantee it."

Nadia walked over to assist Lori with Ian's injury. When she got there, she noticed in the dim light of the house a tear trickling down her face. "You okay, Lori?"

Her friend nodded as she attended to McGill. Without taking her eyes off the Scotsman she said, "I am really tired of Ian getting hurt. Who is this Al-Qaedi person?"

Wolfe pulled out his cell phone. "Someone we need to stop."

Starlight illuminated the country road Al-Qaedi followed. His frustration growing by the second the further he walked. There were no additional houses along the path. Suddenly off in the distance, headlights could be seen approaching.

Standing in the road, he held a pistol and pointed it at

the approaching vehicle. The headlights illuminated him and the car slowed. When the car's driver realized what was happening, they slammed on the brakes and stopped ten feet from the Iranian.

Before the hapless soul inside the car could react, Al-Qaedi rushed to the car window and fired the pistol.

Chapter Forty-Five

SOUTHWEST MISSOURI

The sun peeked over the eastern horizon to reveal multiple black Chevy Suburbans with blacked-out windows parked in the circle drive of the mansion. Several FBI forensic team members swarmed over the abandoned Ford Excursion while others searched the house, treating it as a crime scene.

Sitting on the tailgate of one of the large SUVs, Ian McGill watched as one of the FBI agents redressed his wound. "You act like ya've done this before, laddie."

"Yes, sir. Four years as a Marine medic."

"Then I'm in good hands."

The agent smiled. "I understand you're ex-SAS, sir."

"Aye. Twenty-five years."

"During my two deployments, I met some of your comrades. Some of the best men I've ever had the pleasure of serving with."

"Aye, laddie. They are."

Wolfe walked up to the two men. "Al-Qaedi's fingerprints are all over the interior of the Excursion. He's the one who got away."

McGill said, "Bloody coward."

"Like I've said, he never gets his hands dirty."

"Aye, you've mentioned that." McGill paused. "What's next, Michael?"

"Now that we know he was definitely here, a national BOLO has been issued again. They haven't identified the five bodies yet."

The FBI agent placed a bandage over his sutures and said, "You need to have a real doctor take care of that, Sergeant Major."

"Aye, laddie, first thing tomorrow." As the FBI agent headed toward the house. McGill returned his attention to Wolfe. "I understand JR's office was bombed right after we left."

"Yes."

"He okay?"

"Yeah, he had a few cuts from flying glass, but the police car kept the officer, Sean, and JR from being shredded by the debris."

"What's next, Michael?"

"JR found an email from a lawyer in St. Louis alluding to a search for the real estate agent who worked with Nadia and me. I think I need to start there."

"What am I supposed to do, twiddle me thumbs?"

"No, according to Joseph, you'll be assisting the FBI in determining who these men are."

McGill frowned. "In other words, a desk job."

"You could say that. Besides, you and I are the only two who know Al-Qaedi on sight. Until he is caught, we need to split up. Nadia and I are heading to St. Louis to have a chat with the lawyer."

"How you gonna find him?"

"FBI already has his office under surveillance."

The time approached ten a.m. as Wolfe and Nadia passed the town of Rolla, halfway toward their destination. She turned in her seat toward him. "Want me to drive?"

His mouth twitched. "You're just as tired as I am."

"Yeah, but I've been catnapping for the past two hours."

"You hungry?"

She nodded. "Starving."

"Let's find a café and get some breakfast."

"Coffee would be good, too."

"My point."

They found a small café in the town of St. James. As they waited quietly for the waitress to bring their order, they sipped coffee. After a few moments, Wolfe broke the silence. "McGill told me you were responsible for taking down four of the men."

She did not answer right away, studying the coffee in her mug. Finally, she said, "Yes."

"You okay with it?"

She looked up at him. "Michael, I did what had to be done."

"I understand that. But it's been a while since you were in a similar situation."

"I've never been in a situation like that before, Michael. But yes, I'm fine."

The food arrived and silence fell over the table again. After Wolfe paid for their meal, they walked toward their Jeep in the parking lot. Halfway there, he said, "You did good, Nadia. I'm proud of you."

She grasped her husband's hand and squeezed.

At exactly fifteen minutes past one p.m., Wolfe and Nadia followed four FBI agents into the office of Dan Morales. The lead agent, Shirley McDonnell, stood in front of the elderly lady who manned the desk in the lobby and said, "FBI, please show us to Dan Morales' office."

The woman stared wide-eyed at the female agent and then pointed to a door, which opened at the same time.

Morales said, "What's the meaning of this intrusion?"

The female agent replied, "Are you Dan Morales?"

"Yes. I demand to know what this is about."

McDonnell looked at her accompanying agents. Three of them surrounded the lawyer and escorted him back into his office. She, Wolfe, and Nadia then followed everyone into the room and Wolfe shut the door.

Morales squirmed. "Are you going to inform me what this is about?"

McDonnell said, "Dan Morales, you are under arrest for violation of US Code 18, subsection 2339A—providing material support to a known terrorist."

Morales' mouth opened, but he did not say anything.

Wolfe wandered over to the lawyer's desk and started rifling through the paperwork lying open. He found something and picked it up. After skimming it, he handed the piece of paper to McDonnell.

She read it, frowned, and instructed her agents, "Gather all the files." She held the page so the attorney could see it. "Care to comment on this, Mr. Morales?"

The attorney twisted to see Wolfe, whose wardrobe consisted of jeans, a polo shirt, and a bomber jacket. "You don't look like an FBI agent. What is this all about?"

Wolfe walked over to the man after receiving a nod from McDonnell. "You are being charged with aiding and abetting a man named Mohammad Al-Qaedi. That aid resulted in the death of four police officers in Springfield, Missouri. Plus, the destruction of a building valued at over three million dollars. Since Al-Qaedi is a known international terrorist, one I have been tracking for months, that makes you an accomplice. As a lawyer, you have to realize you are in a precarious position."

Morales only glared at Wolfe.

"Apparently, you do understand the seriousness of the charges being brought against you by the US government, Mr. Morales. So, I will ask this only once. Where is he?"

"I have no idea who you're talking about."

"I'm sure you are a smart man, but that was not a smart answer." Wolfe stepped aside. "Agent, he's all yours."

As the FBI agents led the attorney toward his office door, he looked back at Wolfe. "Wait."

Wolfe clasped his hands behind his back. "Yes."

"I don't know where he is right now, but I can tell you where he will be at nine tonight."

After making his statement, Morales was escorted from the office by two FBI agents. McDonnell and another female agent remained behind. McDonnell turned to Wolfe and asked, "How do you want to handle the information he just gave us?"

Glancing at his wristwatch, Wolfe said, "As much as I would like to be there, I think it's time the FBI takes over. I've accomplished what I needed to do."

"What's that, Michael?"

"Exposing how dangerous Al-Qaedi can be. It is going to take more than a few individuals to take this man down. You need to set the wheels in motion, Agent McDonnell."

She smiled. "I'll be happy to."

The Next Morning

Wolfe opened his eyes to see the digital clock on his nightstand displaying the numbers 11:23. He blinked several times and realized Nadia still lay asleep next to him. He shook her gently, which caused her to roll away from him.

She groaned. "What time is it?"

"Almost noon."

After sitting up on the side of the bed, he placed his elbows on his knees. He then supported his head with the palms of his hands and closed his eyes. Not five seconds later, his cell phone vibrated and danced on the nightstand surface.

Checking the caller ID, he answered, "Hello, Joseph."

"Have you seen any news today?"

"No. What happened?"

"The lawyer sent the FBI into a trap. The building where he told them Al-Qaedi would be blew up after they raided it. Ten FBI agents were lost when the building collapsed."

"Shit."

"A total of fifteen civilians were in the building as well. All of whom were members of the mosque where Al-Qaedi hired the five men."

"I take it Al-Qaedi was nowhere to be found."

"You would be correct."

Wolfe remained quiet for several moments. "How the

hell did he get from Christian County back to Detroit so fast?"

"The FBI is asking the same question."

"Will they let me talk to the lawyer?"

"That's why I'm calling. Ryan Clark wants you to have some alone time with the guy."

"Where is he?"

"In a holding cell at Joint Base Andrews. There will be a Gulfstream arriving at the airport for you in an hour and a half."

"We'll be there."

The call ended and he looked over at Nadia, who now sat on the edge of the bed.

She returned the look with one eye open. "I take it you and I are going somewhere."

"We need to be at the airport in an hour."

"Michael, let's seriously think about retiring after this."

Chapter Forty-Six

JOINT BASE ANDREWS

Dan Morales greeted Wolfe from his chair in the interrogation room with folded arms and a smirk. The retired Marine shut the door and continued to stand. He tilted his head. "Not sure why you look so confident, Morales."

"I haven't been given access to a lawyer yet. My rights are clearly being violated, and you will be named in the lawsuit I intend to file."

"Knock yourself out on that one, Danny. I take it you haven't been told about the new charges filed against you by the Department of Justice."

The smugness disappeared.

"You are being named as an accomplice in the deaths of ten FBI agents and fifteen civilians."

The man glared at Wolfe but remained silent.

Wolfe continued. "You see, the place where you said Al-Qaedi would be was booby-trapped. After the explosion, the building collapsed, killing everyone inside. As far as the

FBI is concerned, you are as guilty as the person who planted the bomb."

"I want a lawyer."

"That's the other news I've been asked to relay to you. You have been reclassified as a domestic terrorist. If convicted on all the charges filed, you are looking at multiple life sentences served consecutively."

"I want a lawyer."

"Tell me where Al-Qaedi is, and they might let you have one."

"I know my rights."

Wolfe's mouth twitched. "Yes, everyone is aware you know your rights. But what you don't know is that the US government is thinking about deporting you."

"I'm a US citizen. They can't deport me."

"Are you really, Morales? Think about it."

The man's brow furrowed.

"Your parents lied to you. They entered the US illegally when you were three months old. They paid a lot of money to get your birth certificate forged. You are not a US citizen." Wolfe paused for a moment. "Plus, due to the fact you lied on your law school application, they are considering revoking your degree, which means you'll lose your license. Not that you would be able to keep it anyway, but the hole you're in keeps getting deeper."

Sweat popped out on Morales' forehead as he stared at the tabletop. Wolfe finally sat across from him and waited. Finally, the attorney narrowed his eyes and said, "What's in it for me if I tell you?"

Wolfe shrugged. "Not sure there is anything, except you'll know you told the truth."

"Then, why should I talk?"

There was a knock at the room's door. Wolfe stood and opened it. Nadia appeared and handed him a file folder. She winked, turned, and left. Wolfe returned to the table, sat, and leaned back as he studied the contents of the folder. "Hmmm."

"What? What's in the folder?"

Wolfe looked over the top of the file. "FBI found your bank accounts, the ones you keep secret from your wife. You've got quite the fortune there, Danny. Unfortunately, since the source of this income is suspect, the Department of Justice had the IRS seize it."

Morales' face grew crimson, and he slammed his hands on the table. "That's illegal. I earned the money through hard work and legal fees."

Wolfe stood and leaned over the table, supporting himself with the palms of his hands. "Danny, I have two words for you. Tough shit."

"That was my retirement money."

"You don't get it, do you? You're already retired. You will be spending the rest of your days in a maximum-security federal penitentiary. I'm sure you're familiar with the conditions in those places. If you survive a year, you'll be lucky." Wolfe tucked the file under his arm. "Let me know if you change your mind."

He reached the door and opened it. Morales said, "Do I get a lawyer if I tell you?"

"Yes."

"He's on a boat heading up the St. Lawrence River toward the Atlantic."

"Name of the boat?"

"Shining Star."

This revelation caused Wolfe to momentarily pause. "Did you say the *Shining Star*?"

Morales nodded.

Wolfe asked, "How's the arm?"

"It was barely a scratch. Why is everyone so damn worried about it?"

Wolfe grinned. "We care about your well-being, Ian." He paused for a brief moment. "Do you remember a ship called the *Shining Star*?"

"Bloody hell, yes. Why?"

"Apparently, Al-Qaedi is on it, heading for the Atlantic."

"Son of a bitch."

"Coast Guard told me it would enter Lake Ontario late tonight."

"Are they planning to stop it?"

"Not in the waterway. Too big a chance at closing the passage. They want to wait until it gets into more open water."

"Are we invited to the party?"

"If you can get your lazy ass to Washington DC ASAP, we are. You and I are the only individuals who can positively identify Al-Qaedi. They'll stop the ship before it gets to the Gulf of St. Lawrence, preferably before it leaves the estuary. This is going to be a joint effort with the Royal Canadian Navy."

Wolfe and McGill landed at Canadian Forces Base Bagotville less than 120 miles north of Quebec City. As the two men stepped off the FBI Gulfstream, the blades of an SH-60 Seahawk from the USS Oscar Austin started rotating faster. Wolfe carried a duffel bag and the gun case containing his Barrett. McGill carried only a duffel bag.

They rushed toward the US Navy helicopter, ducked slightly under the blades, and climbed the air stairs.

Once everyone was situated in their seats with their headphones on, the pilot said, "Welcome aboard, gentlemen. We have about an hour's flight time to the deck of the USS Oscar Austin. The HMCS Ottawa is waiting there as well."

Noticing the young pilot's rank, Wolfe asked, "Where's the *Shining Star,* Lieutenant?"

"About thirty nautical miles southwest of Quebec City."

"Good."

"We'll be onboard ship long before interception."

The pilot remained quiet the rest of the journey. After gently setting the Seahawk on the flight deck of the destroyer, he said, "I'll be your pilot for the upcoming festivities."

Just before taking his headset off, Wolfe said, "Looking forward to it, Lieutenant."

The two men disembarked, ducked, and, once clear of the rotor blade wash, straightened. They were met by a tall man in an FBI windbreaker and a naval officer displaying a gold oak leaf on his shirt collar. Neither man introduced himself nor gave the impression they were happy to see them. The naval officer said, "Follow me."

When McGill and Wolfe were standing in a small below-deck conference room, the naval officer said, "I'm Lieutenant Commander Sikes. I've been told both of you can identify the individual we are to take prisoner."

Wolfe and McGill nodded.

"I've not been briefed about your qualifications." He frowned. "That makes me nervous, gentlemen. Not knowing how you will react during a possible crisis."

Wolfe tilted his head and motioned toward his partner.

"This is Ian McGill. He was a sergeant major in the British SAS when you were learning to read, sir."

The naval officer started to say something when McGill piped in, "Standing next to me is Michael Wolfe, one of the best Marine snipers ever produced by your country's military. If you're worried about how we will react in a firefight, don't. We've been in more than a few together, laddie."

The FBI agent briefly tried to hide a smile with his hand but instead offered it to Wolfe. "So, you're the sniper Rick Flores keeps talking about?"

As the two men shook, Wolfe said, "Yeah, I know Rick. He likes to embellish stories at times."

The FBI agent glanced at the naval officer. "Frank, lighten up. I've heard stories about our Mr. Wolfe here. All of them good."

Sikes contemplated McGill. "So, you were with the British SAS?"

"Aye, laddie."

"How long?"

"More years than I wasn't."

The naval officer offered his hand. "Welcome aboard, Sergeant Major."

The Next Morning

Wolfe concentrated through his binoculars at the now-anchored cargo ship *Shining Star* floating off the starboard bow of the *USS Oscar Austin*. "Its flag of convenience is Panama, but it's owned by an Italian shipping conglomerate and based out of the Port of Calais."

Lt. Commander Sikes glanced at Wolfe. "How'd you know that?"

"Ian and I had a run-in with this particular ship and its captain, over a year ago. It was doing the same thing then, ferrying a terrorist around."

McGill folded his arms. "The captain at the time was an arrogant little prick named Patrick O'Shay, nicknamed, Paddy. If he's still captain, he'll nary be happy to see Michael and I again."

Wolfe took the binoculars down. "My guess is he's still captain. Otherwise, why would someone like Al-Qaedi be on board?"

The FBI agent, who had finally introduced himself as Kevin Ramos asked, "Is he the one who planted the bomb in Detroit that killed ten agents?"

Wolfe brought the binoculars up again. "One and the same." He paused for a moment as he studied the comings and goings on the ship's deck. "Kevin, can you see if you can get confirmation on who the captain is?"

"I called it in ten minutes ago. No response yet."

"Lt. Commander, from the activity I see on the deck, it appears they're preparing to launch an inflatable boat. Until we have permission to board the *Shining Star*, you might want to get a helicopter up to discourage that kind of behavior."

"Good idea, Mr. Wolfe."

Chapter Forty-Seven

ABOARD THE SHINING STAR

Captain Patrick O'Shay glared at the two warships blocking his passage to the open Atlantic. With hands on hips, he said to the man on his right, "Thought you told me there was no way the Americans or the Canadians could know where you were. It appears they both know."

Mohammad Al-Qaedi glared at the captain. "This is your fault."

"How could it be my fault? You're the one the American FBI is searching for."

The Iranian remained silent as they kept tabs on the activity aboard the two warships. "I am surprised they have not boarded yet."

O'Shay raised his binoculars to his eyes. "Best you get off the ship now. You might not get another chance."

"How?"

"We have a few inflatables available. Take one of them. I'll say you hid amongst the crew and then hijacked the ship."

"This is what I get for trusting a nonbeliever."

With a swift, practiced move, O'Shay produced a Sig Sauer P365 XL from his jacket pocket, stepped back two feet, and pointed it at Al-Qaedi. "I've been assisting the likes of your kind for a decade. Do not question my motives, or I'll shoot you right here and give you to the Americans."

The terrorist sneered. "You are a coward, O'Shay. The minute the situation grows intense, you profess innocence to protect your own skin."

"I suggest you get off my ship. Right now."

"You are being well paid to take me to Calais."

"Not that well paid."

"What do you plan to do, shoot me?"

"The thought is tempting."

Al-Qaedi stormed off the ship's bridge.

O'Shay returned the gun to his pocket and once again raised the binoculars to his eyes. "Now, if I can convince the Canadians he's a stowaway, maybe I can get out of this."

Kevin Ramos ended the call on his cell phone and said, "You called it, Michael. Patrick O'Shay is still the captain of record for the *Shining Star*. The holdup about boarding the ship is because we're in Canadian waters. The Mounties have to authorize the action."

Sikes returned to the bridge. "The captain of the *Ottawa* just signaled we are a go for boarding." He faced Wolfe and McGill. "You two ready?"

Wolfe nodded, and McGill said, as he followed Wolfe off the bridge, "'Bout bloody time."

As Wolfe boarded the SH-60 Seahawk, Agent Ramos said, "The Canadians will handle security." He pointed toward a Sikorsky CH-148 Cyclone taking off from the helipad on the stern of *Ottawa*. "From what I was told, there will be a contingent of both Canadian Joint Task Force 2 members and Royal Canadian Mounted Police. They'll rappel down before we board."

McGill said, "I've worked with the Task Force 2 chaps before. We'll be in good hands when we get there."

After strapping in and placing the earphones on, Wolfe concentrated on the *Shining Star* as the Seahawk took off. He could see ten individuals rappelling down ropes dangling below the big Sikorski helicopter as it hovered above the deck of the cargo ship.

McGill tapped Wolfe on the leg. "Michael?"

"Yeah."

"Think Paddy will be happy to see us again?"

"I'm looking forward to his reaction."

With a grin, McGill said, "So am I."

After rappelling down to the deck of the *Shining Star*, Wolfe and McGill were met by a Royal Canadian Mounted Police officer. "You Wolfe and McGill?"

They said in unison, "Yes."

"Follow me. The captain is not being very cooperative."

When the contingent entered the bridge, Captain Patrick O'Shay stared at the new members of the boarding party and said, "Ah, bloody hell. Not you two again."

McGill grinned and said, "Last time I saw you, Paddy, you were being accompanied by a group of lads from MI5. How come you're still a captain?"

O'Shay crossed his arms. "I was found innocent."

"Bullshit. Ya probably lied your way out of it. But this time, I think ya screwed the pooch. Al-Qaedi is wanted both in the UK and the US. You're not going to lie your way out of it this time."

Wolfe walked up to O'Shay and growled, "Where is he, Paddy?"

"Where's who?"

"Mohammad Al-Qaedi."

"You're daft. No one on board by that name."

The sergeant with the Mounted Police who met them at the helicopter motioned for Wolfe to join him outside the bridge. When they were out of earshot, he said, "A few members of the crew are reporting seeing a dark-haired man on board over the past few days. No one was introduced to him. One man told us he's staying in one of the guest berths below deck. We've searched them all, but there's no sign of him."

Wolfe's brow furrowed. "Sergeant, remind your men, the man we are after is extremely dangerous."

"Already did."

"Remind them again." He paused. "What's the water temperature this time of year?"

"About seven degrees Celsius. Why?"

"That's about forty-five degrees Fahrenheit. How far to shore?"

"About two kilometers in either direction. Why?"

Wolfe calculated the odds. "He could make it, but it would be difficult."

"Swim to shore, in these waters? More like damn near impossible."

"Yeah, well, I've witnessed more than a few 'damn near impossible' achievements by Al-Qaedi. He needs to be stopped, once and for all, or more bodies will pile up."

Another Mountie approached the sergeant and whispered in his ear. When he finished and walked away, the

Mountie tilted his head and studied Wolfe. "You the sniper we were told about?"

"Yes."

"There's an inflatable missing, and one of the crew said he observed a dark-haired man jump off the stern. I'll call the Cyclone back. Ever use a C14 Timberwolf?"

"I'm familiar with it."

"Can you use it?"

Wolfe did not hesitate. "Yes."

"Follow me. We're going hunting."

Mohammad Al-Qaedi lowered the small inflatable boat off the stern of the cargo ship. The rumble of an approaching helicopter encouraged him to hurry. He let go of the rope attached to the raft, watched it fall onto the water, and then swung himself over the side rails.

He hit the surface and immediately sank. An involuntary gasp caused him to inhale a quantity of cold brackish water. Fortunately for him, the ship's propellors were idle as it waited to be boarded. Surfacing, he swam for the dinghy and managed to climb aboard, coughing up water and gasping for air. The ambient air temperature and his soaked clothes contributed to the sudden onset of involuntary shivering.

Years of surviving near-death mishaps and unexpected changes of fortune gave him an edge. Without thinking about it, he immediately started paddling the small boat away and downstream from the *Shining Star*.

The Sikorsky CH-148 hovered one foot off the stern deck as Wolfe and the Mountie sergeant, whose name Wolfe learned to be Andre Benoit, scrambled aboard the aircraft. At the same time the door closed, the helicopter began gaining altitude. It swung out to the *Shining Star's* port and circled toward the northern shoreline.

Wolfe used binoculars to scan the water to the left of the helicopter while Benoit repeated the process to the right. Keeping his altitude at fifty feet, the chopper pilot swung the tail rotors around and headed back toward the middle of the estuary. Once they approached water behind the cargo ship, Benoit said, "I've got something about a half klick downriver from the *Star*."

Wolfe moved to the side of the chopper where the Mountie sat and scanned the area mentioned. "Small dinghy with a man. That could be him."

Benoit instructed the pilot to close in on the small boat. The helicopter screamed over it at an altitude of only thirty feet.

Wolfe said, "That's him. Circle around again."

The pilot nodded and did a long sweeping turn back toward the dinghy.

Al-Qaedi stopped paddling as the large Sikorsky flashed overhead. He stopped paddling and followed the aircraft as it flew north and then swung around to return. With the realization he would probably not escape this time, he withdrew the Taurus G3 pistol from his belt and held it at his side as the Sikorsky approached. The helicopter now flew at a lower altitude, and he could see the down wash disturbing the surface of the estuary. With a grim smile, he waited until the helicopter arrived almost directly above him. He then aimed the gun and pulled the trigger.

The pilot jerked the collective to the left and banked the helicopter away from the gunfire. He yelled, "Gun!"

Wolfe picked up the C14 Timberwolf sniper rifle. He had not told Benoit the exact truth. He was more than a little familiar with the weapon. "Can you give me a stable platform at an altitude of three hundred meters?"

"I can, but the wind at that height over the river can be a little unpredictable."

"No problem. Do the best you can."

Wolfe turned to Benoit. "I need to confirm this is Al-Qaedi before I fire."

"No problem on my part. He fired first."

The pilot said into his microphone, "At three hundred meters and one fifty downrange."

"Wind direction?"

"Out of the northwest, forty-two kph."

"Got it." Wolfe did the math in his head and knew he had a 335-meter shot with a stiff crosswind. He made the adjustments to the scope and raised it to his shoulder.

Benoit opened the side door, and Wolfe secured himself with a safety strap. The helicopter swayed slightly and then corrected itself. He set the crosshairs on the figure in the boat below. The scope magnified the man's image and revealed a defiant scowl as he stared directly up at Wolfe.

"Confirmed, target is Mohammad Al-Qaedi."

Benoit focused on the boat below. "Take your shot, Marine."

Chapter Forty-Eight

SOUTHWEST MISSOURI

Two Months Later

Nadia entered the hangar and walked over to where Michael worked on the Beechcraft's right engine. He finished tightening the sparkplug and said, "I'll be done in a few minutes."

"Not why I came out. Joseph is on his way over."

"It's the middle of the week. What's he doing in town? Did he say why?"

"No, he just asked if we would be here. When I said we were, he indicated he'd be right over."

"Huh." He wiped his hands with a shop rag. "Wonder what this is all about."

"I don't know. Should we tell him?"

"Probably a good time."

"I have the letters written. All you have to do is sign yours."

Wolfe continued to wipe his hands with the rag as he stared at her with a blank expression.

She sighed. "Michael, if you've changed your mind, we can postpone this until you are truly ready."

"No, we need to move on with our lives. As you've said more than once, it's time we stop acting like we're still in our twenties."

She placed her hand on his arm but did not say anything for a few moments. "Let's see what Joseph has to say."

"That sounds like a good idea." He followed her out of the hangar.

Wolfe poured a cup of coffee for the man who now occupied a seat at their breakfast bistro table. When he placed it in front of his friend, the older man said, "Thank you, Michael."

After Wolfe sat, Joseph looked at Nadia and then at the retired Marine. "I wanted to make sure you two heard it from me before the news media gets it all wrong. I've turned in my resignation to President Griffin."

Wolfe sipped his coffee. "Why now?"

"It's time. Originally, I intended to stay only a year or less. But my ego got in the way, and I actually enjoyed the experience."

Nadia said, "There's a however coming. Isn't there?"

"Yes. Mary was recently diagnosed with breast cancer. We decided to come home so we can concentrate on getting her cured. Besides, we're both tired of the Washington DC scene. The constant pressures and the intense pace can get to you after a while."

Putting her hand on his arm, Nadia offered him a sympathetic smile. "What's the prognosis?"

"Good. They caught it early, and she's in excellent spirits."

"I'm glad to hear that."

Quiet returned to the table as each of the three individuals sipped coffee and settled into their own thoughts. Finally, Joseph broke the silence. "Which brings me to the reason I'm here."

Wolfe raised an eyebrow. "Kind of figured you had another reason."

"The president is going to name Jerry Griggs to the position of National Security Advisor."

"Congratulations to Jerry."

"I told the president you two would probably retire soon, and he has requested I ask you to stick around for a while."

Nadia took a deep breath. "Why?"

"The country is entering a tumultuous period. External terrorist threats are slowly receding, but domestic ones are gaining strength. The president would like to be able to call on your services should he need to."

Wolfe tilted his head and slowly shook it. "No, Joseph. Nadia and I have discussed it more than once. The time has arrived for both of us to step aside and let others take over."

"I told him that's what you would probably say." He took a sip of his coffee. "Unfortunately, there aren't too many individuals with your and Nadia's skill set."

"Be that as it may, Joseph, the answer is still no."

The man who resembled the actor Morgan Freeman gave them a slight smile. "Trust me, I understand. Would you like an update on Mohammad Al-Qaedi?"

Wolfe shrugged.

"I'm going to tell you anyway. After you sank his raft,

the Canadian Navy picked him up. By the time they got there, he was in an advanced state of hypothermia."

"I hope he didn't survive."

Joseph clasped his hands together on the table. "Officially and for public consumption, he didn't. Unofficially, he is in the custody of the Canadian Navy. The Brits are in negotiations to have him extradited to England for crimes against the Crown."

"What about the DOJ?"

"They want a piece of him but feel it would be politically wiser to let the Brits have him."

"Why?"

"Because they are afraid someone within the DOJ would leak the fact he's still alive. If it became widely known he survived, no telling what his followers would do."

"Sad, but they're probably correct. However, his time has passed. I'm not sure his followers have the same goals anymore. Can the Brits keep it under wraps?"

"Yes." Joseph paused. "I'm curious, Michael. Why did you sink the inflatable?"

"The helicopter's motion kept causing me to miss."

"Bullshit. You've made much tougher shots than that one."

Wolfe's mouth twitched. "I'm a sniper, Joseph, not an assassin."

"There's a subtle difference, but I understand what you mean." After another sip of coffee, Joseph raised his eyebrows. "If you two retire, what will you do?"

Nadia placed her hand on her husband's arm. He returned the gesture with his hand on hers. "We have a few ideas. But for now, let's just say we plan on being busy."

Joseph grasped his coffee cup. "I'll miss working with you two."

The conversation lasted another hour before Joseph left. As Michael gathered the coffee cups and placed them in the dishwasher, Nadia said, "Are you going to get bored in retirement, Michael?"

"No. As I was sighting in on Al-Qaedi with the rifle, I remembered the nightmares I used to have during the first Gulf War. I didn't want them to return. My first shot missed because the helicopter jerked during a strong gust of wind. I took it as a sign. So, I targeted the inflatable. Did Al-Qaedi deserve to die? Probably. But I no longer care to make those types of life-and-death decisions."

She walked over to him and placed her arms around his waist and her head on his chest. He returned the embrace as they fell into a prolonged silence.

Finally, he said, "When's your doctor appointment?"

"Three."

He checked the clock on the breakfast nook wall. "It's almost one."

"I know."

"You sure you want to take the chance the baby will be normal?"

"Yes. It will be normal, Michael. I'm only forty-one, and I've kept myself in good shape. I just don't want to tell anyone yet. Besides, who would we tell?"

"Well, there's Lori and Ian."

"I've already told them." She lifted her head from his chest and looked up. "How is the great Michael Wolfe going to handle being a father?"

"Don't know. I may very well find it to be the greatest challenge I've ever faced."

Next in The Michael Wolfe Saga

vinci-books.com/cloakofdeceit

Their names are on the list—and someone's crossing them off

Michael Wolfe thought he left the shadows behind. But when a global kill list surfaces with his name on it, he and Nadia must fight to survive a game designed to erase them.

Turn the page for a free preview…

A Cloak of Deceit: Chapter One

WASHINGTON, DC

Present Day

William Fischer, better known as Will to his friends, did not resemble the stereotypical Hollywood spy. But at one time, he roamed the streets of Europe as one of the more successful operations officers the CIA ever produced. These days, if someone needed to know details about matters inside the hallowed halls of the George Bush Center for Intelligence located in Langley, Virginia, all they needed to do was ask Will. Since retiring, he maintained contacts both inside the building and outside. Most of these contacts would meet him in various diners, taverns, or dive bars around the DC area. After decades spent abroad, he seldom ventured out of Maryland, Delaware, or Virginia.

On this particular Monday evening, Fischer sat alone at a table in a small Italian eatery five blocks from his house. He justified his habit of walking to and from the café by claiming the exercise did him good. With his bill settled and a half-full glass of the Irish ale demanding his attention, a slender woman sat across from him. He recognized the crystal blue eyes and the blonde hair that fell riotously around her face and shoulders.

Lowering the glass from his lips, he smiled. "Well, lass, it's been a while."

"Yes, William, it has. You haven't changed."

"Nonsense, I'm older and fatter."

"Maybe, but you still keep your rusty-brown hair unruly." She leaned forward. "I always loved the way you refused to trim those bushy eyebrows and your walrus mustache. Just like I remember."

He studied her through the smudged lenses of black horn-rimmed glasses. "You didn't come all the way to North Potomac to tell me I haven't changed, Sam. Why the visit?"

A gentle smile appeared on her lips. "Can't an old friend just stop by and say hi? Besides, I've missed you." She studied him a moment. "I've always loved your wardrobe. It's what I call thrift shop chic: rumpled corduroy sport coat, khaki pants two inches too long, scuffed loafers, and a wrinkled white oxford shirt."

"They're comfortable and you're stalling." He paused, clasped his hands in front of him, and leaned forward over the table. "Look at my manners. Can I get you something?"

"No. I'm not here to eat. I ran across something someone in your position might find useful." She palmed a small object on the table and slid it toward Fischer, keeping it hidden by her hand. "Do not keep this in your house. Use the information wisely."

Covering the object with his own hand, he slipped it off the table and placed it in his front pants pocket. "How bad is it?"

"Explosive. Just having this material could be dangerous for you. Read the information and you'll understand why."

She hesitated. "I'm giving it to you so you can warn the appropriate individuals."

After a couple of chuckles, Fischer lowered his glass and set it on the table. "Sam, my life has been in danger ever since I set foot in that damn building over in Virginia for the first time."

Samantha Edgar placed her hand on his arm. "Not as much as having this info. You need to watch your back carefully."

"You know something I don't?"

"Nobody knows more than you do, Will. That's the problem. Have you spoken to Joseph recently?"

The older man shook his head. "Not since he retired. Why?"

She started to say something but caught herself.

He drained his glass and returned it to the table. "Never figured you to be a worrywart. What's wrong?"

She stood. "I've already said too much. Watch your back, Will." She turned and disappeared into the crowd inside the bar.

The waitress strolled by. "Can I get something for your friend?"

"No, she just stopped by to say hello. Thanks for asking."

"My pleasure. See you tomorrow night?"

He stood. "I certainly hope so."

The warning from the former CIA case officer who just left his table left him a bit unsettled. Having not seen her since his days in Ukraine, the sudden appearance and emphatic warning seemed a bit odd.

Shaking off the feeling, he debated taking an Uber home, but who in their right mind would agree to a five-block ride? He walked out of the restaurant and gathered his thoughts. In his many years working for the agency, he had been threatened more than once. Most threats were simply nothing more than someone blowing off steam. But for someone like Samantha Edgar to go out of her way to hunt him down and give him a warning? He slipped his hand into his pants pocket and felt the small flash drive. His curiosity about the information on the computer storage device grew stronger by the second.

He walked back to his house, constantly looking over his shoulder.

A lifelong bachelor, Fischer lived in the Washington, DC suburb of North Potomac west of the busy I-270 corridor leading to Frederick, Maryland. His modest ranch-style home, having been paid off for years, held the mementos of a long career as a CIA operations officer. His current source of income came from being a consultant. A fancy way of saying he charged a lot of money for information others needed.

He took pride in the fact his information was always good, and his regular clientele depended on his expertise.

Fischer followed his normal daily routine during the next fourteen days. These activities included phone calls and poring through the pages of the most influential online news feeds around the globe. Being multilingual, a fact few of his friends or clients knew, he kept up with world events and the clandestine efforts to change them. The only exception to his regular habits, staying inside his house. Apart from an excursion to a bank and the mailing of a package to an old colleague, he did not venture out.

After fourteen days of using Grubhub and DoorDash,

the warning from Samantha Edgar faded into his subconscious, and he once again took a stroll to his favorite Italian hangout. The minute he stepped out of his house, he noticed an unfamiliar vehicle parked across the street. After a moment's hesitation, he considered going back inside. He then remembered his neighbor across the street recently purchased a new SUV, and this must be it. With a quick shake of his head, he set out for the diner. Being paranoid did not become him.

The uneventful walk to the diner and the subsequent safe return home brought a feeling of normalcy.

After unlocking the front door, he stepped inside and relocked it.

Searing pain and then blackness engulfed him as he slid to the floor.

A bright light stirred him back to consciousness. He blinked several times in an attempt to shade his eyes. His efforts failed as he realized his arms were bound to a chair.

A deep voice growled from behind the light. "I hope you enjoyed your nap."

Fischer knew not to say anything.

"I suppose you are wondering why this is happening, aren't you, William?"

The voice sounded familiar, but he could not place it at first. He remained quiet.

"Well, I'll answer your unasked question. You need to find another hobby besides being a noisy chatterbox about agency affairs."

"I find it fascinating."

"You might find it as such, but it's unhealthy for you."

"Is that a threat?"

"A promise."

Fischer took a deep breath. "What do you want?"

"Information."

"About?"

"Someone gave you information you shouldn't have. Where is it?"

"I have no idea what you are talking about."

The slap made his ears ring. "Wrong answer."

"Who are you?"

"I hope you aren't expecting an answer."

"Thought I'd try." The last statement confirmed he knew the speaker.

"Well think about *this*. You need to give me the information back, and I need Joseph Kincaid's location?"

"I have no idea what you're talking about."

"I'm sure you do. I couldn't find it here in your house. Last chance, where is Kincaid?"

Fischer shook his head.

"Very well. The next time you hear from me, you won't like the outcome, Will."

"Sticks and stones, mate."

No reply. The front door clicked shut. Then, as silence filled the room, so did the smell of natural gas. He tugged harder at his bound limbs. They did not budge. An hour later, the hands of a cuckoo clock on the wall of the living room reached eight and twelve. The resulting explosion shattered the tranquility of the quiet neighborhood in North Potomac.

A Cloak of Deceit: Chapter Two

SOUTHWEST MISSOURI

The sound of tires approaching outside the open hangar caused Wolfe to stop working on his aircraft's port engine. Directing his attention to the asphalt drive, he grabbed a shop towel to clean his grease-covered hands. He replaced the cowling of the exposed engine on the Beechcraft B55 Baron and walked out of the hangar.

A gun-metal-gray Range Rover Sport slowed to a stop and an elderly man dressed in a navy blazer, white oxford shirt, pressed khaki chinos, and scuffed loafers exited the vehicle. The guest, who resembled the actor Morgan Freeman more than a little, waved. "Good morning, Michael."

"Mornin', Joseph. This is a pleasant surprise."

"Hope you're not too busy."

"Nope. Want some coffee?"

"Yes. Plus, I need to speak to you and Nadia."

Wolfe raised an eyebrow. "About?"

"Let's talk inside."

They walked the fifty yards to a custom-built home

north of the hangar. The two buildings were located on the northern end of a sixty-two-acre plot of land. Once inside, Wolfe brewed a pot of coffee while Joseph sat at the breakfast nook table.

"Nadia will join us after she gets Ben down for his nap."

"How is the young tike? Isn't he about four years old now?"

"Just turned and he's doing great." Wolfe leaned against the kitchen counter. "How's Mary doing?"

"We received good news from her oncologist. The tumors are gone, and she appears to be in full remission."

"That's great news."

"Yes. We have to keep monitoring it, but she's in good spirits."

Nadia came into the kitchen, and Joseph stood to give her a hug. "Did I overhear Mary's in remission?"

"Yes."

"That's a relief." She settled into a chair at the table. Wolfe placed a cup of coffee in front of her and one before Joseph.

He sat across from his friend and held his mug with both hands. "Okay, what did you need to talk about?"

"Do you remember my friend, William Fischer?"

Wolfe nodded.

Joseph produced a key and an index card from within his navy blazer. He laid them on the table. "A week ago, I received these in a package with the return address of a UPS Store in North Potomac. There was a note inside telling me if anything happened to him, I was to collect the contents of a safe deposit box." He pointed to the key. "Using that key and the instructions on the card. By the way, I didn't find his name anywhere on or inside the envelope. I knew Will sent it because of a code word he and I used back in the day, printed at the top of the note."

Picking up the key, Wolfe said, "I take it something happened to Will."

Joseph continued. "A gas explosion destroyed his house two days ago, with him inside. Police are calling it an accident. However, one of my contacts within the agency told me Will's body was found tied to a dining room chair. Michael, it was no accident."

"Doesn't sound like it."

"Another thing, Will mentioned in the note I was not to retrieve the contents. I'm too well-known in and around DC."

Looking over his coffee cup, Wolfe took a sip and said, "There's a protocol for gaining access to a safe deposit box, Joseph."

"I'm aware of that. The index card has instructions on the process."

"So, you want me to go to Washington, DC and retrieve whatever's in the safe deposit box."

"Yes."

"I'm retired, or did you forget?"

"I'm aware of your current status." He paused for a moment. "I wouldn't ask you if the circumstances were different. But, right now, you and Nadia are the only two individuals I trust to retrieve whatever's in the box."

"You know an awful lot of people, Joseph. Surely, there's someone else?"

"The individual I spoke to indicated the CIA has changed over the past year. Many in current management are self-absorbed and only interested in their own advancement. The people in the field don't know who has their backs at the moment."

Wolfe examined the key again. He glanced at Nadia. "Okay with you?"

"We owe Joseph a lot, Michael."

"Yes, we do. Very well. When do you want me to leave?"

"As soon as you can file your flight plan." He paused a brief moment. "There's another reason I prefer you do this, Michael. You can fly into a small place like Potomac Airfield, and no one will know you're in the Washington, DC area."

"Fine with me." He studied the index card for a few moments. "What's in the safe deposit box?"

Joseph shook his head. "Not sure, but it appears he might have been murdered over the contents."

"You want me to check out his house?"

"I don't advise it. From what I've been told, it was leveled in the explosion and resulting fire. Probably not worth the chance of being seen by someone or having your image captured by a security camera."

"Then I can leave early and get back the same day."

"I was hoping you'd do it that way. When do you think you could be back?"

"Depends on how long it takes to obtain access to the safe deposit box, but I would say late afternoon."

"I'll be here when you get back."

He left at dawn and made a fuel stop in Lexington, Kentucky. Michael Wolfe arrived in the Washington, DC area by eleven a.m. A rental car provided by Enterprise waited for him at the airport fixed-base operator's office. An hour later, he presented the safe deposit box key and his ID to a TD Bank branch representative.

The young lady nodded and went to a file drawer next to her desk. She pulled the card to the box. "This is unusual. I'm supposed to ask you to recite a nine-digit number."

Wolfe shrugged. "It's Washington." He recited the numbers from memory.

She chuckled and said, "Perfect. I'll take you to the box."

When they both inserted their keys, the door opened, and Michael pulled out the long rectangular box.

"I'll be right outside when you're done." She exited the secure area while he placed the box on one of the pullout shelves scattered among the drawers. Inside, he found a bubble-wrapped object. He removed the protective outer plastic and found a 128-gigabyte flash drive. He stuck it in his pocket and returned the box to its appropriate slot. Stepping out of the secure area, he thanked the young lady and returned to his rental car.

At exactly 6:13 p.m., he touched down on his 3000-foot asphalt runway and taxied into the open hangar. Joseph leaned on the front quarter panel of his Range Rover and waved as Michael taxied past.

After shutting the Baron down, he exited and handed the flash drive to Joseph. "Nothing in the box but this."

Holding it up in the fading light of mid-October, Joseph said, "Let's see what's on it."

Nadia stood on the back deck of their home. As they approached, she said, "What'd you find?"

Joseph held up the flash drive. "Would you do us the honor of seeing what's on this?"

Five minutes later, she stared at the laptop screen and said, "It's encrypted."

Wolfe chuckled. "How long is the encryption key?"

"Looks like nine digits."

He recited the numbers he gave the lady at the bank.

She entered the numbers into the encryption key. "Nope. Now what?"

Wolfe pursed his lips and turned his attention to Joseph. "Was Fischer paranoid?"

"No, but he took security seriously."

"Huh." He remained quiet for several moments. "Try the numbers backward."

Nadia nodded and typed the numbers. The contents of the drive spilled onto the laptop's screen. They saw an Excel spreadsheet, a Word document, twenty jpg files, and an MP3 audio file.

Joseph leaned back in the chair and furrowed his brow. "Huh." He stared at the screen for a few moments. "Nadia, let's have a look at the pictures."

About the Author

J.C. Fields is a multi-award-winning and Amazon best-selling author. Many of his fourteen published novels have been awarded multiple gold, silver and bronze medals in the Reader Favorite International Book Awards contest.

Over the past several years, many of his short stories have been featured on the YouTube Podcast Fear From the Heartland, a part of the Chilling Tales for Dark Night network.

After a decade as an independent author, he signed a publishing contract with Vinci Books. Vinci Books is a world-class publisher created to offer independent authors the best of self-published and traditional publishing.

His passion for helping new authors reach their dream of publishing is reflected in his involvement with local writing groups and serving on the boards for the Between the Pages Writers Conference and the Ozarks Creative Writers Conference.

He lives with his wife, Connie, in Southwest Missouri.

Acknowledgments

Seven years ago, I embarked on a quest to achieve a dream held since high school. To be an author. I consider the book you hold in your hand a milestone. *A Matter of Payback* is my tenth novel. Thank you, kind readers, for your support and enthusiasm over the past few years. In addition to you, the readers, I have to thank a talented group of individuals who have assisted me in achieving this lifelong ambition to become a fulltime writer.

Sharon Kizziah-Holmes, owner of Paperback Press, has been my publishing coordinator since my first novel, *The Fugitive's Trail*. Over the course of these past seven years, she has been a steadfast supporter and someone I can count on to tell me if I am screwing up. She is also the one who has to deal with the final formatting issues on my eBooks, paperbacks and hardbacks. She has saved my sanity more than a few times over the years.

I also have to thank and tip my hat to my critique group, Shirley, Sharon, Lori, Heather and Conetta for their honest and sometimes brutal feedback when I submit material. We have been together almost three years and they know when I am not producing quality work. They definitely tell me.

I have a new editorial staff in place for this novel. Kate Richards, does the heavy lifting and developmental editing. Nanette Sipe and Shirley McCann provide the last lines of defense doing final proof reading. Thank you all.

Paul J. McSorley, returns as the voice of Michael Wolfe.

His talent as an audiobook narrator continues to grow with each novel he produces. Paul is also the creator of a successful YouTube Podcast called *Fear From the Heartland*, which I am privileged to be a contributor. I believe much of my success has been the collaboration between the two of us on my novels and short stories.

And again, last but not least, my wife Connie. She is my rock, the love of my life, my best friend and my largest supporter. She keeps me grounded and on track. I cannot imagine where I would be without her.